PRAISE FOR JANE L. ROSEN

"I'm tempted to write this blurb in all-caps boldface: I LOVED THIS BOOK! It is a smart, sensitive, and incredibly satisfying romantic comedy, studded with fun insider tidbits about New York City. Count me as Jane L. Rosen's biggest fan—and make your summer sweeter by reading *A Shoe Story*."

—Elin Hilderbrand, *#1 New York Times* bestselling author of *28 Summers*

"Read *A Shoe Story* and fall in love—with its heroine, Esme Nash; with its bighearted cast of characters; and with New York City, whether for the first time or all over again." —Katie Couric

"Jane L. Rosen has a forever fan in me."

—Emily Henry, #1 *New York Times* bestselling author of *Book Lovers*

"*Beach Read* meets *The Notebook* in [*A Shoe Story*, an] utterly absorbing Greenwich Village tale of first loves and second chances."

—Jo Piazza, *New York Times* bestselling author of *We Are Not Like Them*

"[*A Shoe Story*] is Jane L. Rosen's best book yet. . . . Her sense of humor, excellent character depictions, fabulous dialogue, and strong sense of place make this story extra sole-ful (can't help myself)."

—Zibby Owens, editor of *Moms Don't Have Time to Have Kids*

"Readers will identify with *A Shoe Story*'s heroine, Esme Nash, as she grapples with figuring out if what she once desired is still the life for her in this charming, clever, and irresistible tale. Trust me, you'll want to walk a mile or more in Esme's shoes."

—Elyssa Friedland, author of *Last Summer at the Golden Hotel*

"Perfect for fans of Rosen's *Nine Women, One Dress*, *A Shoe Story* shows us the power of the right shoe to change our mood, or even our lives."

—Brenda Janowitz, author of *The Liz Taylor Ring*

TITLES BY JANE L. ROSEN

A Shoe Story

Eliza Starts a Rumor

Nine Women, One Dress

A Shoe Story

JANE L. ROSEN

BERKLEY
NEW YORK

BERKLEY
An imprint of Penguin Random House LLC
penguinrandomhouse.com

Copyright © 2022 by Jane L. Rosen
Readers Guide copyright © 2022 by Jane L. Rosen
Penguin Random House supports copyright. Copyright fuels creativity,
encourages diverse voices, promotes free speech, and creates a vibrant culture.
Thank you for buying an authorized edition of this book and for complying with
copyright laws by not reproducing, scanning, or distributing any part of it in any
form without permission. You are supporting writers and allowing Penguin
Random House to continue to publish books for every reader.

BERKLEY and the BERKLEY & B colophon are registered
trademarks of Penguin Random House LLC.

Library of Congress Cataloging-in-Publication Data

Names: Rosen, Jane L., author.
Title: A shoe story / Jane L. Rosen.
Description: New York: Berkley, [2022]
Identifiers: LCCN 2021050944 (print) | LCCN 2021050945 (ebook) |
ISBN 9780593102114 (hardcover) | ISBN 9780593102121 (trade paperback) |
ISBN 9780593102138 (ebook)
Subjects: LCGFT: Novels.
Classification: LCC PS3618.O83145 S56 2022 (print) |
LCC PS3618.O83145 (ebook) | DDC 813/.6—dc23/eng/20211015
LC record available at https://lccn.loc.gov/2021050944
LC ebook record available at https://lccn.loc.gov/2021050945

Printed in the United States of America
1   3   5   7   9   10   8   6   4   2

Book design by Daniel Brount

This is a work of fiction. Names, characters, places, and incidents either are the product of
the author's imagination or are used fictitiously, and any resemblance to actual persons,
living or dead, business establishments, events, or locales is entirely coincidental.

To Warren,
for thirty years, my north, south, east, and west.

Give a girl the right shoes and she can conquer the world.

—MARILYN MONROE

I hope you're not wearing those shoes with the red bottoms;
they won't think you're hungry enough.

—A NEW YORK CITY CABBIE TAKING ME TO MY FIRST-EVER
MEETING AT A PUBLISHING HOUSE

PROLOGUE

Every pair of shoes tells a story. The white lace and satin heels that never made it down the aisle—possibly a tragedy, perhaps a great escape. The discovery of mismatched pumps—one black, one blue—a comedy of errors. That pair of sneakers hanging from a wire on the corner of Mulberry and Grand—a coming-of-age tale. The black-and-white saddle shoes circa 1950 in the window of 2nd Time Around—a lifetime of adventures.

If every pair of shoes tells a story, imagine the journeys had by an entire closetful.

Here is one such story—that of a young woman named Esme Nash stepping out in Greenwich Village over twenty-eight steamy days of summer, hoping that life can be changed as easily as a pair of shoes.

Actually, Esme's shoe story begins seven years earlier, in the bucolic college town of Hanover, New Hampshire. . . .

ONE

The Red-Bottomed Shoes

Esme Nash strolled across the Dartmouth Green, committing each sight, sound, and smell to memory. Set to graduate the next day, she had approached every moment of her last weeks of college with this sense of impending nostalgia. She'd savored her last scoop of Morano Gelato on Main Street, her last latte at the library coffee shop, and her final grade (an A+ on her senior thesis in art history titled "The Seven Muses of Gustav Klimt").

As she breathed in the scent of fresh-cut grass, Esme wondered if she would soon start feeling just as sentimental about the smells of NYC. She was pretty sure that New Hampshire would win the olfactory contest but thought New York might take the lead with her other senses.

Esme reached her destination, the Hinman Mail Center, to pick up the package that her mom had now asked her about at least six times. The last package, she noted sentimentally, of her college career. She was also hoping to purchase a poster tube large enough to safely transport the life-size replica of her favorite Klimt painting, *The Kiss*, which had hung on her walls since first-year student move-in day. The golden masterpiece had followed her throughout her four years on campus, and she wasn't about to leave it behind as she started her next big adventure.

Though Esme Nash grew up in a small town in upstate New York, she had always yearned to live in a big city, specifically Manhattan. In a few days' time her dream of doing so would become reality, and she was still pinching herself.

She handed the package notification to the mail clerk and pulled out her to-do list while she waited. Esme loved a good to-do list, or more specifically crossing things off one gave her a sense of control, however out of hand things were.

The frazzled mail clerk returned carrying a shoebox-size package wrapped in brown paper with her parents' return address in the corner. Esme immediately shook it, while the overwhelmed clerk searched for the delivery log.

"It's shoes!" she exclaimed to no one in particular.

"Wait, you have to sign for it," the clerk called out, still searching.

The box most likely contained a pair of Birkenstocks, her practical mother's ideal for walking in graduation. Maybe she had gone with black patent leather straps as opposed to nubuck, to mark the grandeur of the occasion, but Esme knew that would likely be the extent of her extravagance.

There *was* a small chance, though, that the box contained a pair of vintage Christian Louboutin pumps, specifically Pigalles, named for the risqué district in Paris. A used pair of the classic red-bottomed shoes were Esme's dream acquisition, and she and her mom had turned searching for them into a never-ending thrift-shop treasure hunt. They had spotted a few scuffed and scraped red soles in her size over the years, but Esme was determined not to settle for a single scratch that she had not personally inflicted on their shiny red bottoms.

Could her mom have hit the jackpot just in time for her college graduation?

"Sign here!" the clerk shouted.

Everyone was spent by the end of the semester, and this woman was clearly no different. Esme passed on asking for the poster tube. She didn't see any and was not up for waiting around for another search, too anxious to get back to her room and tear open her package. She signed her name, thanked the clerk, and shook her box again. On the way back to her dorm, Esme allowed herself to dream that the box actually contained the sophisticated black patent pointed-toe pumps with the sky-high heels and the trademarked bright red soles. The latter detail was the equivalent of a secret covenant for a future filled with glamour, excitement, and promise.

She pictured wearing the shoes after graduation, on the first day of her prized internship at the Hudson Payne Gallery. She imagined standing in them at the day's end, peering out the window, anticipating the arrival of her boyfriend, Liam Beck. From there they would wander along the narrow downtown streets, holding hands, before ducking into their local haunt for a bite to eat and a glass of merlot.

Liam and Esme had begun concocting their future plans in the earliest weeks of their relationship. Once she discovered that he shared her New York City dreams, Esme fell even harder for the clean-cut, handsome, baseball-playing Alpha Delta from Cape Cod, who she had first imagined to be just a fling. Their vast differences— him at his happiest shotgunning a beer, her at her happiest in the galleries of the Hood, Dartmouth's campus art museum—shrank in comparison to their similar life goals. Never mind that when he kissed her, even after nearly three years of dating, her heart still raced.

She pictured herself kicking off the red-bottomed pumps to climb the gazillion stairs to the fourth-floor Greenwich Village walk-up the two were set to share, even though her mother had gone on and on about the cow and the milk whenever she had brought up "living in sin."

"It's about being practical," Esme had explained, "so that I'll have enough money after rent to buy my own milk!" Practicality her mother understood. Exorbitantly expensive high-heeled shoes, not as much.

Esme couldn't take it anymore. She leaned the package atop one of the ivy-spattered brick walls that marked the old New England campus and ripped off the outer paper to reveal *Happy Graduation* gift wrap and a bright pink card.

Open the card first! she heard her mother insisting.

In typical Maggie Nash fashion, the note was long-winded and filled with praise for her only child: the joy she had given her, the endless pride she had in all of her accomplishments, and a lot of talk of the future and all the changes that were coming for them both. That part left Esme curious regarding her parents' plans for their fast-approaching empty nest.

It ended with:

A gift for walking into your future.

Love, Mom

Those are some lofty words for a pair of Birkenstocks, Esme thought eagerly.

Just as she was about to rip off the wrapping for the big reveal, her phone buzzed. She hoped it was her mom, excited to share the moment with her in real time. But the words *Rochester General Hospital* flashed across her screen, sending her heart pitching to her stomach.

"Hello."

"Is this Esme Nash?"

"It is," she managed.

"This is the intake nurse from Rochester General Hospital. Are you a relative of Henry and Margaret Nash?"

"I'm their daughter."

"I'm afraid your parents have been in an accident."

Esme walked across campus like a zombie, straight to her car, and got in. She didn't cry; she didn't call or text anyone to tell them what had happened. She just turned on the ignition, gripped the wheel, and drove straight home. Six silent hours later she arrived at Rochester General.

While the Dartmouth College Class of 2009 was walking in their commencement ceremony, Esme was sitting in a folding chair outside the ICU waiting to hear the results of her father's third surgery. The hospital social worker approached to discuss burial plans for her mother, before convincing her to go home and get a little sleep. She listened, thankful that someone else made a decision for her after a night of unimaginable ones.

Esme made her way through the hospital parking lot to her car and got in. As the door closed behind her she heard a scream—a loud, piercing, and painful scream. It took her a minute to realize it was coming from her own mouth. The box wrapped in *Happy Graduation* paper peeked out from the floor of the passenger seat, causing the notable accomplishment—college graduation—to enter her mind before floating out again as if it were completely insignificant. She reached for it and tore off the paper, revealing a light brown shoebox with Christian Louboutin's signature scribbled across it in white, the word *PARIS* added auspiciously in one corner. Her hands trembled as she shook open the lid. She pulled out the red felt dust bag and then the shoes—brand-new black patent Pigalle pumps with one-hundred-millimeter heels and the signature red-bottomed soles. She clutched them like a life vest, lay down on the front seat of her car, and whispered, "Thank you, Mommy," before falling off into a fitful sleep.

TWO

The Orange Crocs

SEVEN YEARS LATER

Esme Nash adjusted herself in her seat on the Greyhound bus, wiggling her butt to and fro, while gently pressing her knees into the seat back in front of her. Her intention was to nap for at least the first half of the seven-hour ride to New York City. She wondered if she was too old to sit in this childlike position but couldn't imagine falling asleep sitting upright.

At thirty I will sit properly, she told herself. *One more year to slouch.*

She thought about the name her mother had given her—Esme. Unlike her dad, who tended to fly by the seat of his pants, her mom, like Esme, had always been a planner. Maggie Nash had chosen the name for her future daughter way back in high school, after reading Salinger's short story, "For Esmé—With Love and Squalor." Now, a few days after her father had passed away, making her an orphan like the Esme in the story, she felt a misdirected anger toward her mother. Maybe if she had named her Heidi or Gidget, she would be yodeling in the Alps right now or surfing the waves in Malibu instead of sitting, orphaned and alone, on a Greyhound bus.

She closed her eyes as the bus whirred out of the Rochester depot. Even though she had been up half the night and refrained from having a cup of coffee before the 8:00 a.m. departure, sleep, once again, eluded her. One would think it was from excitement, but Esme knew that it was most likely nerves. She had not left her hometown of Honeoye Falls, or even the Rochester area, in seven years, except for a few trips to New Haven to take her dad to a spinal cord specialist at Yale. Those trips had been a complete waste of time, as the doctors there had the same diagnosis as the ones back home: Henry Nash would never walk again. They also had no scientific explanation for why her father didn't speak. He had not said a word in the seven years between the accident and his passing.

On the previous morning, Esme had sat on the floor of her father's bedroom staring down the last relic of caring for him: a pair of orange Crocs she had bought to wear exclusively in the house, when it had gotten to the point when germs were his biggest enemy. They were all that was left after the men from Home Pro Medical Supply had carried the monitors, the oxygen tank, and, finally, the hospital bed out of the house. She had picked up the Crocs carefully, as if their namesake might inhabit them and take a piece out of her. In truth they already had.

When sitting there, alone on the floor, she admitted to herself that she wasn't doing well. For the first time in a long while, she'd seriously considered calling the grief counselor who had helped her after her mom had died, though she wasn't quite sure this was grief. It felt more like depression. Most of all, she felt demoralized, as if she had no idea what to do or where to be or, quite frankly, who she was anymore.

She had known from the start that death was the endgame for her father—science and the percentages all pointed to it, but she hadn't expected to slowly lose herself as well. With each passing day, the things that were once important to her had slipped away. While getting her hair cut for his funeral, she realized it had been ages since she'd even gotten a trim. She couldn't remember the last time she had shaved her legs, let alone bought a new pair of shoes, and she had let all the art-mag subscriptions, which had once made her feel so hip and up-to-date, lag. She really didn't like who she had become, aside from the fact that she hadn't given up on her father. Henry Nash had become unrecognizable as well; once the funniest person in the room, he died the complete opposite.

Someone at her dad's service had handed her the name of a therapist, and while she had dismissed it at the time, calling now seemed to make sense. She did not know what to do next, and the thought of tackling her minutia-filled to-do list made her want to cry.

She was wearing the cardigan sweater she had worn to the funeral. It was her mother's, and since she had not taken it off for days, she was concerned that she might need to wash it, rinsing away the last hint of patchouli and vanilla that somehow still lingered on it after so many years.

She'd reached into the pocket of the sacred cardigan and felt for the therapist's card, part of the trove bestowed on her at the funeral by mostly well-meaning people proffering unsolicited advice. She read each out loud before flicking them one by one across the room in the general direction of the trash bin like a kid flipping baseball cards.

First up, a card from a real estate agent, obnoxiously placed directly into Esme's pocket, followed by a painfully nasal "Call me when you want to sell this place."

Esme had responded confidently, "I'm never selling my parents' house."

She'd pedaled her legs up and down, to loosen the seal that was forming between her thighs and the vinyl floor, before flicking the real estate agent's card across the room as well. She'd followed that with cards for a medium, an organizer, and a gutter cleaner.

The last was the source of her only laugh in weeks—as if Esme's paralyzed father had been cleaning the gutters for the past seven years, and now that Esme was "orphaned," employing someone to perform this service would be at the top of her list.

The last two cards were for the therapist and a dog-sitting company.

"When my husband died I started fostering dogs," her elderly neighbor had advised before handing her the card. "It was the best thing I did for myself to heal."

At the time, Esme had taken the card for Waggy Tails with an optimistic smile that was completely fake. The last thing she wanted was to take care of another living, breathing thing; yet in the aftermath, she didn't flick it across the room. Instead, she put it back in her pocket.

She'd fiddled around with the therapist's card between her fingers while breathing in and out purposefully in her father's aseptic bedroom. The act was meant to calm her, but the air still smelled medicinal and it did the opposite. She dialed the number, coaxing herself not to hang up as it rang. A machine picked up.

"This is Dr. Aronoff. I will be out of town through the month of August. Please call nine-one-one if you are feeling like you may hurt yourself or—"

Esme hung up before the rest of the message played.

She was not feeling suicidal. In fact, she was not feeling anything. Just empty, alone, and untethered.

Untethered being the worst.

She'd picked up the Crocs and closed the door behind her, anticipating leaving it closed forever.

Then, as she shoved the orange Crocs onto the top shelf of her bedroom closet, the infamous graduation gift from her mother caught her eye. She had pulled the shoebox down every once in a while in the first years after her mom died, but the sight of it always left her in tears. Tears may be an understatement. The act left her sobbing uncontrollably, not just because they were the last gift from her mom; the shoes represented the exact moment when the clock stopped on her life.

She had never been able to look at the box without crying ever since. But then, when she pulled the box down off the shelf, sat on the floor of her closet, and slipped on the shoes, she reacted much differently. She waited for the tears to flow, but none came. It felt as if something in her had switched—specifically, as if something in her had switched back *on*.

Esme barely remembered dialing the number for Waggy Tails, but obviously she had, because there she was, her sacred Christian Louboutin shoebox in tow, on a Greyhound bus headed to New York City to care for a dog named Elvis for the next twenty-eight days. She was hoping to arrive refreshed and ready for anything.

She again begged sleep, but none came.

She gave up and pulled out her phone to make a new to-do list. An old one, from before her dad died, popped up.

- Change PT appt.
- Send in insurance claims.
- Refill meds.
- Ambulette for Thursday.

She permanently deleted the old list from her phone and began a new one—a hopeful hodgepodge of everything she wanted to do and see in New York. It had been ages since she had felt hopeful about anything.

Esme had hung on to hope for as long as she could over the years while caring for her father, but any lingering optimism was eventually beaten out of her by the emotional and physical stress of it all. Her life had become a roller coaster: from too much sleep to sleep deprivation, isolation to complete lack of privacy, feelings of usefulness to feelings of pointlessness. A cacophony of contradictions. She was heartbroken that her father had died, she truly was, but she was happy to be stepping off the roller coaster.

She tried to consider this August in New York as a new adventure, though many of the things she had been meant to do in the city post–college graduation were still on her mind. She made note of them, before listing everything else that she hoped to do and see, including viewing a few of Klimt's old muses who now hung in a museum on the Upper East Side. Reading it over quashed her anxiety and replaced it with excitement—an emotion equally counterproductive to sleep. In the end she drifted off in spite of it all, dreaming of exploring the city with her new furry friend, Elvis. In her dream she was wearing the red-bottomed shoes.

THREE

The Brand-New White Converse Chuck Taylors

Esme woke as the New York City skyline peeked out from the rain-spattered window, and she embraced the feeling of hope. As the silhouette of the city came into focus, she pictured her favorite scene from the movie *Annie*, which she and her friends had watched so many times in middle school that they wore through the tape. Her friends always argued over who would be Annie, or Miss Hannigan, or even Daddy Warbucks, but Esme was only interested in one part—the just-off-the-bus girl with her big solo. When she showed up in the film, Esme would jump off the couch, throw her arms in the air, and belt out, "'NYC, just got here this morning, three bucks, two bags, one me!'"

That's how long she'd been dreaming of this day. Even though she was arriving years behind schedule and not really in the mindset to belt out show tunes, she allowed herself to hum the melody as she exited Port Authority. She stepped onto Eighth Avenue and into the pouring rain, laughing at herself for thinking that she,

Esme Nash, would be greeted by the Rockettes sashaying up Forty-Second Street.

She pulled up her address for the next month and announced it to her cabdriver.

"Two-fifty Mercer Street in Greenwich Village, please."

"OK, lady," he said while slamming shut the window between them and screeching away from the curb. She smiled. At least the cabbie didn't disappoint.

During the harrowing trip downtown, Esme buckled up and thought of the first time she and her parents had visited New York City, over Christmas vacation many, many years before. They had done all the things you were meant to do in New York at Christmas—FAO Schwarz, the top of the Empire State Building, a Broadway show, skating at Rockefeller Center—but Esme had one special request. She wanted to try sushi. At that time there were no sushi restaurants where they lived upstate. They headed to a little place in the Village called Ichiban that the concierge at the hotel had promised was the real deal, and assured her reluctant dad that it wouldn't kill them.

It wasn't the not-fishy taste or the texture or the perturbed look on her mother's face when her father ordered his third sake martini that surprised her, it was the people at the restaurant. They weren't the same people she had seen in the audience at the Winter Garden Theatre or on the observation deck of the Empire State Building. These were real New Yorkers. It was the first time she realized that people actually lived there. That *she* could actually live there.

Now, as the metered fare rose, she stared out the window until suddenly the city became a village—her village for the next twenty-eight days. She crossed her fingers that the cabbie would stop while they were still in the exceedingly pretty part. And he did.

"Here you go, lady. Two-fifty Mercer."

She looked up at the tall brick building on the tree-lined street that would be her home for the month of August. The sun came out as she stepped from the cab. The windshield glistened, the birds chirped, and somewhere in the sky there may have been a rainbow. But Esme didn't notice such things anymore.

She did notice the stifling August heat that the rain did not succeed in tempering. She silently belted out one last stanza from her favorite childhood song.

"Too hot, too cold, too late, I'm sold, again, on NYC!"

As she paid the taxi—fourteen dollars plus a six-dollar tip, which prompted a sincere "Thanks, lady!"—a uniformed man, whose name tag read MIGUEL, came running out to help with her bags.

"Need a hand?" he said without waiting for an answer. She followed him into the lobby.

"Who are you here to see?" he asked.

Esme completely forgot the woman's name—but remembered her charge's name. "I'm here to dog-sit—for Elvis in apartment Eight-D."

"Oh, great. I've been in and out of there taking care of him. Sweet boy. Ms. Wallace left real quick. I think she was headed for rehab, but I'm not entirely sure for what."

"I don't know much about it—other than they needed someone right away," Esme replied, reminding herself never to tell Miguel anything.

"How long will you be here for, if you don't mind me asking?"

"Twenty-eight days."

"See, I was right . . . rehab!"

Where she came from, *rehab* would have been whispered. He said it like her employer was vacationing in Bora-Bora.

He walked Esme to the front desk, where he gave her the keys and had her sign a form left by the Waggy Tails people.

"Elvis is a friendly boy. You'll love him. I already did two walks today—so you're good until bedtime. Everything you need is written down up there, except that he loves when you scratch him behind the ears, and he loves the dog run in Washington Square Park."

On the ride up, Esme realized she had no idea what kind of dog was awaiting her. As she unlocked the door, she braced herself to be knocked down by a mastiff but was greeted instead by a little mop of a thing who was very happy to see her and couldn't have cared less that she was a stranger. She erased all previous thoughts of him protecting her in the big city and made a mental note to add *buy pepper spray* to the list she'd typed up on her phone on the Greyhound.

The third item on the list—*bump into Liam Beck while looking my best*—should have been moved to the number one spot, as speculation of her former boyfriend's whereabouts had been ransacking her thoughts ever since embarking on the "what could have been" tour. While that wasn't how she had billed this adventure when convincing herself to drop everything to skip town and spend a month in the Big Apple, it had quickly turned in that direction.

She used to believe that Liam was her soul mate, mostly on account of the fact that she never stopped thinking about him. Now she wondered if that were true, or if it was more likely that her soul had atrophied at the time of her parents' accident, freezing her feelings for him just where she had left them. Either way she knew one thing—she hated the way it had ended between them and wanted badly to apologize. She wondered if he thought of her, and if so, was it with longing, animosity, or sympathy? Sympathy being the worst.

Surely the title Poor Esme *does not have to follow me for the rest of my life!*

She surveyed the apartment, then sat at the table and read through the list of instructions. Her favorite was:

Elvis will bring you his leash in his mouth when he wants to go out.

"You're a smart little guy, huh?" she asked while scratching his ears.

She was happy to have someone to talk to, even if he didn't talk back.

She dragged her suitcase into the bedroom. The bed looked delicious—high and fluffy and white—like a giant marshmallow. Elvis interrupted her unpacking with his leash in his mouth. She happily obliged.

"Just a short walk," she told him, as it had said on the instructions for evening. "Tomorrow, I promise, I will take you to the park!"

FOUR

The Dirty White Converse Chuck Taylors

As Esme and Elvis left the apartment the next day, she was instantly taken by the morning light jutting in and out of the buildings and trees. The quick-moving angular shadows reminded her of the colorful tube kites that danced with the wind in front of car dealerships and grand openings back home. She watched as people on foot, on bikes, and in cars, moved in and out of the light. Illuminated. The realization that she was no different than them both delighted and distracted her.

This is my grand opening. She smiled hopefully before stepping off the curb into a big black puddle.

The curbside lagoon that, within a week of being a Manhattanite, Esme would easily traverse with grace now left her new white Converse soaked and dirty. She didn't let it douse her mood. She recognized that even seeing the dancing light was a step in the right direction, albeit a damp one.

She had a feeling that if she were to let Elvis lead he would walk her right to the dog run, but she pulled up Google Maps just to be safe.

"Just give me a second to get my bearings, Elvis."

She realized she was now talking to the dog in public, but figured, *Hey, it's New York—who would notice or care?* She typed *Washington Square Park* into Google Maps, and it popped up above the last two depressing destinations she had searched for in Rochester: the mortuary and the funeral venue. She swallowed the lump in her throat associated with their memories.

The contrast between standing on a Greenwich Village sidewalk mere days after standing at her parents' new and old graves was indeed surreal.

"Just keep moving," she said out loud. To an observer it may have looked like she was speaking to the dog, but she was most definitely speaking to herself.

On her roundabout way to the park, the bright red door of a quaint little bookshop where Waverly Place met Tenth Street summoned her. Over the past years, with too many hours inside watching, worrying, and caring for her father, books slowly replaced shoes as her biggest passion. Books took her places, while shoes reminded her that she had nowhere to go. As she browsed the tiny store, she weighed her choices. Diving into a new novel would definitely land her in her comfort zone. A book could be her dinner companion, as it had on the nights she didn't join the nurses for dinner. They usually ate on snack tables in her father's room while watching *Gilmore Girls* or rom-coms on the Hallmark channel. Aside from their taste in television, they all had one other thing in common. They were each desperate to get Esme out of the house, often using the movie plots as a subtle tool to push her to have a life. *Subtle* may be the wrong word. They would say things like "Esme! You are wasting your best years sitting in this house. You were not the one in the accident—your parents were. Go on a date."

Esme would answer back, "My life is not a Hallmark movie!"

Yet here she was, living inside the plot of one. She wrote the synopsis in her head.

Esme Nash spends a month in the quaintest part of Manhattan just around the corner from the life she was meant to be living seven years earlier, before fate stepped in the way.

She put down the novel she was contemplating buying and asked the shopkeeper to recommend a tourist book that wasn't too touristy.

She ducked in and out of a few more stores before picking up a "bagel with a smear," as the *New York like a Native* book proclaimed was the proper way to order one, from the take-out window at the Greenwich Village outpost of the "Iconic sanctuary of sturgeon, Katz and Son."

"*SCHMEAR*," the man behind the counter impatiently corrected her.

She recited the correct pronunciation over and over in her head while he prepared her bagel.

Her heart jumped when she saw the famed arch of Washington Square appear in the distance, leaving her with a long-forsaken feeling: joy. It caused her eyes to well up a bit. She blinked the tears away, and she and Elvis picked up the pace, each equally excited to get to where they were going.

Once in the park, Elvis was clearly in charge, only allowing her to stop for a second to gaze at the giant fountain, watch a juggling unicyclist recite "Gunga Din," and gape at a woman hand-feeding the squirrels. He pulled her straight to the dog run, where she unlatched the gate and let him off his leash. Once inside, he was greeted by other dogs in a way that made her think they were old friends. She felt oddly jealous: it had been so long since she'd been welcomed like that. She sat down on a bench and pulled out her lunch. Within minutes she made an old friend as well.

"Next time you should try the whitefish or the baked salmon salad," an old man said, eyeing her bagel.

Esme smiled, wiping cream cheese from the corner of her mouth, as the man pointed to the name printed on her lunch bag—*Katz & Son*.

"That's my store—well, it was. I sold it five years ago to the Toscani Brothers. Have you heard of them?"

"I haven't," she said, adding, "I'm not from here."

"I can see—by your reading material."

She blushed at the sight of the tourist book peeking out from her purse. She was hoping to present herself in a more indigenous fashion.

The old man continued. "They're the biggest family-run supermarket chain in New York—one of them ran for mayor a few years back."

The chatty old man sat down next to her and reached out his hand. "Sy Katz."

Esme wiped off the remainder of the schmear from her pinky and reached her hand out in return. "Esme Nash. Nice to meet you."

"You, too."

He continued talking as if he were standing at a lectern, not sitting on a park bench.

"The Toscani children wanted to do something a little different, something more hip. Somehow, they found herring hip. I never got it, but I liked the kids, especially the one girl; she had the brains and the palate for it. I taught her everything I know. Well, mostly everything. Can you keep a secret?"

Esme laughed. "Go ahead. I have no one to tell."

"That can't be true, a pretty girl like you. I left out one little ingredient in the whitefish salad so that people would miss me when I'm gone. I want them to say there's something missing here; it must be Sy Katz, but really it's a little bit of kippered salmon."

"Your secret is safe with me, Sy Katz."

She pulled out her book and felt immediately awful for doing so. It wasn't like she had so many people to talk to. Thankfully it didn't dissuade him in the least.

"You know, it's a tricky business, smoked fish. There is a delicate balance between smoke and salt. I personally took a little nibble of every fish and felt its consistency between my fingers before I chose it. It's a science, but you can't really teach it."

"Like a nose in the perfume business," she said, shoving her book back into her bag.

"Exactly. You're a smart girl, too. Where are you from?"

"A small town outside of Rochester, Honeoye Falls."

"Never heard of it. But I like the name, Honey Uy!" They both laughed at his enthusiasm for the last syllable. "Are there falls?"

"There are. The Honeoye Falls are right in the center of town."

"Sounds beautiful."

"It's very quaint." *And small and suffocating.*

"What brings you to town?"

"I'm dog-sitting for Elvis."

As if on cue the dog came barreling over.

"Ohhhh. Catherine Wallace's dog. How long is she away for?"

"Twenty-eight days—now twenty-seven."

As she said it, she wished she'd said a month.

"Rehab?"

Ugh, I'm really throwing this woman under the bus, she thought.

"I don't really know much about it."

"Apparently, the saying that you can never have too many shoes may be wrong," Sy quipped. "My guess—she's got a case of Imelda Marcos Syndrome."

Esme couldn't help herself, curiosity trumping privacy.

"Shoes?" She sat at attention.

What are the odds that I would end up in the home of a shoe-obsessed woman?

"Oddly enough, I was once guilty of the same affliction—but not to that level, thank goodness," Esme admitted.

"It's not that odd—half the women in this city think nothing of sacrificing a paycheck on a pair—though not to Catherine's extent. She has a serious issue, I believe. I've seen the shopping bags at her side to prove it."

"C'mon. That can't be a real thing."

"Compulsive-buying disorder. I once knew a gal who was obsessed with buying oyster plates. And she was kosher. Never even ate an oyster."

It was hard to know if he was trying to make her laugh or not. But she did, and it felt good.

"In any case, that's a great gig you got yourself. I'm in between jobs," he circled back. "I signed a noncompete for ten years with the Toscanis. On my one hundredth birthday, I'm going to open a big fish store right across the street from my old one."

"Really?"

"Maybe. Until then I'm just going to keep coming here every day with Scout. Here, boy. Scout, this is Esme Nash. Give her your paw, Scout."

Scout did no such thing.

"I try to teach him stuff, but I didn't get him till he was nine, and you know, old dogs and new tricks don't go well together. Elvis is younger. They're thick as thieves."

"I can tell." Esme beamed, already feeling attached to her prodigy.

"His mother doesn't socialize much, though. Big entertainment lawyer, always has her nose in a contract or something. But she doesn't fool me. Most of us here, I would say, are on the lonely side—she's no different."

Esme nearly admitted to fitting in perfectly but decided against it. While this man clearly wore his heart on his sleeve, hers was still deeply buried. He revealed enough for them both, and she was happy to listen.

"I shouldn't have agreed to retire at ninety. It seemed so far away until there it was. I didn't know it would be so sad to be old. I was never lonely when I was working. You see that young man over there?"

He gestured to a guy in his fifties, wearing a leather jacket and holding a leash—his Montreux Jazz Festival baseball cap doing an inadequate job of taming his unruly locks.

"Do you recognize him? He was a rock star. His band broke up years ago. He told me that walking that dog saved his life, that if he didn't have to walk him, he might stay home all day."

Esme tried to make out who the mystery man was, but his hat was pulled down too low, and she wasn't particularly adept at recognizing rock stars.

Scout came back over and nuzzled the old man's leg. Sy patted his head, proclaiming, "Man's best friend! We have an appointment—have to cut our visit short. It was nice meeting you, honey from Honeoye Falls! See you soon, I'm sure."

Esme would usually cringe if someone called her honey, let alone honey from Honeoye Falls. She might possibly even say something biting in return. But today she liked it. It felt, to her, like kindness. Kindness laced with a heartache that left her curious about the old man's life.

She smiled and said sincerely, "Hope so!"

She resisted the urge to pull out her book again and just took it all in.

FIVE

The Lanvin Black Patent Leather Mary Janes

On the way home from the park, Esme took a different route, not so much on purpose; more because even with GPS she found Greenwich Village to be completely confusing. When she saw the sign for Bank Street, she started walking west, like a homing pigeon, toward the gallery where she had nailed an interview all those years before.

She arrived at the familiar spot and peered inside. The soaring walls were coated in the brightest white and covered in the poetry paintings of John Giorno. Esme remembered sitting in the dark her first year of college, watching slides of his works flash on the screen at the front of a cavernous lecture hall. Her NYC-born-and-bred roommate was also enrolled in History of Modern Art 101. She'd leaned over and whispered in Esme's ear that Giorno had been lovers with Andy Warhol, Robert Rauschenberg, and Jasper Johns. Esme had never even heard of John Giorno, and her roommate was privy to his illustrious sex life. An *I've seen it all before* vibe seemed to follow her everywhere she went. It was in that moment that Esme realized she would need to work twice as hard to keep up with the other kids at Dartmouth. Top of her class back home, Esme was not used to such a challenge, though not scared of it.

She put her nose up to the gallery window and squinted to read the only painting in clear sight. It read:

DON'T WAIT FOR ANYTHING.

She took it as a sign that she should march right in and introduce herself. She stepped back to check her reflection in the window. It filled her with insecurity.

She remembered her interview at the Hudson Payne Gallery, for which she had dressed in a chic city outfit that her roommate had loaned her, right down to her shoes. She had answered every question like a pro, when in actuality it was the first proper interview she'd ever had. At the time, her only experience had been as a docent at the Dartmouth campus museum for a few semesters and one month interning for the artist Robert Longo. She knew he and the head of the museum had sent along stellar references, but she couldn't help but feel that her roommate's killer pair of Balenciaga boots was the actual reason that she had aced the interview. Her confidence had sprung from her feet.

She looked down at her feet now and nearly cried. There was no way she was going inside. She couldn't get back to Catherine's apartment soon enough.

Will it ever be possible for me to find that self-assured girl again?

Once home, she fed Elvis, took a warm shower, and scoured the kitchen, landing on half a bottle of chardonnay in the fridge and a vast collection of take-out menus. She splurged on sushi from a place on Sullivan Street—hoping to feel like the New Yorkers she had seen in the Japanese restaurant all those years ago. When her dinner arrived, it took her nearly five minutes to recognize that the buzzing sound filling the room was from the doorman downstairs announcing her food delivery, and another two to figure out that she had to hold the button down while she spoke in order for him to hear her. It wasn't the gossipy doorman Miguel, who now seemed to be a saint compared to the grumpy one on the other end of the intercom with zero patience for her ineptitude.

Even with the wine, the big meal, and the long day behind her, she tossed and turned in the marshmallow bed. She remembered what Sy had said—about the woman whose apartment she was living in and her obsession with shoes. She had already peeked into her bedroom closet, where she had found a paltry showing in the shoe department, though her absent employer and Esme did look to have the same size foot. She threw in the towel on sleep and decided to suss out the situation.

Elvis padded behind her as she walked around, opening doors: the towel closet, the laundry closet—no shoes. She rummaged around the floor of the coat closet for a bit, pulling out a cute pair of equestrian-style rain boots and an old pair of UGGs. *Not impressed.* She was about to give up on Sy's shoe theory when she came upon the pantry behind the kitchen. She took a deep hopeful breath and opened the door.

"Sweet Mary Jane!" she proclaimed, grabbing an iconic Lanvin black patent pump and running her fingers over its gathered toe and trademark instep strap.

"Elvis, your mama has a problem indeed!"

Elvis looked up at her like he wished he were sleeping, while Esme wondered if she would ever sleep again. It was as if she had stepped into her very own version of Narnia.

Catherine Wallace had turned her walk-in pantry into a shoe closet. The floor was carpeted in a pale gray with a single silver pouf placed directly in the middle, like a sacred throne for putting on one's shoes. The entire perimeter was shelved, each side color-coordinated by category: heels, flats, boots, and one great big beautiful rainbow of silk and satin dress shoes. Esme grabbed a pair of black Prada sandals adorned with ostrich feathers, sat down on the pouf, and slipped them on. They fit perfectly, which filled her with utter joy, followed by complete panic.

I may never leave this closet.

She stood and looked at her regal feet in the mirror, picturing herself spinning around a dance floor with Liam, who she had been thinking about more and more since arriving in Manhattan. It wasn't like she'd never thought of him over the years—she had—but it was usually when she lay in bed desperate to stop her mind from running in awful directions. She would replace her reality with fantasies of bumping into Liam on imaginary business trips in imaginary hotels in imaginary cities. The mini rom-coms that she dreamed up were much more conducive to sleep than real life.

A pair of Gucci ankle boots whose picture she had recently ripped out of a magazine—a practice she had mostly given up on—caught her eye. They were classic in every way except for the single line of pearls encrusted around each heel. Perfection. She carefully put away the Prada heels and tried on the booties. From there everything got a bit frenetic—though she was mindful of putting each pair back where it belonged before trying another. Pavé crystal-covered Salvatore Ferragamo sandals with his iconic flower heel; Dolce & Gabbana silver plateau platforms embellished with ruby-, emerald-, and amethyst-colored stones; Golden Goose sneakers whose $450 price tag seemed outrageous until she slipped them on and felt as if she had actually discovered the Golden Goose; and a pair of SJP Tuscan-leather pumps inscribed with the words *Hello* and *Lover* on the toe box of each.

If you know, you know; if you don't, you may not be worthy of entering the closet.

About twenty pairs of shoes later, with many more still to go, Esme's mood slowly turned. She sat on the pouf and let the real tears that had not come at the funeral or its aftermath flow. They were not for her dad, or even for her mom, who she still missed like crazy every single day. They were for Esme. For Esme and her feet, for whom she had once had great aspirations. She cried for her lost twenties and for the former promise of her high school senior superlative title: most likely to succeed. She cried for the long-gone confidence that had once allowed her to step into that art gallery and land her dream job. And she cried for the shattered dream of moving to a city with the boy she loved, who she imagined was now a very grown-up, accomplished, and possibly even sophisticated man.

She swung her leg to the side to comfortably unlatch the delicate buckle of the black-and-white tulip-detailed Miu Miu platforms she had gleefully stepped into and decided it was time for bed. She had no desire to continue down the familiar road of gloom and doom—she was tired of feeling sorry for herself and just tired in general. As she slipped the last pair of Catherine's shoes back into place, she spotted them on the shelf above. Her hands began to shake.

Just go to sleep, Esme, she thought, but it was too late.

She picked up a pair of black patent leather red-bottom Louboutins identical to the ones that her mother had bought her for graduation and turned them over. Their red bottoms were scratched and scuffed in a way that indicated they were worn, while hers still remained pristine. She thought about the evolution of her shoes, or lack of evolution, really. If her life had not skidded to a halt, her red bottoms would have been scuffed with memories of productive days at the gallery and fun nights in the city. Her shoes were in the same condition as they had been when she received them. The memories came flooding back.

When Esme arrived at the hospital on that awful day, the intake nurse who had phoned her took her by the arm and led her into a curtained room for privacy.

She slowly explained: "Your father suffered a catastrophic spinal cord injury and is in surgery. He's in very good hands."

The nurse took a long beat before continuing. Esme wondered if it was for her own sake or for Esme's.

"I am so sorry to have to tell you this, but your mother, I'm afraid, is gone."

"Gone, where did she go?" Esme asked, shocked that her mother would leave her father in the hospital alone.

Suddenly, the nurse's soft words seemed cruel. She stopped mincing them and came right out with it. "Esme, your mother is dead."

Esme's feet fell out from beneath her, and the next thing she knew she was sitting in a chair sipping apple juice with a candy striper rubbing her back. The look on her face—pity—rattled Esme. No one had ever looked at her that way before. The intake nurse returned.

"How are you feeling?" she asked softly.

"I'm OK," Esme lied.

"If you feel up to it, you can see your mom now; we kept her here in case you wanted to. Do you?"

Esme nodded her head but was not at all prepared for what she was about to see or the indelible memory it would deposit on her brain. As they walked through the ER, more eyes looked at Esme with pity. She really didn't like it.

"We cleaned her up as best we could, but she is still intubated," the kind nurse said.

Esme didn't fully understand until she saw her mother with her own eyes. A plastic tube jutted out of her throat, only adding further useless pain, she imagined.

As if reading her mind, the nurse said, "They tried to resuscitate her, but the paramedics told me she most likely died instantly upon impact. A broken neck. Your father suffered similar injuries, but below his neck at the C5 vertebra. The difference in his height saved his life."

"Who hit them? Do you know?" Esme pleaded.

"No one. As far as we know, they swerved into a tree. It may have been a drunk driver, but it's just as likely that he swerved to avoid an animal of some sort. We should know more when your father wakes up."

The words felt like they were running out of the nurse's mouth into one of Esme's ears and out the other without stopping to register in her brain. It must have been some kind of survival mechanism, she figured. Images were not as easy to dismiss.

The nurse gave her a once-over. "You're just a kid. Is there anyone else to call—any other family?"

Esme was an only child born to two only children. If there was someone else to call, she couldn't think straight enough to make a suggestion. Though numb with shock, she felt a crushing sensation of someone slowly choking her, squeezing their hands around her neck, only allowing for small slivers of air to pass through to her lungs.

She breathed in a sliver and said, "It's just the three of us." She shuddered and corrected herself. "The two of us, now."

"I'm so sorry," the nurse said, taking Esme's hand in hers with more pity, and added, "And I'm sorry that I called you a kid."

"It's OK." Esme took a deep breath, quietly observing, "I was one this morning."

The nurse put her hand on Esme's back.

"I'll leave you alone with your mother for a few minutes. When you're done, come out, and I'll take you to the surgical waiting room. I'm so sorry."

That last vision of her mother was the first thing Esme's mind brought up when thinking about her for years afterward. She was gray and cold to the touch. It didn't seem like she was there, but Esme spoke to her as if she were, just in case.

"I love you, Mommy" was all she could get out before sobbing and laying her head on her mother's chest. The weight of it all pinned her down. She tried to say more, tried to pull herself away and speak to her mother's face, but the pain of knowing that this was the last time she would see her was too much. She was aware of the nurse waiting outside the door and wondered how long it would be before she would come in to see if Esme was OK. If it weren't for Esme's natural tendency to please, she might never have left the room. She promised her mother that she would take care of her father no matter what it took, just as she knew her mother would have done herself. And she kissed her goodbye. Once she stepped out of the room, she ached to go back in—but what would be the point? It would never be enough.

Outside, she was alarmed to see that same intake nurse in a heated discussion with two police officers. The hair on the back of her neck stood straight as a weird sense of panic filled her belly. She went back in to the safety of her mother for what would be the very last time.

SIX

The Baby-Blue Satin Jimmy Choo Slingback Pumps

Esme was deeply asleep on the floor of the shoe pantry when she heard her phone ringing in the next room. She startled, jumped, and banged her head on the lowest shelf of shoes, knocking a few to the floor. She was still rubbing her temple when she found her phone in the bedroom and answered it with jangled nerves.

"Hello, hello."

It was her father's night nurse, a.k.a. her current BFF, Selena Beaumont. Selena had first shown up at Esme's doorstep about two years earlier. At the time, it would have been hard to tell who was more thrilled to see who. Unlike the *Gilmore Girls* nurses, as Esme had lovingly taken to calling them, she and Selena were the same age. That fact would have been enough to bond over under these unusual circumstances, but they nearly stayed up all night finishing each other's sentences. Selena was saving for med school by working insane hours as a night nurse, so her life was similarly on hold, albeit for much different reasons than Esme's.

"Are you OK? Do you need a nurse?" Selena asked comically.

"Don't tease me! I would be so happy if you came here!"

"I wish. I already started a new job."

Selena hadn't taken a vacation since they met aside from once to visit family in New Orleans. Esme had toyed with going with her but couldn't bring herself to leave her dad, even for a few days. Caring for him was most definitely a two-person job, and insurance barely paid for one. She had always wanted to go to New Orleans. Ironically, now that she was free to go anywhere, she yearned for roots more than wings.

"I banged my head, hold on, give me a second," she said, inspecting herself in the mirror. She was fine, physically at least. She sat down on the bed for what she imagined would be the third degree followed by an analysis of what she should do differently. Selena was often giving Esme her two cents, and she didn't imagine the distance between them or the fact that her father had just died would change anything.

She was right. After Esme was done describing the neighborhood, the apartment, and the sushi she had ordered in for dinner, Selena, in typical Selena fashion, let her know just what she was doing wrong.

"You need to meet people, Esme. The only person you mentioned speaking to was the doorman."

"I just got here. I did meet a nice man at the dog park."

"Single?"

"Most definitely." She neglected mentioning that he was ninety years old.

"That's good, but no more ordering in dinner. You should go out every night. I found a great article on eating out alone in NYC. I'll send it to you."

"I am in mourning, you know."

"You only have twenty-eight days there, put the mourning on pause—like you did living over the past seven years."

It was harsh but true, Esme thought.

Selena softened it a little. "You can properly mourn when you get home. This is meant to be an escape."

What Selena said wasn't all that outlandish. Aside from the fact that Esme had cried herself to sleep on the floor of the closet, she wasn't feeling that sad since arriving in New York. She had experienced the five stages of grief for her father long ago. Denial, anger, bargaining, depression, and acceptance. Acceptance being the most difficult.

She had known that her father would never walk again from the start, but she thought for sure he would talk. Understanding that he wouldn't took much longer to accept. At first she spoke to him constantly, coming right out and asking him about the night of the accident, but eventually she gave up on that and moved to lighter topics.

Dad, would you like me to change this bandage for you?

Dad, isn't this soup delicious?

Dad, it's so nice out, do you want me to open the window?

As time went on, meeting his unexplained silence with her own was less painful than the alternative. What she felt right now was mostly relief—relief and guilt for feeling relieved. She was sure that in due time the finality of it all would hit, and she would go through the five stages of grief again, but for now she decided to be in the moment. After all, what was waiting for her back home—or, rather, what wasn't—would still be waiting there in a month.

Selena brought the conversation back to a pleasant subject. "So, how's the dog?" she asked in a consolatory tone.

"Good. A little mop-like thing."

Esme looked around the bedroom for Elvis. She covered the phone with her hand and yelled, "Elvis, come here, boy!"

Nothing.

She looked under the bed, in the bathroom, and headed back toward the closet. Selena was chatting away about the pros and cons of dog ownership while Esme was irrationally panic-stricken, looking for Elvis. Given her record when it came to her nearest and dearest, she was sure that he'd been cursed by the few ounces of love she'd bestowed upon him over the past twenty-four hours, causing him to have a doggie aneurysm and die on the spot. She headed back to the closet, where she immediately screamed. It was worse. Elvis was sprawled out on the floor of the shoe kingdom chomping on the one-hundred-millimeter heel of a Jimmy Choo baby-blue satin pump as if it were a Texas rib eye. Its mate sat dead in the corner; apparently it had been his appetizer.

"Oh my God. I have to go."

She grabbed the shoes and screamed "Bad boy!" to which Elvis took off with his tail between his legs. Esme inspected the damage, which was considerable, and then googled the cost of a replacement. It was more than a week's dog-sitting salary. She typed *Best shoemaker Greenwich Village*, threw on shorts and sneakers, and dragged a remorseful Elvis from under the bed and escorted him out the door.

Once outside, Elvis immediately perked up and started walking in the direction of the park. Esme, feeling guilty that she had yelled at him, allowed the detour.

"Just a short visit," she said, "and then we are off to face the music."

Esme unleashed Elvis inside the gates and sat down on a bench. The other dog mamas and papas were busy chatting one another up. She could tell from the snippets of conversation that they were all quite friendly. She imagined herself joining in.

Hi, I'm Esme. I have absolutely nothing to add to the conversation, but I can stand here and smile and nod.

She opened up the article Selena had sent on her phone. "Dining Solo in NYC." The third spot on the list, the Mercer Kitchen, was close by. The magazine said it was a great place to people-watch and maybe even spot a Kardashian. Not exactly her comfort zone—which made it a perfect choice.

Esme hadn't gone out much over the years while caring for her dad, but when she did it was usually to the Honeoye Falls Inn, which was not an inn but the local watering hole. Everything about it was just what you would expect, and the polar opposite, she imagined, of the scene at the Mercer Kitchen.

The Honeoye Falls Inn, with its beer-soaked floors, jukebox, and perpetual line at the pool table, mostly catered to local alcoholics and kids home from college. Esme hadn't frequented the bar much in high school, nor did she run there on the first night home on school breaks to meet up with the old gang. Ironically, when she could have been carefree like that, she was too uptight to know it. The act of always pushing herself to run faster, work harder, score higher didn't leave much room for drunken revelry.

Maybe, if her life hadn't turned upside down, she would have stopped at the inn when visiting her parents as a postgrad over Thanksgiving or Christmas to throw back a beer or two with high school friends. And maybe she would have enjoyed herself, even though she had wanted so badly to get out of her small town, and even though the image of her designer shoes sticking to the beer-stained floor made her cringe. She was not in that category anymore. She was now in the category of people who never left Honeoye Falls—the barstool regulars basking in the smell of stale beer and crushed dreams. This included the bartender—a.k.a. the ex-captain of the high school wrestling team whose glory days did not last much longer than his all-county championship, and the former head cheerleader who waited tables at the diner next door and

sometimes stopped in before going home to the child she had reluctantly had on her own at eighteen. While neither of them ever had
much in common with *Esme Nash, Most Likely to Succeed* before, the
new Esme Nash occasionally hooked up with the bartender at the
end of his shift or commiserated with the former cheerleader over
their unexpected turns in life.

That was pretty much the extent of her social life. She abhorred
people feeling sorry for her more than loneliness and pushed away
nearly every friend she'd ever had. She was more comfortable wal-
lowing in the smell of stale beer and crushed dreams.

Elvis took a break from getting his butt sniffed and jumped up
on the bench next to her to smother her face in what she deemed to
be apology kisses. She was thankful he'd been on the receiving end
of the butt sniffs. She didn't even notice Sy and Scout arrive until
they were upon her.

"Fancy meeting you here!" Sy proclaimed, from what she imagined to be a stock of old-man sayings.

Elvis jumped down to greet Scout, and Sy immediately took his
spot. Esme was happy to see them both and smiled to show it.

He patted Elvis on the head. "Good boy!"

"Not today. Look what he did to Catherine's shoes."

She pulled one out of her bag to show him. He inspected the
damage.

"Oy vey. Don't fret. I know the maven of shoe repair!"

"You do? Where?" She whipped out her phone to take it down.

"You'll never find it. I'll take you."

"You're probably right. Everyone says the city is a grid and so
easy to figure out. I've had an easier time in a corn maze."

"That's because the grid starts above Houston Street, wrapping
around the West Village. The streets around here, like Bleecker and
West Fourth, are all pre-grid."

"Well, it's more interesting, but it's much easier to find Fifty-Third and Third than Bleecker and West Fourth."

"You'll never find Bleecker and West Fourth," he said. "They don't meet."

"My point exactly!"

"Come with me. I'll give you a tutorial on the way."

"Are you sure? You just got here!"

"Eh, I'll be back again tomorrow. Let's go."

Esme and Elvis and Sy and Scout set out for the cobbler, with Sy shouting out interesting facts about the neighborhood along the way and Esme taking it all in.

"Eleanor Roosevelt lived right over there in the forties, at number twenty-nine. And Robert Zimmerman stayed at the Washington Square Hotel, right over there, on his first visit to New York. Do you know who Robert Zimmerman is?"

"I do—Bob Dylan," she proclaimed, silently thanking her dad for his tendency to shout out classic rock trivia over the songs playing on the car radio when she was a kid.

"Yup. This place was a haven for poets and artists and beatniks in berets. They were a bit crazy, but it was definitely a step up from when it was a potter's field—hundreds of bodies are buried underneath this park. More than a few poor souls were hung from those trees, too."

"Not quite the peace, love, and bohemia it's known for."

"Very true, it's changed a lot since then. Even the street names have changed."

He noted the history of each one they passed. Esme loved every minute of it.

"Waverly to Christopher was called Factory Street, and West Fourth was Asylum Street."

Esme joked, "That's fitting because it's maddening that a street named West Fourth crosses a street named West Eleventh!"

Sy laughed. "Guess what Bleecker Street was named?"

"I have no idea."

"I'll give you a hint. It's my personal favorite."

She thought for a minute and came up with "Fish Street?"

"Close. Herring Street!"

"Ha!" She looked around, taking it all in. She was so happy to be there. "I'm sure the whole city has changed a lot over the years," she remarked.

"It has and it hasn't. New York is stubborn. It's filled with ghosts who won't let you forget who and what came before you. No matter how it changes, New York is still where it's at. It will always be where it's at."

"You must miss the good old days though, no?"

"Not really. People wax nostalgic about the good old days, but it's really the romance of being young that they miss. Everyone is sentimental for the city of *their* carefree youth."

They walked on, chatting all the way. Sy was so consumed with his tour guide responsibilities that he didn't even notice that Esme had stopped dead in her tracks a half block before. He walked back to meet her where she was staring up at a brownstone building.

"What's up there?" he asked.

"My carefree youth," she mumbled, before explaining, "This is where I was supposed to live after college. Twenty-eight Barrow. Third floor."

"Ah, the story behind the mysterious young lady who appeared out of nowhere at the dog park one day."

She sat down on the stoop and told Sy, in as few words as she could, how she was meant to live there with her old boyfriend Liam, but her parents got into a horrific accident, killing her mother and paralyzing her father. She always said those words without lingering over them, stating the facts with zero emotion. She may as well have been saying, *I'll try these in a size seven.* Her story was usually met with shock followed by sympathy, but Sy's reaction was a bit different from most. She guessed that at ninety he had seen and heard just about everything.

He gave her a consolatory pat on the shoulder and said, "Such tsuris for a young woman," before bounding up the stairs like a teenager, seemingly more interested in her future than her past.

"Which apartment?" he asked.

"Three-A. But it was seven years ago."

"Liam Beck? He still lives here."

"No way."

"Should I buzz?"

"No! Oh my God! No!"

Esme jumped up and hightailed it down the street. Sy did his best to follow her. When he finally caught up, he had a lot to say.

"Esme, I get that something awful happened to you, but it's in the past now. Maybe you want to comb your hair and put on some rouge before you see him, but you must see him."

Esme fought the sudden urge to check herself in a mirror and said, "I'm sure he is happy and taken. I don't need to blow up his life twice. And besides, I'm pretty sure he hates me."

"Oy. This is history repeating itself."

He grew very quiet as they walked down the street. Esme couldn't take it anymore.

"Tell me your story, Sy. C'mon, I told you mine."

"OK. But only because it should serve as a warning to you. A lesson from an old man to a young woman in what not to do in life."

"I'm ready."

"You sure? It's a long one."

"Nothing but time."

"OK, so . . . It was Rosh Hashanah 1942."

"1942!" Esme laughed.

"I told you—long story." He smirked in a way that made her picture him as a young man. "I had skipped shul to work on my sailboat docked down in Sheepshead Bay. I'd bought it and refurbished it with this real nice fellow Mel Schott, who I'd met at Sea Scouts."

"Sea Scouts?"

"Yes, it's like Boy Scouts, but on the water. That's how Scout got his name. Everyone assumes *To Kill a Mockingbird*. Anyway, Mel had the money, I found the boat, and we fixed it up to flip it. I was real jazzed about the whole thing and excited to leave my mother with some cash before I went off to the war. I had signed up for the Coast Guard, at just sixteen."

"Sixteen!"

"I lied about my age, which wasn't unheard of back then. Everyone wanted to fight the Nazis. When I see a sixteen-year-old kid now, I can't imagine such a thing—and my poor mother letting me go."

Esme shook her head in amazement as he continued.

"So Mel showed up that afternoon with his neighbor, a girl named Lena Leven. When they first walked up, I was kind of sore about it. He said he'd be coming with a friend, and then he went and brought a girl with him. I was annoyed and not so nice about hiding it. Lena could tell, and it somehow made her more determined to be useful."

He stopped on the corner. "I'm hungry, you?"

"I could eat."

"OK, let's make a pizza detour."

"I can go for a piece of pizza."

"It's a *slice*, not a *piece of pizza*. New Yorkers don't have time for such long-windedness."

"Says a man who began his story in 1942."

"Touché." Sy laughed.

They walked over to Carmine Street, and Sy directed her to a bench across from Joe's Pizza.

"Watch the boys," he said, before returning with two slices.

The warm, gooey pizza may have been the best she'd ever had.

"Pretty good, huh?" he said as if reading her mind. "For a buck extra they add the fresh mozzarella—you like?"

"Mmmmm. So good, thank you."

"My pleasure. Where were we?"

"With Lena and Mel on the boat. 1942—"

"So Lena had never been on a sailboat before," he continued. "But she took to it like nobody's business. Once we got far enough out and the wind slowed down, I took out some sandwiches—dark pumpernickel bread with butter and sliced smoked salmon—that I'd made back home. Lena was so hungry from all the work and the sea air, I guess, that she ate two. I had never seen a girl eat like that. Even though she was famished, she ate like a lady. She took small bites and wiped the corner of her mouth with a napkin after nearly every one."

Suddenly self-conscious, Esme reached into the bag to grab a napkin, laughing as she wiped tomato sauce from the corner of her mouth. Sy laughed, too.

"Manners and etiquette were a whole different ball game back then. Even the poor kids in my neighborhood were taught all that stuff, right along with math and English."

Esme smiled with a mouth full of cheese.

"She had a beautiful smile—like you. A beautiful mouth with thin pink lips. And jet-black hair so thick that the wind didn't even muss it. And her eyes, her eyes were the color of a purple sky during that sliver of time between day and night."

"The violet hour!" she exclaimed, familiar with the enchanting time of day.

"Exactly."

Esme pictured a young Elizabeth Taylor as Sy continued.

"I remember thinking that I wished I'd brought dessert. I never eat dessert, but I always leave room for it."

"Really? I would eat dessert first if I could."

"I have more of a salt tooth than a sweet tooth."

He took a break to eat his pizza while Esme fed Scout and Elvis little pieces of her crust. When he began again, he seemed sadder, almost bereaved.

"Lena and Mel were from another world, an entirely different Brooklyn than I was from. My friends and I used to chip in to buy a twenty-five-cent Spaulding to play stickball. When the damn thing would roll into the sewer, we would have to save up for weeks for a new one. She had a horse—her own horse! I knew that I should steer clear of her, especially since I was set to be leaving soon, but by day's end I was smitten. I had no idea that there was a much greater roadblock ahead of us than our different lots in life."

His face dropped, and though they had only just met, Esme could tell that his whole mood had turned. He stood up and collected their mess, folding the napkins neatly as if they were clean before throwing them out.

"You done?" he asked abruptly.

"Yes." She sensed she should drop it but couldn't help herself. "What was it? What was the roadblock?"

"Next time. Scout's losing steam, and the shoemaker's right down the block."

Esme could tell it was Sy who was losing steam. She resigned herself to the fact that she was not hearing the end of his story just yet and followed him down the street.

SEVEN

The Even-Dirtier White Chuck Taylors

Stepping into Berger's Stitch and Shine was like stepping back in time. The linoleum floor was clearly original, as was the proprietor, a woman named Hadassah Berger, or Mrs. Berger, as she preferred to be called. Polaroid pictures of famous people and their shoes were thumbtacked to the walls, making up a collection to rival Andy Warhol's. Sy sat in one of the only empty folding chairs that lined the narrow shop for those waiting their turn, while Esme tried to make out who was who. He pointed out a picture of former mayor Ed Koch holding a pair of loafers, and one of Allen Ginsberg in a pair of muddy boots.

"Bet he wore those to that hippie concert in the Catskills."

"Woodstock?" Esme laughed, and laughed again, thinking that her only friend in New York City predated even Woodstock.

She noticed a picture of Village resident Matthew Broderick and started searching for his wife, the ever-reigning Queen of Shoes,

Sarah Jessica Parker, while Sy began pumping her for information about Liam.

"Enough with all this ancient history, I have some more questions about this Liam fellow."

There was no way that Esme was giving up on the rest of his story, but she would give him some time to recover before bringing it up again.

"Fire away," she said, while craning her neck up to the top row of photos: Liv Tyler with a pair of red satin pumps, a young Tim Robbins with cowboy boots, and Rachel Maddow with a pair of wing tips. She sat back down and scanned the crowd, hoping to spot a celebrity in person, one worthy of reporting back to Selena on their next call.

"Why did you and Liam split?"

It was a good question. One that Esme had thought about often over the years, daydreaming about an alternative universe in which she had accepted Liam's offer to give up New York City and all of his plans to be by her side. She would picture him coaching baseball at Honeoye Falls High by day before coming home to the little woman and her disabled father every night, a smaller life than either of them had dreamed of. One she knew he would eventually resent her for.

Liam and his parents had come to her mother's funeral, with a few other college friends and the contents of her dorm room in tow. Most of that day was a blur to Esme, who had felt more like a puppet on a string than a human being navigating the greatest loss of her life, but she remembered her conversation with Liam clearly. Back at the house, they escaped to her childhood bedroom, where she could see, even through her grief, that he was filled with anxiety. Liam had put many summers into his plan to move to New York. He had literally been working toward it since the eighth grade, and there was much more hanging on it for him than the acquisition of designer shoes. She couldn't bear to take him down with her. As painful as it was for her, she cut him loose right away. Her heart tightened as she spoke as directly as possible.

"Liam, I appreciate that you came here, really I do, but it would be much easier for me if you went to New York as planned without me. I have to stay here and take care of my dad."

She wished she were saying it in the token way one does when they offer up something that they don't really mean, but she meant it. He answered it as if she didn't.

"I knew you would say that, Esme, and I already spoke to HR at Miller/Meyer. They said due to the circumstances I could defer the training program for a year. Maybe you can do the same thing?"

She refused to let him ruin his life, and if he did it anyway, she knew he would regret it—regret her. She pulled strength from a place she didn't even know existed and stood firm.

"This is not a year kind of thing; this is my new life."

"I could come here on weekends?"

If he came on the weekends she would have something to look forward to. She wanted to give in, wanted to agree to the lesser punishment in what was feeling like a life sentence, but she couldn't do it.

"That's not going to work, either; you will be working crazy hours, and besides, hearing what's going on in your life while I'm changing bedpans wouldn't be fair to either of us."

"There will be nurses to do that."

They both knew that wasn't the point and that she was most likely going to face unthinkable challenges.

He patted the seat next to him on her bed for her to sit down. She was so tired. She knew one touch from him would crush her resolve. She wished she were the kind of person who could take him up on his offer, but she loved him too much for that. She had no idea how she would get through this without him, but she would have to. She shook her head, locked her legs, and pressed her feet into the shag rug, determined not to cave. He held his phone up in the air.

"Look, I can rent an apartment right in town, much cheaper than New York City, that's for sure. One of them even has a pool."

She knew how stubborn he was. She would have to be mean or he would never leave.

"Yes, because there are so many pool-worthy days in Rochester," she quipped.

She dug her thumbnail into the palm of her hand to try to redirect the pain of losing him, too. With everything spinning out of control, she needed to do this one thing on her own terms.

"Liam. I'm sorry to tell you this with all that's happened, but I've been having second thoughts about us moving in together."

"Well, that's OK, because I can take that apartment and you can live here—with your dad."

She looked him right in the eyes. "I'm sorry, Liam—I didn't say that right. It's not the apartment. I'm having second thoughts about us."

He looked like someone had punched him in the stomach—immediately green and short of breath. He barely eked out the words "Since when?" when one of her mother's friends came to the door, miraculously saving her.

"Esme, Reverend Connolly wants to speak with you."

"OK, thank you."

Liam stood up, wiping quick tears from his eyes. She turned to him.

"You have a long drive ahead of you. You should go."

He shook his head in disbelief.

"Just go, Liam. Please don't make this harder than it is."

It was rushed and cruel—the breakup equivalent of a drive-by shooting.

It also may have been the exact moment when she felt the wall go up around her heart.

"I couldn't ask him to abandon his dreams for me," Esme told Sy.

He nodded in complete understanding.

"You're young. There's still plenty of life left for you both. Maybe together."

"I'm sure he's moved on by now."

"Don't forget, he is still living in that same apartment."

She hadn't forgotten, even for a second. Now she was the one who had had enough talking about the past. It was obvious, but Sy asked her one more question anyway:

"Does he come from a good family?"

"Why do you want to know that?"

"It's important. If I'm going to encourage you to get back with him, I want to know he's from good stock, and not to point out the obvious, but you are a little lacking in the family department."

She had loved Liam's parents, and they knew her before her life had imploded. She had visited them twice on the Cape, where Liam grew up. She could have leaned on them when need be—and need be a lot.

If she were to meet someone's parents now, she could only imagine the prep that would go into it.

Don't ask about Esme's parents, they are both dead.

Perhaps even *Mom, Dad, this is my damaged new girlfriend who will probably stand at the door waiting for me every night consumed with worry that I've been hit by a car or abducted by aliens or found myself in the epicenter of an earthquake, and she will pass all that trauma on to our future children.*

She didn't bother revealing these concerns to Sy.

"He's from good stock," she said with a bit of melancholy, adding, "But I came here to find myself, not him."

"Next!" Mrs. Berger shouted, sending a wave of panic through Esme and ending the conversation, for now. They stepped up and faced her at the counter. She was a round woman with red rouged lips and a line of foundation weaving in and out of her chins. Lucky for Esme, she was happy to see Sy.

"Sy Katz!" She leaned over the counter and looked at his feet. "Still wearing those Hush Puppies circa 1970, I see."

"If it ain't broke . . ." He smiled in a flirtatious way that made Esme wonder about their history.

Sy pulled out the war-torn Jimmy Choo pumps and placed them on the counter as if they were standing in front of the great and powerful Wizard of Oz.

"Esme is here from out of town—she's dog-sitting for the month, and this little guy mistook them for a *Choo* toy!" He pointed to the label and added, "Maybe he can read!" His smile widened, and his cheeks blushed as he relished his own joke.

Esme imagined he must have been holding on to it since the dog park—waiting for the perfect audience. She laughed, and he even got a chuckle from Mrs. Berger, who piped in with her own punch line.

"He can read, but he can't spell."

Her mood soured as she inspected the damage. She eyed Elvis from where she stood, waving her finger at him. Elvis bowed his head and quickly hid behind Esme.

"I know that dog. This isn't his first offense."

"A little warning from Catherine would have been nice," Esme complained to Sy, happy to deflect some of the blame.

"I can repipe them and rewrap the heels, they'll be good as new," Mrs. Berger promised.

"You're kidding!" Esme exclaimed, obviously relieved.

"Not at all. I'm glad someone got enjoyment out of these shoes—they were a Princess Di favorite, you know. The woman who owns them treats them like they belong in a museum. Shoes are meant to be worn!" She looked over the counter at Esme's dirty sneakers.

"You look to be about the same size. Help yourself to anything in that broad's closet and bring them back to me if they need cleaning."

"I couldn't," Esme said, meaning it.

"Well, you're never going to get anywhere exciting in this town in a pair of dirty white sneakers." She handed her a ticket, adding, "Ready on Tuesday," followed by a loud and dismissive "Next!"

"She really took a shine to you," Sy said with a smirk as they left.

Esme laughed. "You're on fire today!"

"Not bad for an old guy, huh?"

Outside, the August heat felt more oppressive than before. Sy ruffled both Elvis's head and Esme's before bidding them adieu.

"What about the rest of the story?" Esme protested.

"You know where to find me," he responded, adding, "So long for now," before heading home for what Esme imagined was a well-deserved nap.

EIGHT

The Bottega Veneta Quilted Magnolia Lidos

Esme laid out her black capris, a black silk tank, and her Nine West gladiators in anticipation of keeping her promise to Selena to go out on the town. They were similar to a wrap sandal that had been a Meghan Markle go-to when she had first been photographed dating Prince Harry, and even with nowhere to go, Esme had been thrilled when she found them. Before discovering the Temple of Sole, she'd actually thought her shoes were all that. Catherine Wallace's den of iniquity had tempered that joy.

Esme was all for the shoes stealing the show. Her taste in clothes was simple and basic. Not basic in the disparaging way that hipsters use the word, but basic in a minimalist way. She possessed a personal style that did not bow to trends. A button-down oxford shirt, straight-legged jeans, black capris, a few white tees, and her favorite little black dress were her mainstays. It was a wardrobe that, while not expensive, fit in just fine in the city. Her roommate from college said that, aside from not owning a blue-and-white-striped marinière, she dressed like a French girl. She had actually seen one of the fashionable tees in a cute shop around the corner and was thinking of treating herself to it.

She had already thrown back a shot from Catherine's massive bottle of Casamigos tequila for courage and was halfway through rereading the list of go-to spots to dine alone in New York when her cell phone rang.

"Hello, is this Esme Nash?"

"It is. Who's this?"

"It's Catherine, Catherine Wallace. Waggy Tails gave me your number. I'm calling to check on Elvis."

"Oh. Hi, Catherine. Nice to meet you. Elvis is great. We went to the dog park twice already, and he is eating well."

She thought of the shoe incident but decided to refrain from mentioning it, worried that it might be triggering for someone with a shoe addiction.

"I felt awful leaving before you got there, but it couldn't be helped," Catherine continued.

"Don't worry, I understand," Esme said in a way that implied she knew the deal. And apparently Catherine had been living in the building long enough to know that nothing was a secret around Miguel the doorman.

"Let's not mince words. Miguel told you why I was away for the month?"

Esme was conflicted, not wanting to rat out Miguel but happy to skip the awkward explanation. She went with the latter. "Yes, sorry, he did."

"I figured as much. Well, I imagine you have snooped a little and found my stash. Feel free to help yourself."

"Really? I couldn't."

"Please, it's actually better for me in the end if you do."

Mrs. Berger's words—*you're never going to get anywhere exciting in this town in a pair of dirty white sneakers*—ran through her mind. She wondered if her Nine West sandals would have garnered a similar reaction. As much as Esme liked them, she imagined they might not cut it at the swanky Mercer Kitchen.

"Thanks so much. I just may take you up on that."

There was an awkward pause in the conversation. Esme filled it with a question.

"So, is there anything else I should know about Elvis?"

"Not really. He loves when you scratch him behind the ears. And when I leave him alone I usually give him a bone, so he doesn't get into trouble."

Now you tell me, Esme thought, but said, "That's good to know. Thanks."

Another awkward silence. Esme didn't think it was right to end the conversation, but she was at a loss and badly wanted to move on to the shoe selection part of the evening.

"Anything else?" she asked cheerily.

Catherine laughed. "Sorry. They let me call to check on my dog because I was anxious about him. I guess I'm trying to milk the phone allowance for all I can."

"I'm game," Esme obliged. "So how's it going?"

She laughed again. "Please, if I talk anymore about myself, my head may explode. Are you from the city?"

"No, way upstate—just outside of Rochester. This is a real adventure for me—thanks."

"What do you do, besides dog-sit?"

"I'm trying to figure that out, actually. I've spent the past seven years taking care of my dad. He died last week. I was meant to have started at the Hudson Payne Gallery back then. I'm thinking of getting back into that."

"Oh, I'm so sorry about your dad. I hope Elvis is giving you a lot of love; he's good at that."

"He is. He definitely misses you, though," she said, thinking Catherine needed to hear it.

"Thanks. He is kind of my best friend. OK, they're motioning for me to hang up. I will check in again next week."

"Nice talking to you. Good luck!"

"Thanks. You, too."

Esme excitedly entered the sacred shoe pantry to transform her outfit from basic to brilliant. There were too many options to choose from, so she spun herself around a few times, pin-the-tail-on-the-donkey style, and stopped. Her eye was immediately drawn to a pair of magnolia square-toed quilted Bottega Veneta mules. She had seen them before, in that exact color, on the pages of *Vogue* in the waiting room of one doctor's office or another. She remembered lighting up at the image of the classic quilted shoe that somehow managed to exude both sex and class. At the time her enthusiasm had been quickly extinguished by her reality. Wearing them out in NYC would literally be a dream come true.

She slipped them on—perfection!

The *click-clack, click-clack* of her heels on the hardwood floor sounded like castanets, encouraging her to do another shot of tequila in their honor before heading out the door.

A s Esme traversed Houston Street, crossing from the Village to SoHo, the pavement changed from cement to cobblestone, along with the whole vibe of the neighborhood—from bohemian to haute couture. She gazed into the windows of Dolce & Gabbana and Balenciaga before finally arriving at the number three spot on the "Dining Solo" list, the famed Mercer Kitchen, housed in the equally famous Mercer Hotel. Dozens of paparazzi fanned out into the street, waiting for someone who she had probably never heard of but every other millennial pushing thirty probably had. It didn't seem like the kind of place frequented by the cast of *Gilmore Girls*, one of her only reference points as of late. She shook off the memory of the endless evenings watching TV alongside nurses and her tormented father and entered with all the confidence of a girl in thousand-dollar shoes.

The subterranean restaurant could best be described as industrial chic. Black, slick tables contrasted with exposed brick walls. A cloudy glass panel overhead revealed fuzzy silhouettes of sandals and heels and loafers of the people walking on the sidewalk above. She took in the room; everyone was wearing black.

The maître d' directed her to the bar area, where she angled her way to an open stool. On one side sat a man with his back toward Esme who was clearly enthralled with the woman to his right. Judging by her body language, the infatuation seemed one-sided. To Esme's left sat the only two not in black: blond and brunette thirtysomethings with Texan accents and a host of shopping bags at their feet.

The blonde asked the cute bartender, "Would it be at all possible for you to charge my phone?"

"We're really not supposed to, but I have a secret place," he said. He took her phone and charger and disappeared with it.

The brunette snickered as soon as he was out of earshot. "I have a secret place, too. I wonder if he could find it."

"You're such a tramp, Holly, and he's wearing a wedding ring."

Holly held up her equally betrothed finger.

"So? I doubt he's really married. The bartender I slept with here last summer said the whole waitstaff wears fake rings to discourage the patrons from fraternizing with them. Flirting is good for business; follow-through, not so much."

"All hat, no cattle."

"Exactly."

Esme held back a laugh and perused the drink menu. It may as well have been written in a foreign language. *Raspberry Lychee Bellini, Concord Boulevardier, Dante's Negroni.* She had no idea what anything was. The bartender, who had returned from his errand, seemed to notice.

"If you don't like anything on there, I make a mean mojito."

She smiled. "That would be perfect, thank you."

He got to work smashing mint with a mortar and pestle. It was as close as she had gotten to food all day. She grabbed a handful of bar nuts and thought about ordering the tuna pizza with wasabi cheese that the article had touted as "a must." In the meantime, the ladies to her left were being hit on by a couple of European suits, who invited them to a table. The brunette said goodbye to the bartender with a wink and a promise.

"I'll come back for my phone." *Wink.*

He smiled back at her very sincerely, but not in a flirty way. He was pretty good-looking, this bartender. Esme took note of his wavy black hair, dark eyes, and whitening-strip smile. He looked a bit like George Clooney. Not the current version, habitually besuited beneath a crown of more-salt-than-pepper hair, but the younger, shaggier, less-intimidating version. He flashed his nondiscriminating Crest-whites at Esme as he placed down her drink.

I guess that smile is for everyone, she thought cynically.

"Here you go, my special mojito."

Special mojito, special hiding spot—Esme was beginning to think she might dislike him.

"What's so special about it?" she asked, contemplating her decision.

"It's a secret recipe that I learned in Cuba."

Of course he did. Yuck. She was feeling awkwardly alone with the ladies on the left gone and the man on the right with his back to her, so she continued the conversation, even though he seemed to be a tool. If there was one thing that she still knew, it was people. She was a great judge of character, and guys like this, red-blooded and able to muddle mint, were rarely for real.

"When were you in Cuba?" she asked.

"I went for my junior year abroad at Brown and got sidetracked— I fell in love."

"With the country or your wife?" she asked, acknowledging his ring. The word *wife* seemed to jar him, leaving her to believe that the women to her left had been correct about his ruse.

"Both," he answered earnestly.

"So did you drop out of school?"

"I finished eventually. I'm starting law school in the fall at NYU. It worked out well. I'm much more in touch with myself now than I was at twenty-two."

Esme physically shuddered at the dreaded *in touch with myself* comment. She had no clue as to who she was anymore or who she wanted to be.

The man on her right kept flying into her space, while a husky type with strong cologne and a pornstache slid onto the stool on her left. She looked down at her shoes, silently apologizing for the uneventful night, when the new guy barked his order at the bartender.

"Two shots of Patrón Platinum, please."

Young George Clooney, as she had now christened him, had a real flair with his pour. He began from about two feet in the air and only lifted the bottle up at a small angle before tilting it back down and pouring the second shot. It wasn't Cirque du Soleil, but it was entertaining. The husky man passed the shot to Esme and introduced himself.

"Here you go, bellissima. No one should drink alone."

She surprised herself with a witty comeback. "No one's really alone at a bar in Manhattan."

"Let's we toast to that," he said with a hint of broken English. He lifted his shot to hers. She complied. His name was Marco, and he seemed like a harmless enough man to do a shot with. His *bellissima* comment made her think he was Italian, but it turned out that he was from one of her favorite cities, Lisbon.

For some reason she introduced herself as Catherine and said she was an attorney who lived in the Village with her dog, Elvis. When she said it, she felt good about herself, accomplished. Not that she had ever wanted to be a lawyer. The Portuguese man seemed like he couldn't care less about her professional status, but Young George Clooney caught it and seemed duly impressed. Before she knew it she had done two more shots, and she couldn't understand where her tuna pizza with wasabi cheese had got to.

She asked the bartender, "Is my pizza almost ready, you think?"

"You didn't order one," he said with genuine concern. "I'll put one in now if you want."

She shook her head; she wasn't sure what she wanted. Her stool at the bar was beginning to feel like it was aboard the *Titanic* in rough seas. Just as she was ready to jump ship, Marco excused himself to go to the men's room.

"Go nowhere," he commanded.

As soon as he was out of sight, she quickly disobeyed. She dropped some cash on the bar, eyed the exit, and made her way toward it, concentrating on her every step in the magnolia quilted heels as she did. Once up the stairs and out the door, she willed herself in the direction of Catherine's apartment and the comforting promise of the porcelain goddess that she feared was her destiny. She was very worried about the shoes and considered removing them and walking home barefoot but realized that was crazy, even by New York City standards. The night air felt good on her face. She was grateful for the small breeze and the fact that she was only a few blocks from home.

The first steps were tough; she rested against the side of the hotel and envisioned making it back to the apartment. She was angry with herself for not paying attention to her tequila intake. She despised drunkenness and vomiting. College was the last time she remembered being in this unfortunate position. Liam would joke that she would rather stick a sock down her throat and roll around moaning in agony for hours than throw up. She was afraid there weren't enough designer socks in all of SoHo to influence the outcome of her evening's excesses on an empty stomach. Out of the corner of her eye she noticed the cute, albeit full-of-himself, bartender dumping a pail of ice onto the cobblestone street. She stood up straight, determined to walk by him with dignity. She was just seconds from a clean getaway when the Portuguese guy grabbed her arm.

"Hey, bella, where are you off to?"

She answered with locked lips, scared of what opening them would release.

"Heading home—bye—thanks." She smiled a closed-mouth smile and focused on her departure. He didn't let go of her arm.

"Bye, thanks?" he asked, clearly annoyed.

"Yes. Nice meeting you," she added, hoping to soften whatever rejection his tone indicated that he was experiencing.

"Where I come from, if you buy a woman a few shots you expect a little something in return."

Despite her fear of vomiting, she now wished she was one of those girls who could do it on command, thereby giving him a little something in return, but she wasn't.

"I have a room right in the hotel. Come up for a nightcap?" he added, still holding her arm. She was in no shape to argue and just wanted to keep heading home, but she started to worry that he might follow her. She considered hailing a cab, but the thought of getting into a moving object felt quite disagreeable. Panic set in, just as the sidewalk began to spin and the bartender approached, saying everything she wished she'd been able to.

"I think the lady said she wanted to head home."

Marco's hand grasped her tighter as his pornstache replied, "None of your business, man."

"It is actually my business. It's everyone's business."

"Oh, so the man I tipped for her drinks is also her knight in shiny armor," he said.

"It's *shining* armor," the bartender answered with a mocking smirk.

A good thing for Esme, as Marco released her arm. Not such a good thing for Young George Clooney, as Marco reached that same arm back as far as he could and slugged him with it. Esme didn't know if the bartender saw stars, but she surely did. They were the last things that she remembered before passing out on the sidewalk.

NINE

The Morning-After Flats

Esme woke up cursing Catherine's window treatments as the sunlight pierced her hungover eyes like tiny daggers. She was usually quite in control of her drinking. If she were to do an inventory of her morning-after regrets, they would likely amount to three, present morning included. Her hair smelled of vomit, her teeth felt as if they were covered in orange shag carpet from a Motel 6, and for the first time in her life, she couldn't remember how she got home.

Elvis jumped onto the bed and curled up on the pillow above her head. She pushed his front legs a bit farther down, over her eyes like a sleep mask. Perfect. Where had he been all her life? She dozed off for a bit and awoke with the same disgust she had felt before, minus the sun's daggers. She didn't want to face the bathroom mirror but knew she would have to.

I can't lie in bed with a dog on my head forever, she thought. *Or can I?*

Maybe that's how Catherine Wallace spends her weekends. Elvis definitely seemed game.

She brushed her teeth in the bathroom, where the smell of coffee lingered, triggering a desperate yearning for a cup. She weighed her options: going out into the searing sun and getting one, or begging the coffee shop on the corner to deliver. That would be a true native New Yorker move, but it felt a bit pathetic, and from what she remembered about the night before, she had just about reached her limit on pathetic. She decided she would put on her sunglasses, find a pair of morning-after flats, and hit the street.

Everything hurt, from her pounding head to her aching toes. She knew the cure for both. Two Advil and a pair of fur-lined blue velvet Gucci slippers that she had lusted after in magazines for years. She never imagined having an occasion to wear them, and now, in the August heat, a quick jaunt to the coffee shop would just have to do. She headed to the closet for her fancy morning-after flats. She may have felt like crap, but her feet would look like a million bucks—or at least the even grand that their price tag reflected. Once again, she smelled the distinct aroma of fresh-brewed coffee as she stepped into them.

Her nose dragged her to the kitchen, where, like some sort of Christmas miracle, a nearly full pot of fresh-brewed coffee sat. Her reaction quickly morphed from excitement to panic. She heard noises coming from the living room and racked her brain.

What happened last night?

The confrontation with the Portuguese guy began to come back to her, and she felt a chill of fear run down her spine. She peered around the kitchen door.

"Hey, good morning," Young George Clooney, the bartender, said, smiling while taking stock of Catherine's books.

Elvis, who Esme would now deem the most fickle dog in the world, was curled up by his feet.

He held a book in his hand, his index finger stuck in the middle like a bookmark. Her panic turned to relief and then back to panic. She was relieved that it wasn't the guy from Lisbon but was quickly mortified by her lack of memory. She had always thought that being too drunk to remember what happened was some kind of sorority-girl myth. At least she could console herself with the fact that she was still wearing the clothes she'd gone out in.

"Wonderful collection of books." The bartender pointed to a row of political biographies and legal tomes. "I thought you were joking when you told that guy you were a lawyer."

"Why would I joke about that?"

"It's actually a common barstool phenomenon. People often sit down and make up whatever the hell they want."

"Well, not me. I'm a lawyer," Esme stated, with an obvious air of self-doubt.

"I see that—where did you study?"

She shot a quick glance at the shelf where Catherine's diplomas sat. "Undergraduate at Maryland, and Fordham Law," she answered, too loud and too late.

Doubt registered in his eyes. "I'm surprised you didn't mention being a lawyer to me last night, when I first mentioned law school."

"About last night," she changed the subject. "We didn't . . ."

"No, absolutely not."

She was relieved. "But you slept here?" she asked, with a definite tone of disapproval in her voice.

"On the couch. You pretty much begged me to stay. I think you were petrified of throwing up again."

That did sound like her.

"That doesn't sound like me," she said, unwilling to give an inch.

"You were a bit liquored up, and I got this black eye defending your virtue. A little gratitude maybe?"

She saw the slight bruise below his eye. The events of last night were slowly coming back to her.

"I do remember a bit. Thank you for defending my virtue." She looked at the book in his hand, *Profiles in Courage*.

"You were very . . . courageous," she added. He looked down at the book and smirked.

"I see you're a big JFK fan . . . Catherine." He said her name as if it were an accusation. Now she was determined to go forward with her ruse, though she had no idea why.

"I am. I collect books on our nation's thirty-fifth president," she said, silently thanking her fifth-grade teacher, Mrs. Sachs, for making the class memorize their order.

"Interesting. I took a class on Kennedy's letters in college. We went on a field trip of sorts to his library. Have you been?"

Her father used to say, "Don't back up bullshit with bullshit." She took his advice.

"I have not," she answered honestly.

He held up the book.

"Do you think he really wrote it?"

"I do." It said so right on the cover: *Profiles in Courage*, John F. Kennedy.

"Which senator's essay is your favorite?"

Now she had no idea what the hell he was talking about. None. Zero. She was toast. Just as she was about to admit defeat, the phone rang. At first she was relieved: Esme Nash, saved by the bell. But by the second ring she realized that this phone call could all out bury her.

Why do I care so much what this guy thinks anyway? What is wrong with me?

The bartender brazenly grabbed the phone. "Wallace residence."

He listened and shook his head a few times before holding it out for Esme.

"It's Kurt Vaughn," he said with a shocked look on his face. "He wants to speak to the dog walker."

Esme gave up and reached out her hand for the receiver without explanation. It was clear from Young George Clooney's expression that he was quite pleased with his win. The man on the other end of the phone was inquiring about Catherine's whereabouts—seemingly more out of concern than in the gossipy way others had. He said that he had seen Esme at the dog park with Elvis and was worried that Catherine was ill or something; she hadn't responded to his calls and texts. Esme replied that she was fine and out of town for a bit. She wasn't about to tell this would-be ax murderer any more than that. The bartender was busy googling when she hung up.

"OK, you got me," she said. "I'm sorry."

"Forget about that—was that *the* Kurt Vaughn, and if so, how do you know him?"

"I don't. Who is he?"

"Only the best metal bass player ever!" He showed her what he had pulled up on his phone. Though unimpressed, she recognized the man from the park.

"Yes. That's him. He's a regular at the Washington Square Park dog run. So am I. I'm the dog sitter." She said the last part with a consolatory air.

"I got that." He paused, then continued. "I knew it was an act last night on the way home. You didn't walk like a New Yorker."

"Why? Because I didn't walk down the sidewalk like I owned it?"

"No, because the streets were empty, and even though you could barely stand up, you made us stop at every light and wait for the walk sign. That's unheard of."

Esme rolled her eyes. She was going to insist that he admit his truth, now that he knew hers, but thought twice. The fake wedding band between them made room for a totally platonic relationship, and she was happy for that, and for the coffee. She poured herself a cup.

"There's no milk. Sorry I snooped, I'm hungry."

"Yeah, I need to do a grocery run."

"Want to go out for breakfast?"

Esme couldn't help herself. "Sure," she responded. "As long as your wife won't mind. You have been gone all night."

"My wife is in Cuba. She wouldn't mind anyway; she's not like that."

Final proof of his charade—a Cuban wife who wouldn't mind sleepovers and brunch dates with lonely female strangers. What was he hiding from? Her empty belly overrode her curious mind.

"My treat. I have to pay you back for being my knight in shiny armor." She laughed, adding, "It's all coming back to me."

TEN

The Puma x Fenty Creepers
by Rihanna

On line at the Corner Diner, which was actually in the middle of the block, Esme apologized again for lying. She explained that, in her case, the truth was so much worse than the lie that she was actually sparing him. After hearing an abridged version of her saga, he agreed.

They settled into a sidewalk table where Elvis took cover from the heat between their feet, prepared to feast on any tidbits dropped from above. Over breakfast, Esme switched the inquisition from herself to the bartender but didn't go too deep. She asked him basic things like where he lived (with his mom, in Brooklyn, for now) and where his dad was (don't know, don't care) and what kind of law he wanted to practice (immigration, definitely immigration). They finished up with a great debate on pancakes versus waffles.

Afterward, Young George Clooney, real name Zach Bennet, walked Esme and Elvis over to Washington Square on his way to the bursar's office at NYU. He surveyed the dog run, hoping to spot the rock star in question, but no such luck.

"I don't see Kurt Vaughn, but I do see the Sturgeon King of New York!" he said, seeming equally impressed.

"That's my friend Sy! You know him?"

"Everyone knows him! He's a legend, and arguably the finest purveyor of smoked fish in the world."

Esme beamed. She had a celebrity friend.

"So funny who becomes an icon in this city," she noted.

"There was a time in the nineties when buckling up in New York cabs was the big issue; he was one of the legends, like Joan Rivers, Jackie Mason, and Eartha Kitt, who recorded messages reminding everyone to wear a seat belt. He said, 'You don't have to be a brain sturgeon to know to buckle up for safety. And now it's o'fishal! Buckle up, it's the law.'"

"I can't believe you remember that."

"I was a kid. I had them all memorized."

"Want to meet him?"

She called Sy over, and the two of them hit it off right away. Sy even performed his taxi PSA for them, clearly relishing the attention. Sy barely waited for the gate to close behind Zach before asking her, "I thought it was going to be the guy from Barrow Street?"

"No, no. He's a new friend," she said, adding, "I went out last night. I may need to make another trip to the cobbler."

"Good for you." He laughed, looking down at her feet with obvious disappointment. "I was hoping you would heed Mrs. Berger's advice. Not today, I see."

Esme blushed, glancing at the monochrome beige suede sneakers with the raised midsoles. She was too embarrassed to explain that the shoes on her feet were the by-products of one of the most buzzworthy collaborations of the year, and that she felt beyond cool wearing them.

She laughed (at herself) as they sat down on their usual bench.

"So. He seemed like a nice fellow, handsome enough, that's for sure," Sy noted enthusiastically.

"Don't get too excited, he's married. Well, at least I think he's married. He wears a wedding ring, but I heard a silly rumor that it was just to discourage patrons from—you know. Have you ever heard of that?"

"Heard of it? I invented it! I got divorced in 1958, but I never took off my ring. Before I was married, two, three times a day someone would come in the store trying to make a shidduch—their daughter, their niece, their accountant's niece, the girl who lived across the hall. It was exhausting. And that's not even including the local matchmaker who would slip photos under the front door of the shop every night. I would walk there in the morning and step on the faces of every eligible girl in a ten-mile radius."

Maybe the fake marriage theory was true, Esme thought. Though she didn't want to think about it, really. She kind of liked that she had made a friend and was not in any headspace for more than that. She changed the subject.

"So you were once married?"

"Yes, for a brief time. She was a pretty blonde. Right out of a Hitchcock casting call."

"No kids?"

"No, it was a short, quiet marriage—no children."

"So, why Katz and Son? Who's the son?"

"I am. And my dad before me. My grandfather had a famous appetizing stall in the greatest food-and-spice arcade in Moscow in the 1800s—until they forced him out with the other Jews. He sent my father to America with a few rubles and his recipes. My dad made them and sold them from a pushcart on Hester Street."

Esme worried that he was now starting his story in the 1800s but was glad he was back at it.

He pulled up an old black-and-white photo of his father and the cart on his phone. The words *Kac i Synov'ya* were painted on its side.

"See, he named it for his father, Kac i Synov'ya—Katz and Son—and I did the same."

"Wow, that's amazing."

"It was common then. There were pushcarts everywhere on the Lower East Side—hundreds of them selling anything you can imagine would fit on a cart, even things you can't imagine, until the thirties when Mayor LaGuardia got rid of them. Then my dad opened up a stall in the newly built Essex Market. He set it up just like his father's in Moscow. He was so proud, even said that within a year he would move us from Sheepshead Bay to Manhattan, not that I wanted to leave Brooklyn. He died of leukemia a few months later, right before my bar mitzvah. He hadn't even seemed ill. The doctors said it came from being gassed by the Germans in World War One years before."

"I'm so sorry, Sy."

"It was tough to grow up without my pops. We sold his stall, and my mother made his recipes out of our kitchen and sold them to friends and neighbors to make ends meet. I missed my dad a lot and started to get in a little bit of trouble. That's when my mother started sending me to Sea Scouts. She wanted me to have some positive male influence. One of the leaders taught me everything he knew about boatbuilding. When I enlisted, I had every intention of being a boatbuilder on my return.

"Soon after I got back from the war, my mother passed away and I was all alone. I found the recipes. Making them, tasting them, it was all I had left of my parents. I leased back my dad's stall at Essex Market and stayed there till 1952, when I opened my first store, followed by the one you visited in the Village. The Toscani kids rented out the storefront next door to the Lower East Side shop and opened the café the year I sold to them. I helped make it all authentic."

"Wow. What an amazing story!"

"It's a common immigrant story really, but instead of falafel or tamales or gyros we sold herring. That tamale guy with the line around the corner on Greene Street, his kid will probably open a five-star Mexican restaurant one day using the same recipes. It's the American dream."

"It definitely is. I'm sorry your marriage didn't work out. You would have been a great dad."

"Maybe. It certainly would have helped with the loneliness. After I stopped going into the store, it hit me like a ton of bricks how alone I was. In the end it wasn't the herring I missed so much as the schmoozing. Sometimes I ride the subway for no other reason than to be around people. You know, New Yorkers have a bad rap for being standoffish, but it couldn't be further from the truth. Everyone talks to each other on the subway—*What a cute baby. Is that a good book you're reading? How 'bout them Yankees?* Where else can you have intimate discussions with people from all over the world? I could schmooze there like I did at the store.

"That's why I got Scout, for company. I never had a dog before, didn't think it was fair with my hours. I went in to adopt a puppy, but this little guy kept looking up at me with sad eyes. Turned out he'd been there over a year. I figured two old dogs were perfect for each other."

Esme understood loneliness all too well. At the beginning of her ordeal, she would talk to her friends honestly about the misery of her martyrdom, as she took to calling it, but as time went on, she couldn't bear the phone calls and switched to texting. With just one lie—*Sorry, couldn't get to the phone. How are you?*—the torture was mitigated. Her friends quickly adapted, which made her realize that avoiding lengthy conversations was best for everyone. No one wanted to go into detail about their new job or their new love—or even their new shoes—when the person on the other end of the line had absolutely nothing new to say. Faced with her father's silence, and with no one to talk to but the nurses, Esme became very lonely. That was why she had been so happy to meet Selena. Finding someone her own age to talk to who would understand her life felt like a miracle. Far from home, Selena had felt the same.

Esme patted Sy's hand with hers, and he grasped hers back in a touch-starved way that made her want to cry. If he had no one to talk to, she was sure he also had no one to hold his hand.

She changed the subject. While Esme didn't care about the rock star's fame like Zach did, she was curious about his relationship with Catherine Wallace. There was something about living in a stranger's house that was very intriguing. From the little bit of snooping she had done among the few photographs and many scuff-less heels, Catherine Wallace's life seemed to be quite insular and solitary.

Esme asked Sy casually, "Hey, what's the deal with Elvis's mom and the rock star?"

"I'm not privy to any deal, but they definitely spend a lot of time talking to each other, usually on that bench." He pointed to an empty seat in the corner. "He's the only one she puts down her work for. They're in the same business—sort of. She's an entertainment lawyer and he's an entertainer, if you could call that noise entertainment."

"Yeah, but you said he didn't play anymore. He called her home phone concerned about her—it seemed like more than that to me."

"Do you know what a yenta is?"

"Yes, Sy."

"Good. Then stop being such a yenta and start worrying more about your own love life and less about theirs."

"I pretty much worry about everything. You wouldn't know it by looking at me, but I'm far more concerned with when the other shoe will drop than the ones on my feet."

"Between your nosiness and your Jewish disaster mentality, it's hard to believe you're not a member of the tribe."

"Jewish disaster mentality?"

"Yes, why worry about tomorrow when so much can still go wrong today."

Esme laughed. "That, I can relate to. So, what went wrong with you and Lena? You haven't finished telling me your cautionary tale."

"What time is it?" Sy asked, alarmed.

Esme reluctantly pulled out her phone. "Now? Almost one."

"I gotta go. A friend of mine is taking me and Scout sailing this afternoon. At fourteen hundred hours."

"A friend?" she asked, annoyed.

It seemed Sy Katz had an affinity for leaving her mid-sentence or mid-story. She began to wonder if he did it on purpose.

"Yes." He laughed. "The one fellow who isn't dead or in Florida. He keeps a thirty-two-footer at the Seventy-Ninth Street Boat Basin. Maybe you would like to come with me one day? It's the best way to see the Statue of Liberty."

"I would love that, thanks, but what about the end of the story?"

"Tomorrow—I promise," he declared, followed by his signature salutation. "So long for now!"

And with a little extra spring in his step, presumably on account of the impending sail, he left her hanging. Yet again.

ELEVEN

The Red F*ck-Me Pumps

While Sy didn't finish his story, Esme knew that it was at the forefront of his mind all these years later. She decided to take Elvis for an early-evening stroll down Barrow Street in hopes of casually bumping into Liam on his way home from work. She refused to spend a lifetime looking backward.

She popped on a cute pair of bowed Aminah sandals, powdered her nose, and reset her ponytail. She looked at herself in the mirror and smiled. She looked fine, maybe even pretty.

Yes, definitely pretty.

It had been a long time since she had thought of herself that way. She was well aware how what was inside had an awful way of poisoning what was outside.

Pain doesn't reflect well on one's face, while happiness is the equivalent of an Instagram filter.

She practiced her apology in the mirror a few times before heading out the door. "I'm so sorry for the way I ended things. I didn't know what else to do at the time, but in retrospect I know I hurt you, and that wasn't my intention."

Her well-shod feet may have been strolling up Barrow Street, but her mind was strolling down memory lane. She soon drifted off to the day that they met.

Esme Nash and Liam Beck's "How did you two meet?" stories never gelled. They would recall them in a similar fashion to the disagreeing talking heads in *When Harry Met Sally. . . .*

From her perspective, the first time Esme laid eyes on Liam Beck was on first-year move-in day. She assumed she had him all figured out right off the bat—with his Dartmouth baseball hat pressed down over his buzzed blond hair. He had reached over her head to hold open the door to their hall while Esme and her mom struggled with full hands. She'd instantly noticed his washboard abs peeking out over his gym shorts. He smiled at her in a way that made her feel awkward. While she was an athlete, too—a long-distance runner—she had no desire to be labeled as a jock. She wanted badly to mix it up with the edgier kids and the intellectuals and wanted nothing to do with bros like Liam Beck—though she did allow herself to picture her pointer finger tracing the space between his abs, descending beneath the string of his knee-length gym shorts. Her mother quickly broke the spell, embarrassing her by saying, "He looked nice, didn't he?" just as her dorm room door swung shut.

"*Ugh, Mom, he could hear you,*" she said, jumping down her mother's throat. The pain had immediately registered on her mother's face. Esme was never one to disrespect her mother as many other girls she knew often did. When thinking back now to the few occasions that she had, she felt a magnified sense of guilt.

That first weekend of college was filled with orientation activities, and Esme found herself frequently surveying the room for the cute boy with the abs. She caught his eye just as they were asked to choose partners for a trust exercise. He pointed to her, as if to ask if they could pair up, and she nodded her head as coolly as she could. When they were instructed to fall back into their partners' arms, Esme did so with butterflies in her stomach, and not due to trust. He caught her with ease, and as he lifted her back up, he gently brushed his face against her neck.

"You smell nice, Esme," he whispered in her ear.

"Ivory soap," she answered, shocked that he knew her name and wishing she had answered with something somewhat sexy.

She barely saw him after that.

Esme's first-year roommate, a girl from Manhattan named Chloe Rose, soon filled Esme's head with all things NYC. Like many of the kids from the city, Chloe was above the usual college antics and spent her time brooding in all black and regaling Esme with stories of her decadent youth. Chloe had grown up in the Dakota, which, it turned out, was all one needed to be considered cool. She could have been the most boring girl on the planet, which she wasn't, and everyone would have thought her exciting from that mere fact alone. Esme had quickly learned to revise her answer to the question "Where did you grow up?" from "I'm from New York" to "I'm from a small town outside of Rochester." Her original answer, just New York, was apparently misleading. As if only the residents of the 13.4-mile island of Manhattan had a right to that title.

Soon enough, she had thought at the time, *soon enough*.

Until then, she would just take it all in.

Esme couldn't wait to shed her small-town skin, and when her Dartmouth track team coach suggested a job as a counselor at a high-end sleepaway camp in Maine, she grabbed it. The camp was known for being a summer escape for the offspring of NYC's elite, and the pay was good. Besides that, there had been a strange tension between her parents as of late, and Esme had not been looking forward to a whole summer of being in the middle of it. All the things that her mother had once found endearing about her father seemed to have soured. It had been ages since Esme remembered her laughing at his jokes or his silly antics. Her parents' marital discord aside, she was mostly just excited not to spend the whole summer in nowheresville.

On the first night of camp, after the kids had gone to sleep, the counselors got together in the social hall for a meet and greet. They played childish games like human anagrams and balloon pass. Just as she began to wonder what the hell she was doing there, the cute guy on the receiving end of the neck-to-neck balloon exchange read her mind.

"Want to get out of here?" he asked.

"Absolutely," she answered.

They found a secluded spot by the lake, and not long after the initial niceties, they began to make out. By their first day off duty they were smitten—by the second, clearly a couple.

At the end of the summer they both cried when they said goodbye—him to drive straight to Boston College, her to spend some time at home with her parents before the start of sophomore year. Come fall, she threw herself into her studies and spent most nights talking on the phone with him or planning when she would see him next. On the night before Thanksgiving break, which he was set to spend with her family, he'd called and told her he had met someone else and would not be coming after all.

She was hurt, angry, and embarrassed to have been dumped. Instead of crying, she threw on a sexy outfit, including a pair of red high-heeled pumps, and dragged her roommate to a fraternity party—only the third of her college career—where she purposefully sought out the proverbial big man on campus, Liam Beck. Liam and Esme had barely crossed paths since their first year. He was a night owl (when it wasn't baseball season), and she was an early bird, whether track was in season or not. But even so, she had been fantasizing about him and his abs since she had first set eyes on him, and while this move was completely out of character, it felt like just what the breakup doctor ordered.

It was also Liam's answer to the question "How did you two meet?"

Esme filled a cup of the grain alcohol punch from the orange Rubbermaid garbage pail in the frat house basement, downed it without thinking about the repercussions, and approached Liam Beck, in the flesh.

A few hours later she ran her hand over the line between his abs before searching his bedroom floor for her panties. She remembered the staunch warning from the girl she'd stayed with on accepted students' weekend years before: *Whatever you do, never sleep in a fraternity house.*

She got dressed and quietly escaped down the sticky stairs through the back door of the frat, reputation intact—though only for a minute.

The window to Liam's room flew open, and with a huge grin on his face he yelled out, "Good night, Esme Nash!"

She looked up at him and laughed. Even after being outed, she'd walked home on that crisp autumn night feeling good about her first foray into bacchanalian excess and vowing never to look Liam Beck's way again. Somehow, she felt vindicated with regard to the two-timer camp boyfriend, though she wasn't really sure why.

She spent the next day in the library, writing her first of many papers on her favorite artist, Gustav Klimt, whose reproduction of *The Kiss* still hung over her bed, before returning to her dorm to find a surprising note on her whiteboard: *Call me* with a 508 cell phone number. She looked at it for a solid five minutes before wiping it clear.

On the bus home the next day, she thought about her brazen moves: both seeking out Liam and not giving a crap about him afterward. If it were not for her current state of rejection, a note like that would certainly have sent her into a tizzy. She realized that it was probably some kind of transference, but blowing off one of the hottest guys on campus worked for her. Not so much for Liam.

On Monday, back at Dartmouth, Liam was waiting for her at her dorm. She saw him through the glass of the hall door and escaped back down the stairs to a friend's room to wait it out. After the weekend, she was feeling kind of embarrassed by her out-of-character behavior, unwilling to be one of his booty calls unless it was on her own terms.

The next day, he called out to her when she was walking across the Green. She was wearing earbuds and pretended not to hear him.

When he yelled "Esme!" again, a guy she knew from science lab grabbed her shoulder.

"Someone's calling you."

And that was it. Liam and Esme were together from then until graduation. Even with Esme spending a semester abroad in Vienna studying Gustav Klimt's *The Kiss* in person, they had both remained loyal. It was a trait that Esme truly appreciated after the camp-boyfriend fiasco.

As it turned out, Esme had Liam Beck all wrong. He was still in fact one of the hottest guys on campus, but it was not a title he relished. He was old-fashioned and very much wanted to settle down with one girl. And that girl, it turned out, was Esme.

The memories came to a sudden halt on her fourth trip down

"their" Greenwich Village street, when she saw a familiar blond head approaching in the distance. The mane in question sat atop a well-dressed man in a suit and tie who looked much different than Liam had in college. His familiar gait fully gave him away. He always had a way of walking more akin to a slow jog than a brisk step. As if eternally heading for home plate.

Her heart surprised her by breaking through the fortress she had erected around it and dropping to her well-clad feet. After that, vanity got the better of her. It had been nearly an hour since she had checked herself in the mirror. She was sure that the humid air had frizzed her ponytail and wiped away the fresh powder that had dusted her cheeks. The words that she had rehearsed suddenly vanished, along with her confidence. She scooped up Elvis and did an about-face.

With each step home, as the adrenaline wore off, Esme felt the weight of disappointment replace it.

What if that had been her chance?

By the time she entered the apartment, she was drenched in sweat and self-doubt. Her cell phone buzzed, and she pulled a chair in front of the air-conditioning unit before answering it. Her hello—"Hello!"—must have sounded overheated and stressed, because Selena immediately inquired, "What's wrong?"

"It's a million degrees out, and I just saw Liam."

"Oh, wow. Are you going over everything you said to him? Tell me the whole conversation!"

She knew Selena was going to be annoyed at her but spilled it anyway.

"I didn't say anything."

"Esme!"

"You don't have to be angry at me, I'm angry enough at myself for both of us. I've been looking for him ever since I got here. Literally everywhere I go, I daydream about him. I night-dream about him, too. I blew my only chance."

"No, you didn't. I'm sure you'll run into him again. Why not call him? Say you're in town and want to meet up for coffee or a drink?"

"I can't. He has a new number."

She remembered how excited he was that his company sent him the latest iPhone with a 917 number.

"You could go back on social media."

"So he can see that the last picture I posted was of us at his senior formal? No thank you. It will have to happen organically."

"Well, you still have three weeks to go, and you're in his neighborhood, right? I bet you will bump into him again."

"I hope so. If I go home without seeing him, I'm scared I'll be dreaming about him for the next seventy years!"

"Seventy years? Well, at least you're thinking past tomorrow!"

Esme laughed. Selena knew her too well. Thinking about the future while her dad lay paralyzed in the next room was something Esme had avoided at all costs over the years. Now, the blank slate in front of her was filling her with a different kind of anxiety—one in which there were no more excuses to fall back on. She vowed that if she were lucky enough to see Liam again, there would be no reason great enough to stop her from saying hello.

TWELVE

The Simone Rocha Crystal-Embellished Pool Slides

The next day, Esme arrived at the dog park and planted herself on the usual bench, determined not to let anything or anyone get between Sy and his story. That plan was quickly derailed when the rock star came through the gate and confiscated Sy's seat on the bench next to her. There was no way Sy would talk in front of this guy. She'd have to get rid of him quickly.

He introduced himself, "Hey, I'm Kurt, Kurt Vaughn."

"Hey, I'm Esme, Esme Nash," she said in return, giggling to herself.

He paused awkwardly, looking around as if he had no agenda. Then he dove right in.

"So, how is Catherine doing? Does she check in on Elvis?"

"Yes, she's good," Esme answered, adding fictitiously, "Enjoying her vacation."

He responded in a tone of bewilderment mixed with hurt. "I'm surprised she didn't mention that she was going away. We meet here almost every day."

"Oh, I'm sorry. I didn't realize you two were close. I thought you were just dog park friends."

She didn't mean to insult him, but the look on his face registered that she had. His dog, a husky black Lab, came barreling over with a ball in his mouth. Esme happily changed the subject.

"Who's this guy?" she asked, giving him the perfunctory pat on the head.

Kurt perked up. "This is Memphis. He's not really mine. I just walk him."

Esme was surprised that the rock star moonlighted as a dog walker. It didn't make much sense.

She saw Sy at the gate. Her determination to hear the end of Sy's story outweighed all else. She took the ball from Memphis's mouth and stood to throw it. Just as she hoped, Sy noticed and made a beeline to greet her. They hugged hello, and he pointed to an empty bench. Before following him she politely called out, "Nice to meet you, Kurt!"

"You, too," he responded, less enthusiastically. She knew he hadn't gotten what he wanted from the conversation.

When they were out of earshot, she asked Sy, "That's not his dog. Is he a dog walker?"

Sy laughed. "No, he helps out his homebound neighbor by bringing his dog here every day."

"Wow, so he's a good guy?"

"He seems more interested in Catherine Wallace than that dog, but I guess."

They sat down on a bench in the sun, and Esme closed her eyes and stretched her neck out, soaking it in.

"It feels good," Sy observed.

"It does, when it's not sweltering out."

"I'm a bit older than you, a good bone-warming does me a world of good!"

"Are you and your old bones ready to tell me the rest of the story?" she teased.

"Do you have the time?" he teased back.

"Nothing but." She smiled, crossing her legs lotus-style, in preparation for the long haul.

"Fine, where were we?"

She remembered exactly. She wanted to say, *You were about to tell me the big thing that was keeping you and Lena apart*, but in her heart she knew that was what had made him clam up the last time, so she said, "I don't think we even got to the first date yet."

"Do you want the abridged version?"

"Absolutely not."

"You're a good soul, Esme Nash," he said, tapping on her fancy Simone Rocha slides garnished with delicate crystal flowers.

Sy took a deep breath and explained that he eventually got up the nerve to ask Lena out on a real date—to the movies, *The Maltese Falcon*. He picked her up early so that they could leisurely walk there. He said that he'd never been inside a house that big—and that didn't change because, when he got there, she was sitting on the front stoop waiting for him. He'd been all set to meet her parents, like a gentleman, but she came rushing down the path, quickly ushering him away.

"I couldn't decide if I was hurt or relieved." He laughed, remembering how young and naive he was at the time.

"I'd been to the Midwood Theater before with friends, but that was a whole different scene. My buddies and I would chip in for one ticket and pick straws for who would buy it. The rest of us would wait by the back door for him to let us in. That's where I first saw images of the war in Europe—in the news reels before the picture. At the start of the war, there wasn't much talk about what Hitler was doing to the Jews. You would hear rumblings here and there, evasive posts buried in the back of the paper, a cousin who came here on vacation and suddenly stopped receiving letters from back home, but nothing at all equal to the unimaginable atrocities. Most of my cronies didn't really care about the war until the invasion of Pearl Harbor, but I did because I felt the Germans were responsible for my father's leukemia. I enlisted because I wanted to avenge my father's death, without yet fully understanding what was happening to my people over there. But I'm getting off track—my first date with Lena."

Esme smiled. "Yes. You were headed to the Humphrey Bogart movie, I think."

"I think he was in it—I've actually never seen it!"

Somewhere between Lena's house and the theater he had noticed she was walking a bit funny. When he asked her what was wrong, she admitted that her new shoes were giving her a blister. He suggested they take a break, and they sat on a bench. They talked about a million things—many that he had never said out loud before. He spoke about his dad's passing and admitted how nervous he was to leave Brooklyn, let alone the country, for the first time. Lena told him all about summer camp, what it was like to fly on an airplane, and how hard she always tried to please her very proper mother. By the time they got up, it was three hours later, they had missed the movie, and she was nearly late for curfew. Even though they had such different life experiences, there was a connection that Sy had never felt before with any other human being.

"*Connection* wasn't really the right word," he said. "It was more like a reunion. A reunion of two souls who were destined to be together. Do you believe in that, Esme? Do you believe in bashert?"

"I did once, but not so much anymore."

"Well, you've been through so much—soul-crushing stuff. You will again."

She hoped he was right. While listening to Sy's love story, she sensed an unfamiliar lightness in her own spirit. It felt nice.

He continued.

"I couldn't stay away from her. The next morning I waited at the horse trail by Ocean Parkway with my bicycle to follow along with her while she rode, and the day after that as well. Soon we were spending every waking hour together. I didn't have to turn over the boat till September, when the new owner was returning from his summer vacation, so I took it out every chance I had. Sometimes Mel would come along, but eventually he stopped. He would lecture me that getting so close to a girl right before I was to ship out was an awful idea, that I had to have my wits about me at all times and couldn't be daydreaming about some girl back home, especially this girl, he would say. *It will never happen between you two. Different worlds.* I was real sore at Mel for this, and on account of it all, he stopped hanging around Lena and me so much. At the time I thought he was just jealous, that maybe he had a crush on Lena himself. Who wouldn't? She was everything. When I found out the truth, I was more annoyed at him than at Lena. It was wrong of me, but it was easier that way."

He went on to explain how the days before one goes to the service feel more precious as the time to leave approaches, and how adding Lena into the mix made the time race by. They spent most days out on the boat. He taught her how to chart the waters and currents of Sheepshead Bay, and she turned out to be a very good first mate. It was a hot summer, but being on the bay, with Lena and the breeze and the sea air, made it bearable. Despite the heat, they would always sit or stand as close as possible; the touch of her skin filled him with a sense of peace and belonging he had never felt before.

"When I looked into her violet eyes, I could see her affection for me reflected in them. It was like we were one. She had become an extension of me—like a limb. Maybe Mel had been right. How could I go off to war with a missing limb?"

Some nights they would go to the movies, other nights one of his friends from the Sea Scouts would have people over to listen to records on the phonograph. Lena loved to dance; Sy, not so much, but he did his best, "'cause it made her happy." He told Esme that he had never had a summer like that before or since. It was magical.

About two weeks before he was set to ship out, he and Mel turned over the boat to the new owner and got paid. He was sad to see it go, for sure, but happy to have real money like that, money he had earned. He decided to use a bit of it to splurge on one special night with his girl. He told her that he would be picking her up at her front door at eight o'clock sharp, and he told her to dress up.

Sy hadn't been to Lena's house since that first night. She would always meet him at the bay or at the movies, or even find an excuse to meet somewhere in the middle when going to a friend's house or for dinner. He let it happen because it seemed to be what she needed, but when he really thought about it, he would feel awful and it would get him thinking about what Mel said about their different worlds. That night he insisted on picking her up at home, and she agreed.

He borrowed his aunt's boyfriend's car, a silver Buick Century with white leather interior that the guy had won in a card game, with a sticker price of a whopping $995. When he got to Lena's house, he was happy to see that she wasn't waiting for him out on the stoop like before. As he walked up the path to the front door, prepared to meet her parents, he remembered what his pops had taught him when he was a kid: look someone in the eye when shaking their hand. He wiped the sweat from his palms on his trousers, rang the bell, and held his breath. Lena answered the door and took it all away: his breath, his nerves, everything. His heart dropped to his stomach, and his knees wobbled. He was in love for the first time and thought again about what Mel had said. How could he go off to war with wobbly knees?

"Let's go!" she said.

"I thought maybe you would invite me in?" Sy admitted.

"Oh, you can come in if you want, but no one's home."

He hadn't thought of that. He followed her inside to the living room. He knew the house was big from the outside, but it was decorated so ornately that it felt more like a museum than a home. She asked if he wanted something to drink, but he declined. They sat on the sofa for a long minute. It was gold-colored velvet and had lions carved into its feet. The couch in his house was older than he was and covered in plastic, preserved like a mummy. After about two minutes more of sitting there, he couldn't take it anymore.

"Want to go?" he asked her eagerly.

She jumped up, shouting, "Yes!"

They laughed. They were both impatient types, like two sides of the same coin.

"Everyone says that opposites attract," Sy proffered, "but unless you're sharing a fancy box of chocolates, I never saw the point."

Esme chuckled at his foodie analogy as Sy continued the retelling of his long-ago date.

He was very careful with the swanky car on the drive but let Lena fiddle with the radio, jumping from the Andrews Sisters to Benny Goodman to Xavier Cugat. As they approached the Manhattan Bridge and it became obvious that they were heading into the city, she was too excited to wait. She began asking a million questions about where they were going. All Sy said was it was somewhere really special that he'd heard was all that.

At this point Esme was at the edge of the bench. She could sense that the thing no one had told him was about to become clear. Elvis came over for a pat, and she complied but then gingerly pushed him away, not wanting to break Sy's stride. Luckily, he continued.

"I was taking her to a restaurant called the Brass Rail. There were two of them back then, one in Manhattan and one in Brooklyn. But the Manhattan one was much bigger, taking up nearly a whole city block, and it had a live orchestra. It was *the* place to go. I'd been practicing the Lindy with my cousin Bette, and I was going to surprise Lena with how good I'd gotten at it after dinner.

"When I parked the car on West Forty-Ninth Street, she looked around anxiously. When I took her hand and led her to the restaurant, her face seemed sullen. I asked her if she was OK, and she said a little carsick was all. I said we would order her a Coca-Cola and she would feel as good as new. We entered the restaurant and stood on line behind a few people at the maître d' stand. Within a few seconds the maître d' skipped over all the other people and came right to Lena.

"'Hello, pretty lady,' he said familiarly. 'I'm not used to seeing you here on a Saturday night. What a lovely surprise. How many are you?'

"'Just two,' she said quietly.

"He called someone over and said, 'Bring Miss Leven and her friend to table sixteen right away.'

"We were whisked off to table sixteen, seemingly the best in the house, and I was feeling foolish that I had thought that my first time at the Brass Rail, or any place remotely like it, would be her first time as well. When we sat down I asked the waiter to please bring her a cola. As soon as he was out of earshot, I apologized.

"'I'm sorry,' I said, 'I never should have assumed that this would be special for you.'

"She quickly interrupted. 'No, it's such a special place. It's my dad's favorite restaurant. He eats lunch here nearly every day, or they bring it to his office. And we always eat here or at the one in Brooklyn on our maid's day off.'

"I remember, when she said *maid's day off*, thinking that this would never work between us. And I still didn't even know everything there was to know. She felt so awkward about it all and kept digging herself deeper and deeper. She explained that her maid was off on Thursdays and every other Sunday and that her dad was such a creature of habit that they would go to the same place every time. I couldn't believe they couldn't eat dinner at home without a maid. It was so foreign to me. I thought, Mel was right all along, but I didn't care. When she was done explaining it, she looked down, ashamed; her eyes welled up.

"'I'm so embarrassed,' she said.

"I couldn't bear to see her sad and reached for her hands with the intent of telling her how I felt about her, that I loved her. But as soon as my fingers touched hers, she pulled away like my hands were on fire.

"'*Don't! Don't hold my hand,*' she whispered firmly.

"'Why?' I was so confused.

"'*Because everyone knows me here.*'

"Then I was just insulted. Had I fallen for such a snob? I thought I looked great. I'd even bought a white dinner jacket and new shoes for the night. She realized I was angry and said, barely audibly, '*Sy, I'm engaged.*'

"I was shocked."

He quietly explained her real story, while Esme sat utterly dumbfounded. She had not seen it coming any more than he had.

Apparently, Lena was engaged to a wealthy fellow named Sheldon Schusterman, who lived in the house between her and Mel. He had joined the air force about a year before and was stationed in London. Sy had heard Mel speak of his neighbor Lenny but never his brother Sheldon. Mel had told him about Lenny because he had a hearing problem in one ear and, on account of that, he couldn't enlist. Mel had an exemption as well, but he never said why. Sy only knew that he couldn't enlist and his neighbor was in the same boat. So even though she was just sixteen, Lena and Sheldon were engaged to be married when he returned from the war or on her eighteenth birthday. It was a common thing back then. She was sort of like a war bride, but no one had told Sy about it. At first she said she assumed he knew from Mel, but he didn't, obviously, and she wasn't wearing a ring. Plus she was so young, he never would have thought it. By the time Mel realized what was going on, he confronted Lena, who promised she would tell Sy. But she could never bring herself to.

They left the restaurant and drove back to Brooklyn in silence. After dropping her off, Sy was too upset to go home, so he went down to the bay to sleep on the boat. He knew no one would see him, and at that point he really didn't care if they did.

"At about two in the morning I heard someone on deck and went up to see who it was. It was Lena. She was curled up in a ball crying."

"Oh my God" escaped Esme's lips, breaking the spell again. This time for real.

"What time is it?"

"No way, not again."

"Scout has an appointment at the vet."

"Why? He looks fine."

"It's a checkup—next time I will finish, I promise." He patted her leg and was off.

His goodbyes, Esme noted, were far more succinct than his hellos.

THIRTEEN

———

The Giuseppe Zanotti Gold Gladiators

With each passing day, Esme began to get in a groove, less caught up in the past and more open to her future. Although she still could not wrap her head around giving up her childhood home, she was beginning to consider what taking back her old life plan would look like: moving to the city and getting a job at a gallery to kick off a fabulous career. She redid her résumé to include a brief explanation of her seven-year hiatus from the art world and recommitted herself to her old favorite mantra, *Chance favors the prepared mind.*

She made every effort to familiarize herself with all that she had missed. She spent hours weeding through back issues of *ARTnews* and *Frieze* magazine at the Jefferson Market Library. She even signed up for an NYU lecture on careers in the arts that her new best bud Zach suggested.

It was hard not to dream big in New York. The pulse of the city felt like a pacemaker pumping the old Esme's blood through her atrophied heart. She established a nice routine. Most mornings were spent at the dog park with Elvis, who was truly her main squeeze. He loved her unconditionally, and though she imagined that he, too, was missing *his* true love with absolutely no understanding of where she had gone, he didn't perseverate about the one that got away, like Sy did, or sulk like Zach did about his absent wife, or fantasize about their reunion, as she was guilty of doing herself, with Liam. Although Elvis might be doing all that, too, she realized. Who would know?

On some afternoons, Elvis and Esme would just wander, each time walking farther and farther away from her comfort zone of the circuit to the park and back, acting less like a tourist and more like a native. She began to feel like a Greenwich Village local, knowingly avoiding eye contact with the saliva-spewing woman dubbed the Spitter of Waverly Place and skipping the patch of pavement near the Bleecker Street subway station that on hot days smelled like a urine death zone.

She loved to walk. She would step in and out of the eclectic array of shops in the Village and SoHo in a variety of Catherine's flats and sandals, poring over books or clothing or old records, even though she didn't own a turntable. Sometimes she would stand outside the swanky galleries that dotted West Broadway in SoHo and allow herself to dream again of curating a show by a spectacular artist.

On one relentlessly sweltering day, when she could actually see the steam coming off the pavement and the thought of being outside felt unbearable, she and Zach holed up for a double feature at one of the art house theaters that thankfully still dotted the downtown landscape. In the tradition of iconic New York fictional characters like Don Draper and Alvy Singer, they spent the afternoon escaping the heat, as well as the complicated narratives playing over and over in their own heads. Though Esme still had no idea what Zach's complicated narrative was, she knew it existed. She could practically see the gears of his brain trying to work it all out. She hinted at it every once in a while but still appreciated the hard stop that his marital status (whether fact or fiction) placed between them. This was especially true on occasions like sitting next to him in a dark, cold theater, cuddled up together under his NYU Law sweatshirt, making it hard to concentrate on the plot of the movie.

It was obvious that Zach loved showing Esme around town. He proclaimed that it was his personal mission for the month of August to introduce her to his New York. He said everyone had their own special New York agenda—places and restaurants and dive bars and park benches that made them think: *This is why I live here. This is the reason that I pay too much rent for too small a place that I share with two roommates, a mouse, and a water bug the size of Toledo.* Or, in Zach's case, *This is why I still live with my mother.* He and Esme spent hours reading on the red-painted bench in the secret garden of Saint Luke's, got drunk at a speakeasy hidden behind shelves of cereal at a Seaport bodega, ate at the grilled cheese bar at Murray's, and danced to the music of aging rock stars in the back of Otto's Shrunken Head, where the bouncer wore a cutoff Santa suit over a *Vote Nixon/Agnew* T-shirt. Esme felt blessed to have found the most fun tour guide.

On other days, Esme would set out alone to visit what she considered to be Manhattan's greatest residents: its finest works of art. In typical *old* Esme fashion, she mapped out the whole month's worth of museum visits in advance, carefully setting aside the perfect shoes for each: she picked out a pair of colorful, iridescent Alexander McQueen sneakers in which to admire Kandinsky's *Black Lines* at the Guggenheim; a pair of vintage tan suede Ferragamo loafers to stroll by Edward Hopper's *Early Sunday Morning* at the

Whitney; Christian Dior's version of the ballet slipper, with its thick swath of ribbon fastened around the ankle in a bow, in homage to Degas's bowed *Little Dancer* at the Met; and a dramatic pair of metallic gold Giuseppe Zanotti gladiators to sit for hours on a bench at the Neue Galerie, taking in every inch of her favorite of Klimt's muses, Adele Bloch-Bauer—more commonly known as the Woman in Gold. While she knew every inch of what was still considered Klimt's most famous work—*The Kiss*—both from the replica that still hung on her bedroom wall and from studying the original masterpiece in Austria, she had never seen *this* piece in person. It left her dreaming of returning to Vienna.

On one particular afternoon, after almost leaving barefoot for the Museum of Modern Art due to a combination of too many shoes to choose from and too many works to match them with, Esme got caught up in a group of young students on an art safari. The woman who led them through the museum, searching for Picasso's *She-Goat*, Klee's *Cat and Bird*, and Frida Kahlo's black monkey, seemed to be having the time of her life. As Esme followed along behind them, taking it all in, she became filled with envy, followed by uncertainty. She wondered if the fancy art gallery job that she had once wanted so badly was no longer a good fit for her. Something about sharing art with everyone, as opposed to the elite few who could afford to purchase a masterpiece themselves, suddenly felt more her speed—and more fulfilling. She had loved being a docent at the campus museum at Dartmouth.

After a moment's contemplation, she dismissed her doubts. She had taken her eye off the prize long enough. She knew the best door back into the art world for her was the door of a gallery. Reinventing herself and her approach would delay things even further.

She opened up her phone, right then and there, and created a new to-do list with just two unchecked boxes imperative to her future. She would need to check them both before leaving the city in order to consider her stay a success.

1. Get an interview at the Hudson Payne Gallery.
2. Apologize to Liam.

Even though Esme had been concentrating more on herself and her future, she still thought about bumping into Liam everywhere she went. She swore again that if she were to see him, she would speak to him and apologize—no matter what the circumstance. She daydreamed of spotting him at the seafood counter at Citarella, imagined his face looking back at her through a gap in the stacks of the Jefferson Market Library, and pictured him on the mat next to hers at the hot yoga class she had tried, during which, in her fantasy, she was glistening, not sweating. Until one day, at Berger's Stitch and Shine, he appeared, as if she'd conjured him.

Berger's was divided in half, with a counter for tailoring and cleaning to the left and for shoe repair to the right. Esme was sitting on a cold metal folding chair that felt pretty good on the hottest day of the year, looking a bit disheveled, aside from the navy-blue kidskin Stella McCartney sandals that wrapped around her feet as if they belonged on a Greek goddess. Elvis had plopped down under her chair and almost immediately fell asleep. She was waiting to see if Mrs. Berger could clean up the collateral damage from the incident with the Portuguese guy. On second inspection, it turned out that the Bottega Veneta Lidos had not survived unscathed.

Ironically, she was deep into the Sunday *Times* Modern Love column when a man walked right through the middle of the store, not unlike Moses parting the Red Sea, disregarding the people waiting patiently on either side. Everyone knew that Mrs. Berger didn't stand for such entitlement, and if they were newbies, the sign above her head, SIT UNTIL YOU ARE SUMMONED, made it very clear. The silence that enveloped the room distracted Esme from her article. She looked up as well.

New Yorkers traditionally had each other's backs in these types of situations, but no one bothered yelling "No cutsies!" or "Hey, bud, get in line!" because they anticipated that the entertainment segment of their trip to Berger's Stitch and Shine was about to begin. Mrs. Berger would surely take care of this knucklehead herself.

The man surprised them all, preemptively soothing everyone's anger by turning around and addressing the customers waiting in line. His outfit, a perfectly tailored custom suit worn with polished black wing tips, was that of a wealthy banker-type for sure, but his voice, his voice belonged to her Liam. Esme's hands shook as she held the newspaper over her face, just peeking out from the top. Her heart beat so loudly that she worried everyone's gaze would turn from him to her.

Of course it's the hottest day of the year, she thought, controlling the urge to quickly sniff under her arms. Surely BO would be a valid excuse to break her promise to herself to engage no matter what.

He smiled at the group, and, as Esme had seen them do a million times before, his Adonis-like looks distracted the ladies, and even the men, from hating him. They barely heard his excuse, "I am so sorry to jump ahead, but I'm late for a meeting and have a fashion emergency."

The crowd waited with bated breath to hear the Yiddish version of "No soup for you!" fly from Mrs. Berger's mouth, but none came. She was equally seduced.

"Liam Beck, what did you do now?" she playfully scolded.

Liam Beck, the man, placed a pair of tuxedo trousers on the counter before planting his strong, youthful hand on Mrs. Berger's aged one.

"I just need these let out one inch on either side. Right here, where you took them in last. Too much of my mama's cooking." He laid on the BS charismatically.

"When do you need them by?" she asked in a surprisingly acquiescent tone.

"Thursday?" he formed his hands in prayer. "I have a black-tie benefit Thursday night."

Esme held her breath as Liam turned to leave the store.

Mrs. Berger cried, "Next!"

This prompted the first chair to stand, pushing Esme to scoot right, leaving her in plain and pathetic sight. Her hands shot to straighten her wayward ponytail and wipe any remnants of last night's mascara from under her eyes. She reversed her original stance of speaking to him and said a quick prayer for invisibility instead. As with all of her prayers over the past seven years, it went unanswered.

"Esme?" Liam proclaimed, utterly astonished.

"Hi, Liam." She smiled, adding sheepishly, "Long time."

"Yes, long time." His eye twitched and he looked down at his feet, replacing the suave confidence he had just exhibited with unease.

Esme knew she should stand to meet him, but she wasn't sure her knees would hold her. Plus, there was a strong possibility that she smelled like a truck driver. He stumbled with his next question; the charm he had displayed minutes before with Mrs. Berger was long gone. It was clear he was as gobsmacked as Esme, and the thought filled her with relief, though not enough to stand up.

"Are you living in the city?" he muttered, his tone a little stiff. As if it was his town and she was supposed to tell him in advance of entering, or worse, as if he really did hate her.

"I'm just visiting," she answered, stopping short of blurting out her apology just to get it over with.

"Nice. How have you been?"

"Good, good. How about you?"

"Me? Same old." It was a dumb answer, and they both knew it. It was obvious from his clothes and his black-tie request that there was nothing *same old* about him. She realized her *good, good* was equally ridiculous.

He got it together first, asking, "How's your dad doing?"

"He passed away last month—renal failure."

"Oh, I'm so sorry, Esme," he said quietly.

And there it was. She could literally see the jittery excitement of seeing his old girlfriend extinguished by pity. Even the person seated next to her noticed the awkwardness of their conversation and asked Liam, "Would you like to sit here?"

"He's late for that meeting," Esme chimed in, thwarting the possibility and thankfully changing the tone. Liam laughed.

"Still ever-punctual, I see," he teased, adding, "How long are you in town for? I would love a chance to catch up properly."

He sounded so different. She never remembered him saying a word like *properly* back in the day.

"That would be lovely," she answered back, matching his Queen's English. "I'm here for the rest of the month. I'm dog-sitting this guy."

She patted Elvis on the head, hoping he would break the ice a bit. He barely opened his eyes to acknowledge the introduction.

"Very cute," he said. "I know it's short notice, but are you free Thursday night?"

A do-over where she could look her best, or at least not her worst, and apologize in private.

"I am," she answered, trying to play it cool.

"Great, my girlfriend and I are cochairing a benefit at the Brooklyn Botanic Garden."

The word *girlfriend* rose like a samurai's sword before swooping down and severing her heart. The feeling surprised her.

Of course he has a girlfriend. It has been seven years. What did I expect, that he'd been nursing heartache this whole time?

She barely heard the rest of his sentence, and the standing/sitting thing was getting weirder by the minute. She again realized she should get up and tested her legs to do so. No such luck. She breathed in and answered him, "That sounds great."

"OK, then," he pulled a hand-pressed invitation from his messenger-bag-style briefcase and handed it to her. "Here you go. And feel free to bring a date. We have room for two more at our table."

"Thanks. I'll bring my boyfriend," she said, stabbing him back while clutching the invitation.

Mrs. Berger yelled "NEXT!" again, about three octaves louder than the last time. The nosy woman to Esme's left looked at her impatiently.

"Are you going to go or should I?"

Esme stood and looked Liam in the eye. She glanced at the invitation and somehow held it up without raising her fragrant arms.

"See you Thursday," she said, smiling lightly.

"See you Thursday," he said back. She felt him watching her as she went up to the counter.

FOURTEEN

The Chanel Ballerina Flats with Black Cap Toes

The next morning Esme woke up to a text from Zach, and happily responded.

Central Park?

Yes!!!!

Meet me on the steps of the Met at noon!

Esme nuzzled Elvis awake and announced, "Rise and shine, pup, we're going to a different park today!" The location immediately made her think of *Gossip Girl*. She reevaluated her shoe choice for the day as she dug through the closet, thinking, *What would Blair Waldorf wear?*

As she stepped out of the subway in a schoolgirl-like miniskirt and the signature shoe of the Upper East Side, she looked around

in awe. It was as if she'd been transported to another city. That was
the thing that amazed her the most about New York—how a few
blocks in either direction changed everything. She wondered if the
natives felt similarly.

The Upper East Side presented itself as all one would expect.
Once she'd left busy Lexington Avenue, everything seemed to be
scrubbed down and primped up, as if company were coming. In the
middle of Park Avenue sat what looked like a mile of flowers, flanked
by what Esme imagined to be the palatial residences of Manhattan's
elite. On Madison, the sidewalk sparkled and the pages of *Vogue*
cascaded from store windows onto well-groomed patrons at sidewalk
cafés. And Fifth Avenue was in a whole different league—its buildings stood regally looking out over the park, as if they knew perfectly
well that their view set them apart from the rest of the world.

"Don't poop here," Esme whispered to Elvis as they turned the
corner at Seventy-Seventh and Fifth. She knew better than to talk
freely to him up there. She presumed that the pasteurized people of
the Upper East Side only revealed their crazy while recumbent on
an analyst's couch.

They settled in on the steps of the Met with Esme feeling oh-
so-native and Elvis staring down the hot dog man. Before long,
Zach appeared amid the throngs, his backpack overflowing with
provisions for their day. He woo-hoo'ed for her to follow.

They entered Central Park's eight-hundred-something acres just
south of the Met, where the vibe of the city shifted once again.
Inside the park, the acceptable dress code and behavior of Manhattanites seemed to reset. Esme could smell it in the air and see it on
the faces of the people passing by. It was as if, upon entering, the
cardinal rule turned from *walk faster* to *stop and smell the roses*.

On one side of the park's entrance sat a small playground guarded
by a life-size statue of the three bears. It looked so civilized—only

one slide and a set of bucket swings. She imagined the tall-standing mama bear in the center of the statue saying, *You may enter, but there will be no pushing and no shoving, and you must wait your turn to go down the slide.*

"Even the playgrounds are sophisticated up here," Esme observed.

"Not really," Zach countered. "This is the backyard for thousands of pent-up kids looking to get their ya-yas out. I once saw a boy at the Ancient Playground on the other side of the Met crack his head so badly, I swear I saw his skull."

"Yikes! Did you spend a lot of time here?"

"I did. Most Sundays we would visit my grandparents, who lived right up the street. I have some pretty great memories of them here."

The windy path was bordered with the old-fashioned iron benches that lined the entirety of the park. Each was adorned with a small plaque: HAPPY ANNIVERSARY, NANA AND POP-POP; WELCOME TO THE WORLD, LIA; WE MISS YOU, BRIGGS! For a second, Esme allowed herself to dream of the possibility of having that kind of bench-worthy love in her life, before shuddering at the reality of her anchorless existence.

As they entered the arched tunnel to the Great Lawn, Zach brought her back to the present.

"This was always my favorite part—listen to this echo.

"Helloooooooo, Esmeeee," he bellowed.

"Hellooooo, Zacharyyyyyyy," she played along.

"My father always called me Zachary."

He said it in a way that made her think she'd hit a nerve. She put it in her back pocket to ask him about later—along with what the real deal was on his wife. In all the time they had spent together, their conversations had been mostly benign. For now, she had to concentrate on convincing him to be her fake boyfriend Thursday night.

They found a good spot, kicked off their shoes, spread out a blanket, and unloaded the delicious contents of his bag. It seemed he had brought one of everything, including a delectable bone for Elvis, which he immediately got to work on.

"I had no idea what you would like. Pick first; I eat anything," he said.

She chose a turkey, apple, and Brie sandwich, her favorite.

"This is delicious, Zachary, thank you."

He smiled oddly.

"Does anyone but your dad call you Zachary, or just Zach?" She really liked calling him Clooney the best but thought that would necessitate her explaining that she thought he was good-looking.

"Only my dad—who spent most of his time addressing the fact that I was a great disappointment to him."

She couldn't imagine this smart, kind, thoughtful man being a disappointment in any way but realized it wasn't her approval he was seeking.

"Do you want to talk about it?" she asked, not really keen on discussing fathers but not wanting to appear uninterested.

"Not particularly," he said, providing them both with relief. He briefly explained himself. "Not everyone has a father who they'd drop everything to care for. It may not seem like it to you, but in some ways you were lucky. You have no idea what it's like to live in an unhappy home, to see your mother in tears."

A lump formed in Esme's throat. She put down her sandwich and lay down on the blanket for a bit. She thought about Selena, questioning her on her parents' relationship. She had once asked very casually, "Did your parents have a good marriage?"

Esme had taken a beat before answering. "Yes, very."

Even though Selena was her friend, Esme's gut reaction was to lie, or at the very least exaggerate. Truth was, she didn't know much about her parents' marriage, except that it had obviously grown colder over the years. She could trace it back to that odd time when they were both set to visit her during her junior year abroad in Europe. Only her mom showed up, refusing to explain why. Or maybe before that, if she were paying attention. She wished now that she had pushed her mom on the subject, but at the time she was more interested in showing her around Vienna and having fun than getting to the bottom of it. Of course she had no idea that she would have to live the rest of her life with unanswered questions. She was sure of one thing—it was easier to care for a saint than a sinner. With that in mind, she hadn't been completely honest with Selena.

This time, even though there was no reason to lie aside from self-preservation, she shrugged her shoulders, silently took the Fifth, and moved on.

"I have something for you, too!" she said, as she pulled the invite out of her bag and held it to her chest. "Are you working Thursday night?"

"I am not," he answered suspiciously.

"Do you own a tux?"

"I do."

Zach's background confused Esme. He was like a chameleon—able to fit in with the aristocracy or the working joes. She handed him the card and put her hands to prayer as he read it out loud.

THE BIRD BALL AT THE BROOKLYN BOTANIC GARDEN
An evening of fun, food, and festivities to benefit
the Audubon Society of New York

"Esme. These things are the worst. People are desperate to fill their tables, especially in the summertime. Why do you want to go to this?"

"Because I bumped into Liam yesterday, and he invited me. He invited us, I mean—me and my boyfriend."

"And I'm the boyfriend?"

Esme looked at him with puppy-dog eyes that rivaled Elvis's.

"Well, there is still time to back out," he said, tossing the invite aside.

She picked it up and proceeded. "I can't back out. I have no way of reaching him, and I looked like crap when I saw him. I need a black-tie do-over."

"First of all, I doubt you could ever look like crap, and second, you said you're not interested in him that way anymore, so what does that matter?"

"What does it matter? Honestly, if I were on my deathbed and Liam were to walk in, the first place my mind would go would be to how my hair looked."

"Women are so bizarre."

"No, we've been trained to prioritize our looks for our entire lives. It's exhausting. You have no idea how easy you have it being a man. I probably spend more time on my eyebrows than you did on this entire look you have going on today."

Zach looked down at his wrinkled Che Guevara T-shirt and cargo shorts and laughed. "You may have a point."

"Also, my heart dropped to my toes at the sight of him, so I may have been wrong about not being interested. But, regardless of whether I am or not, I want to apologize to him in person, when I'm not looking like crap. I need a do-over."

"OK, but what do you need me for? You should go by yourself. Why complicate things with a fake boyfriend?"

"Because he has a girlfriend, and I'm pretty sure she's not fake."

"Have you seen her? Like on social media or anywhere?"

Esme remembered the moment she deleted her Facebook and Instagram accounts. It had been a long day, even longer than usual. Her father's nurse had called in sick, and the woman they had sent to cover for her was completely inept. Her father had a doctor's appointment, and everything that needed to happen first—feeding, bathing, and dressing—took twice the time it usually did. When Esme finally got him into the ambulette, there was no way they were making it on time. When they arrived late, they were told the person after them had gone in first.

Esme had spent the time scrolling through her social media—something she had been avoiding, as it always made her feel awful. She had just turned twenty-six, and suddenly other people's lives, or the lives they were showing the world, looked as if they were beginning to click on many levels. Stephanie Wolf was on a business trip to Paris. Georgina Stuart was on vacation in St. Barths with her new girlfriend, who looked like Zendaya, and Esme noted two or three engagements since she had last checked in. She remembered thinking that if she and Liam were still together and had been cohabitating since graduation, they probably would have been on the same trajectory. She was filled with anger and jealousy. The feelings surprised her as, until then at least, she had never thought of herself as an angry or jealous person. She took it out on a girl named Sophie Michelson, whom she had never really liked, and who, according to her bio, was *#livingherbestlife one latte at a time!* Star-eye emoji, painted-nails emoji, and the most infuriating—red-high-heel emoji.

Sophie had posted a picture of her plate from Nobu in New York City with the caption "This fatty tuna is EVERYTHING." It enraged Esme so much that she felt a slow burn fill her chest. Stupid Sophie Michelson was bragging about fatty tuna at the most famous sushi restaurant in New York City while she had just chugged a warm chocolate Ensure from the pouch behind her father's wheelchair because his appointment had gone through lunch.

She typed, *Takes one to know one!*, referring to the fatty tuna, with a misguided sense of vengeance against the girl who was always trying to take off a few pounds. She paused before pressing Enter. It was all too much; she didn't even recognize herself anymore. She deleted the nasty comment and then did the same to all her social media. In retrospect, she was surprised she hadn't snapped sooner.

"No, I'm not on social media. Do you want to check yours?"

"I'm not on it, either. We may be the only ones left." He laughed.

"What's your excuse?" Esme asked.

"Remnants of communism from my time in Cuba, I guess. You?"

She surprised herself with her honesty. "Jealousy, I guess. It was a constant reminder that the entire world was happier than me. I've never swiped left or right, either, have you?"

"No, I missed that whole thing, too," he said, holding up his ring finger and doing a single jazz hand.

He was really sticking by his story, and though Esme sensed there was something fishy about it, she now believed that the marriage itself was real.

"Do you have the rest of the invitation, with the benefit committee on it?" he asked.

Esme stared at him blankly. While this was totally out of her league, it turned out that Young George Clooney, in contrast to his Communist rhetoric, had apparently been to many a fancy benefit, usually on the arm of his grandmother when his grandfather had bowed out. He pulled out his phone and googled, narrating his every move.

"OK. Audubon Society NYC—got it . . . *Home, About Us, Go Birding*—who knew?"

"Not me." Esme smiled, encouraged by his sudden enthusiasm.

Here we go—*Events and Adventures . . . The Bird Ball. Host committee: Mr. Liam Beck and Ms. Morgan Miller.*"

"Morgan Miller? Let me see that."

Zach googled more before turning his phone to Esme with a picture of Liam and his girlfriend, the stunning Morgan Miller. Esme's face dropped along with her turkey sandwich.

"What?"

"Morgan is the younger sister of Liam's best friend, Jed. I met her when I visited the Cape. Their father runs the firm that Liam works at, Miller/Meyer."

She sunk back onto the blanket, surprised by how completely deflated she felt. Zach rubbed her arm and said it was no big deal, but she could tell he was lying. Liam was dating the daughter of the CEO of the company he worked for—the ever-powerful Michael Miller. Esme had pictured him involved with some random girl, not one he had a longer history with than her.

"Why are you so upset?" Zach asked. "You didn't want him anyway."

"Yeah, but I thought if I did, it would be a simple thing—not the equivalent of King Edward abdicating the throne for Wallis Simpson."

"And you're Wallis Simpson?"

"Yes, and Morgan Miller is the entire British Empire."

Zach laughed, hard, while Esme formed a desperate pout.

"Will you please be my date for the Bird Ball?"

"I don't know. What do you think they're going to serve at this thing? I'm thinking quinoa. Is that how you say it? Definitely not chicken."

"You think you're very funny, don't you? You know I could ask someone else."

"Who, Sy?"

Esme giggled at the thought, and the unfamiliar feeling—happiness—made her giggle more.

She pulled out her phone. "Maybe it's time I learned to swipe right."

This got his attention. He went to grab her phone back, and she jumped up, running around serpentine-style until he finally tackled her. Even prone on the ground, she didn't give up, switching hands, pressing it behind her back, over her head, under her butt. Zach's hands were flying everywhere. Whenever they stumbled over her body she felt a jolt of electricity that caused the hair on the back of her neck to stand up straight and her heart to jump. He seemed to feel it too, as he abruptly rolled off her and sprawled out on the ground in dramatic defeat.

"OK, you win. I will be your date for the Bird Ball!"

"Really? Thank you!"

"Don't act so surprised." Zach laughed. "You had to know I wouldn't let you go alone. And in all seriousness, I think that if you leave New York without clearing things up with your ex, you will think about what could have been forever."

She wondered if he was referring to her love life or his own but didn't pry.

"You're the best, Zach, thank you!" She leaned over him and kissed him quickly on the cheek.

"That one was from me," she said before dramatically planting another longer kiss in the same spot. "And this one is from the fishnet Louboutins with iridescent jewels and one-hundred-millimeter heels that have never before stepped out of the house, let alone gone to a ball!"

Zach laughed again, adding, "I don't know how you're going to go back to mere mortal shoes after this."

FIFTEEN

The Fishnet Louboutins with Iridescent Jewels and One-Hundred-Millimeter Heels

The more Esme thought about the Bird Ball, the more she was sure she needed to be wearing the fishnet Louboutins. Even in the apartment with no one watching, they gave her a much greater boost than their hundred-millimeter heels supplied. She was convinced that, like Cinderella, she would not have the confidence to go to that ball if her feet were not adorned in the French designer's version of the glass slipper.

The problem was, the shoes had never been worn. And while Catherine had given her carte blanche to do so, Esme knew that breaking in the red-bottomed soles of a pair of Louboutins was akin to taking a new car out of the lot. She decided that, after walking Elvis to the dog park, she would bring the shoes to Mrs. Berger in advance to see if anything could be done to preemptively preserve their soles. A solution would go a long way to preserving Esme's soul as well. Breaking in someone else's Louboutins was a sacrilege.

But first, the dog park.

Within minutes of Esme planting herself on her usual bench with a sandwich of baked salmon salad on an everything bagel, Sy appeared. She offered him half her lunch, and though he passed, he beamed with pride at her growth in the bagel-topping department. He noticed the shoebox poking out of her bag.

"Oh no, not again?"

"Oh my gosh, no. This is a preemptive visit. If Elvis had eaten these shoes, I think *I* would have had a nervous breakdown!"

"You could've been roommates with Catherine Wallace at shoe rehab," he teased.

"Very funny, Sy! But the truth is better. I'm going to a ball!"

"With the prince of Barrow Street?"

"I'm going with Zach, but it was the prince of Barrow Street who invited me. Don't get too excited, though—he already has a princess."

Sy did his best to imitate a teenage girl. "Tell me everything."

Esme laughed but was determined to hear the rest of Sy's story.

"No way—I will not tell you mine until you finish telling me yours."

"We're on to happy things, and my story doesn't end well."

Esme considered letting him off the hook, for now. She was excited to tell him about Thursday night, but before she could, he began.

"Fine. Where did we leave off?"

"At two a.m. with Lena crying on the deck of the boat."

They both got comfortable and settled in for the long haul.

"Right. So, that night on the boat, everything changed. I told Lena that I loved her, and she told me that she never felt for Sheldon Schusterman the way she did for me. She said that when she saw me even crossing the street toward her, she'd have to press her knees together to steady them."

Esme thought again about her own wobbly knees at Berger's

Stitch and Shine. The thought made her stomach turn. She had no interest in inviting any more drama into her future and was eager to get to the smooth-sailing part of her life. Sy, meanwhile, had hit his stride.

"Me, Sy Katz, making this beautiful girl go weak at the knees! I never thought it possible that she felt half of what I felt for her. But like the kids say today, it was complicated. The two families were very close. Not only were they neighbors, but they were in business together. And, of course, she felt she couldn't break off the engagement while Shelly was still overseas. I understood, but I wanted to give her a ring so that she would have something from me, an assurance of my love. That felt dishonest to her. She promised that she would break it off first and then we could become engaged the minute I got home. She would take care of everything with Sheldon at the right time.

"A few days later I began training. There was a Coast Guard station right at Manhattan Beach, so I got to see my mom and Lena when I had time off. On the day I was to ship out, Lena came down to say goodbye. She was crying. I would have been, too, but all the guys were watching. Nicknames stick quickly in the service, and I could just imagine what a teary goodbye would have gotten me. I held it together until she reached into her pocket and placed this in my hand."

He reached into his own pocket and pulled out a silver compass. Engraved on the back it read *I Am Your North*.

Between Esme's own state of mind and the fact that she knew they didn't end up together, she didn't know how she held back the tears. It may have been the most heartbreaking thing she'd ever heard.

"You still carry it in your pocket? That is the most romantic thing I've ever heard," she managed instead.

"A lot of good it did me." He shook off the gloom and carried on with his story.

"So, after a few months of training on the Great Lakes, the Coast Guard sent us across the Atlantic. We were part of a flotilla of landing crafts; mine was the LCI-83. You've probably seen this type of boat in the movies, flat-bottomed ships with a lowerable ramp rather than a normal bow. They were used to drop troops as close to the shore as possible during an amphibious assault."

Esme nodded; she actually could picture just what he was speaking of from the movies.

"We practiced landings over and over, going out for hours and hours every day and landing the boats on the beach until we got it straight. There was no room for error. I was in two major invasions and four landings—all before D-Day."

"I can't imagine how scared you were."

"There was no room to be scared, either. You know, you change a lot after you've been under fire. You don't smile as much as you used to. Things aren't as funny as they used to be. I changed. A lot. Whenever I saw a German plane shot down, I thought of my father and my family over there. Though at the time we still didn't fully comprehend what was going on. People don't really understand that—the full extent of the Nazi atrocities weren't revealed till the Allies liberated the camps in 'forty-five."

He took a beat before stating, "And that was it, I never saw Lena again."

"Wait, what? I think you skipped ahead, no?"

"To tell you the rest, I'd have to tell you about the war. Men don't like to speak about war—and for good reason. Talking about it means remembering it. And the things I remember may be too much for a young woman like you to hear."

"Don't worry about me. I can handle it, if you want to try."

He smiled at Esme. "I hope *I* can handle it. I've never really spoken about it before."

He adjusted himself in his seat and continued, in a softer voice than usual. Esme was now completely glued to his every word.

"I'll back up and try to tell you things in the order that they happened. Our first stop was the North African occupation of Tunisia, where we landed in a city called Bizerte. It's the northernmost city in Africa, sitting right on the Mediterranean. We were there for a while. I never saw anything like it before or since; it was a big city, nearly the size of Manhattan. It was already leveled to the ground when we arrived. It ended up being a cleanup mission of sorts, because whoever survived had fled and there was hardly a building left untouched. I never thought the same way about my home again after seeing that—never took the roof over my head for granted.

"From there we headed right across the sea to Italy, transporting troops for the invasion of Sicily. During practice landings, we had been taught to bring our vessels about twenty-five feet from the shore to let our men off safely, but I was a bold kid, and I sometimes defied orders, beached my boat, and went with the men. I did that in Sicily. I saw babies roaming the streets without any clothes on, begging for food. We gave them as much as we could, but it was devastating to witness. I saw tough soldiers moved to tears by it. I watched more than one Nazi die, and I have to say, I can still remember the satisfaction I felt inside of me, thinking of my father and how the Germans needlessly gassed him in World War One, causing his death years after he was home.

"A couple of months later, when we took the beach at Salerno, I saw nothing but death. I watched men, boys really, going down the ramp of my landing craft, carrying forty-five pounds of weight on their backs, blown to pieces, and I had no choice but to get the hell out of there as fast as I could, to bring more men. They called it a victory, but it didn't feel like that to me."

Esme was silent. Sy stared blankly.

"You see what I mean?" he said. "What good does remembering all of this do?" He looked shaken up, and Esme felt bad that she had pushed him that way, but he seemed to want to keep going.

"I could have gone home after the Italian landings, but I signed up for another tour. It was a tough decision. My mother was desperate for me to come home, and I wanted to get back to Lena in one piece and fulfill my promise to spend the rest of our lives together, but I felt a huge responsibility to the crew. We had trained for many months to work together and to depend on one another. We all knew what to do in a pinch, each man's life depended on his shipmates. Even though I had a very small part in the assault against the Nazis, I felt I had to do my part. I figured I would make it up to both of them when I got home."

He looked at his watch—usually a telltale sign that he had had enough talking.

"Let's walk toward Berger's," he announced.

A few steps into the park and Esme linked her arm through his. If anyone was watching them, she imagined, they looked like grandfather and granddaughter. She wanted to hear the rest of the story but sensed that she should redirect him.

"What happened after the war?" she asked.

"To get to that I have to tell you what happened in France. The invasion of Normandy on D-Day was the end for me—not like it was for thousands of other poor souls, but I barely made it out alive." Esme was relieved that they were walking arm in arm and not sitting eye to eye. She guessed that he was, too.

"After Sicily and Salerno, we traveled around the boot of Italy, trying to jump-skip the Germans before making our way to Dartmouth, England, to prepare for the invasion of Normandy. *Prepare* may not be the right word. There was nothing that could have prepared us for Normandy. The night before D-Day we were told that we were joining a large operation, but we had no idea of the scale of it until we saw the other ships. There were thousands of them. It was the largest invasion ever assembled, before or since. The thing that shook me the most, at first, was the noise. The sound was deafening: naval guns blasting offshore, machine guns mixed with huge shells exploding on the beach, and planes swooping above, dropping bombs. Over all of it, I could hear my heart pounding in my chest.

"When we arrived at Omaha Beach, I dropped the front gates of the landing craft and watched as the guys plunged chest-deep into the water, this time toward near-certain death. The Germans were plucking them off one by one, like a carnival shooting game; some never even made it down the ramp. Bullets were flying everywhere. I felt like I was watching myself from above do what I was trained to do, but I had no idea how I was even holding my hands steady enough to do any of it.

"Eventually our landing craft struck a mine that blew a hole right through the troop compartment. I closed my eyes and braced for death, but it didn't come. The boat was grounded from the blow, and whoever was able to had gone ashore, stranded on the beach with the rest of the troops. We were like sitting ducks, under constant fire from the Germans on the cliffs, men dying everywhere you looked. There was nowhere to hide. It was surreal, like a horror movie or those video games the kids play—as if they weren't real men, with mothers and children and plans. Our captain yelled above the noise that we could patch up the hull well enough so that when the tide came back in, we'd be able to get her off the beach and back across the channel to England. Lucky for us, the Germans, seeing that we were disabled on the beach, turned their gun-fire elsewhere and stopped shelling our ship. When the tide came back in, the firing started up again, but somehow we were able to get her off the shore.

"That's when a piece of shrapnel hit my helmet and knocked me under the water for what felt like an eternity. It was as if I went deaf. I lifted my head out a few times, but, with each effort, silent bullets bounced off the water, now red with blood, sending me back under. My buddy, another kid near my age from Oklahoma, saw what was happening to me and grabbed me by my collar. As he lifted me up, a line of bullets ripped his head to pieces right in front of my eyes. I felt myself screaming but couldn't hear any sound. I later found out that the initial hit to my helmet had burst my eardrums. I can't begin to describe the fear. I was thousands of miles from home and had just entered hell—immersed in my friend's blood, his face no longer there."

Esme winced at his graphic description.

So much for him worrying that it would be too much for a young girl to hear.

When they got to Berger's, Sy kept walking, and she didn't stop him. It seemed like he needed to finish the story.

"The weight of him with all of his gear on top of me brought me back under, and at that moment, I remember deciding to give up rather than fight my way up again. The deeper I went, the safer I felt. I don't know if I was beginning to lose consciousness, or if my mind was enabling me to die in peace, but I removed myself from the horror around me and went somewhere else. I had seen scared men do this before, but it usually took the form of reciting the Lord's Prayer or, for a Jew, the Mourner's Kaddish. But prayers never brought me much peace. I willed my thoughts to the summer that I had learned how to swim, sweltering Sunday mornings when my pops and I would do cannonballs off the pier of Sheepshead Bay before shooting back out to the water's surface. My father would easily scale the bulkheads and reach for my hand to pull me back out, as I struggled to keep my head above the current. *Take my hand, son*, he would say over and over, before lifting me up with one arm like a human crane. For a minute I was there with him, and in that minute I felt great solace. I could see my father again, I thought, if I let myself go. His muffled voice—*Take my hand, son*—grew louder and louder until it sounded like an order. I was ready to give up, until I envisioned Lena's face: I pictured her being told I was gone, her violet eyes dark with pain and tears. I couldn't take it. I pushed my friend's dead body off me and used whatever strength I had left to propel myself to the water's surface. The voice was not my father's at all, but my captain's shouting.

"Take my hand, son!"

I reached up to him, and he pulled me aboard. As I lay on deck coughing up a mixture of the sea and other men's blood, my senses went dull.

"The next thing I remember was being propped up on the side of the ship as other men shouted jubilantly at the sight of the White Cliffs of Dover, England. I had never seen such a beautiful sight, but I had no words. I hadn't spoken or heard a thing since being pulled onto that boat. I could see in the eyes of the other men that they doubted I ever would. One of my eardrums was busted, and I was shell-shocked."

Esme thought about her father, who had not said a word since the accident, even though there was no physical reason for it. One of his doctors had once described him as shell-shocked, too. Esme had never heard of that before or since, until now, and she shuddered inside.

"Was it PTSD?" she asked.

"People didn't talk about PTSD then. It wasn't even named yet, but I guess that's what I had. The word *shell-shocked* seemed to come with cowardice attached to it, though I knew enough after what I'd been through to know that I wasn't a coward. I was sent to a country estate turned wartime hospital in rural England to recover. I was vacant, like a walking dead man.

"I felt as if I'd lost my mind, and even overheard two nurses confirming it. 'That boy will never be the same.' I didn't speak until I asked for a paper and pen, with the intention of writing to Lena and telling her that I was not the man she remembered and she should go on without me. When I was done pouring my heart out on the page, I tore it up. I took another sheet and wrote that I was not returning home and was making a life for myself in London. I wrote that there was no place for her in it. I knew she wouldn't have accepted the first letter, and I loved her too much to ask her to spend her life with a poor, broken man."

"Just like me," Esme said quietly, barely realizing she had said it out loud.

"What's that?" Sy asked.

"I get why you did that. I did the same thing with Liam. That's why I think he must hate me. You never saw her again?"

"I never saw her again. I imagine that Lena must have hated *me* when she received that letter. Maybe she still does. It wasn't like she didn't know where to find me over the years."

He paused, obviously remembering the reason he had told her the story to begin with. "There was no closure, and I sometimes think that if there were, my life would have gone differently. *You* still have time. You have to clear the air with Liam."

Esme cleared her throat and perked up. "That's my plan."

He held up his hands, signaling for her to proceed.

"Would you mind if I give you a hug first?" she asked.

"Why? To thank me for my service?" He smiled coyly.

"For telling me your story."

"Believe me, it's been a long time since I talked to someone like that. I may have needed it. Lately, I've been thinking of going to a shrink—just to have someone to talk to. I like talking to you better." He smiled.

"Me, too!" She laughed before giving him the hug she had threatened. His shoulders dropped and she could feel the tension slip from his body as she embraced him. She thought to ask him when the last time was that he was hugged but didn't really want to know the answer.

On the way back to Berger's, Esme told Sy more about her big plans for the Bird Ball. He was thrilled that she would be spending time with Liam and equally happy that she had a "nice young man" to escort her.

As Mrs. Berger contemplated the magnificent pair of shoes, Esme swore she saw a tear form in the cobbler's eye.

"The vamp, the heel, the tilt of the footbed! It's like looking at the *Mona Lisa*," she said in a sweeter voice than usual. She instructed them to "come around the back." Then she added "And pick up that dog," in her usual bossy tone.

Standing in the inner sanctum of the Stitch and Shine seemed to make Sy nostalgic for his own shop.

"Will you ever retire?" he asked Mrs. Berger, a hint of envy in his voice.

"Yes," she said emphatically, "just as soon as they carpet the streets of Manhattan."

They all laughed as Mrs. Berger reached into a gold shoebox and pulled out a pair of sole guards that she carefully snapped on to the bottom of each shoe.

"Here you go." She handed them back to Esme, adding, "Our secret—good for the shoe, not so good for the cobbler!"

Esme wanted to hug her, too, but sensed it would not go well.

"Thank you." She beamed, excited beyond words by the thought of wearing the *Mona Lisa* of shoes.

"Please." Mrs. Berger dismissed her gratitude. "Where are you wearing them?"

"To a summer ball for the Audubon Society," Esme answered, hoping to do the shoes justice.

"For the birds?" Mrs. Berger asked, surprised by Esme's feathered calling.

"Maybe for the birds and the bees," Sy piped in, thinking he was quite funny.

He and Mrs. Berger laughed. Esme thought about the ages of her new friend circle and laughed, too.

"What are you wearing them with?" Mrs. Berger asked, genuinely concerned.

"I'm not sure yet."

"I have just the thing," she said before disappearing. After a few minutes, she returned carrying a stunning halter dress with tiny pink flowers appliquéd around the neckline. It went perfectly with both the Louboutins and the venue.

"Here. This Halston dress hasn't been picked up since 1987. Now it's vintage."

"I couldn't," Esme protested.

"You must," Mrs. Berger insisted.

Esme acquiesced and took the dress. "Thank you for doing this for me," she gushed, even though she knew full well that Mrs. Berger was doing it for the shoes.

SIXTEEN

The Steve Madden Metallic Braided Sandals

Esme had clocked many miles traveling down memory lane since first bumping into Liam. She remembered one night in particular that had really shaped the course of their relationship. She wondered if Liam still thought about it.

Esme had visited Liam's home on Cape Cod twice: once in the winter, low season, and once over the Fourth of July, high season. The experiences were the antithesis of each other—like visiting two completely different places.

The first trip took place on an unusually warm March weekend when Liam had been summoned to help set up his family's seasonal bait shop, which had been the Becks' livelihood for three generations. There was barely enough profit in it to support one family, let alone three, so one of the brothers would be trained in the business and the other would have to find his own way. First dibs traditionally went to the oldest son, but this time it was reversed. It was clear early on that Liam, whether through his brains or his arm, was going places that no Beck had gone before.

The Cape and baseball went together like linguini and clam sauce, and while Liam's brother was never very good at sports, Liam was pretty much good at everything. It soon became evident that baseball would get Liam off the Cape and into college. And it did, but not quite in the direct way his dad had expected when teaching his son to become a switch-hitter.

Famous for having the best amateur baseball league in the country, the Cape was the first stop for many college athletes before the majors, and each team held a kids' clinic in the summer. Hopeful that baseball would be Liam's ticket out, his dad had signed him up for the clinic in Chatham, the town where his bait shop was, rather than two towns away in Orleans, where they lived. In Orleans, Liam had lots of friends; in Chatham he had none. At first Liam missed working at the bait shop. He was happier helping people get fish out of water than being a fish out of water himself. That all changed when he struck up a friendship with the runt of the group, a summer kid from Manhattan named Jed Miller.

Liam and Jed became fast friends, and Jed soon invited Liam over to his vacation house, a ten-thousand-square-foot mansion just a hop, skip, and a line drive away from the elite Eastward Ho! country club. If walking into the Millers' palatial home wasn't enough to blow Liam's mind, meeting Jed's mother and father did the trick. Cassandra Miller sashayed in from the pool in a long pink caftan and kitten heels, stepping, as Esme imagined from his description, right out of a Slim Aarons photograph. She literally offered Liam a glass of Kool-Aid that the maid fetched for him. After he drank it, he never looked back.

Jed's father, prominent New York City banker Michael Miller, was quick to warm up to his son's new friend. From their first conversation, he could tell that the boy was cut from a different cloth than his own son, Jed, who struggled in school and spent more time on the bench than on the field in every scenario. Mike Miller knew Jed was not going to follow in his footsteps under his own steam but thought the two together would have a shot. He took the easily malleable Liam under his wing with that intention.

By the summer after ninth grade, Liam was occasionally caddying for Mr. Miller at Eastward Ho! By tenth grade, after a run of good luck on the course, the superstitious Mr. Miller wouldn't play without Liam by his side. He assured Liam that baseball was not his way into the Ivy League—*he* was.

Liam's father was not happy about his son's close relationship with the high-stakes Miller. He felt he should be playing ball all summer to assure being selected for a college team. Liam paid no mind to his father's discomfort and heeded Mr. Miller's advice. In the end he got to college because of connections, but not the kind involving a bat hitting a ball. The situation caused tension between Liam and his blue-collar dad, and that tension remained even after Liam both was admitted to Dartmouth *and* earned a spot on their baseball team.

When Esme and Liam visited the Cape the first time, everything was great. Nothing pulled them away from home, and both his parents and his brother appreciated the family time and getting to meet the girlfriend he was apparently "always going on about." Esme loved hearing his mother say that. She sometimes felt like winning Liam was a prize, and she was happy that he felt the same. Whenever they walked around campus with his big lumbering arm draped over her shoulder, she felt proud. Him telling his mom about her affirmed that the pride was mutual.

Opening the bait shop for the season was a big job, and while Liam pleaded for Esme to stay back at the house and do schoolwork, she insisted on rolling up her sleeves and pitching in. She'd loved every minute of it and left with a warm feeling for Liam's family. It was a perfect weekend.

Esme was excited to return for the Fourth that summer. Her mom took her shopping for new bathing suits, cutoffs, and the cutest pair of Steve Madden metallic braided sandals that went perfectly with her favorite sundress.

The quiet town that she had visited in March was now brimming with action. The summer people had arrived, creating traffic and noise and a livelihood for the year-round inhabitants, who were both grateful for their business and wary of their company.

Traditions for the Fourth were a big deal on the Cape, and Liam was in the tough position of having to choose between meeting his old friends over at Skaket Beach for a keg party with beer, sparklers, and sky rockets, or champagne, lobster tails, and the perfect view of the professional pyrotechnics at the Millers'. Wanting to impress Esme, he went with the fancy blowout at the Millers'. Not wanting to hear his father's lecture on old friends and loyalty, he lied as they left, announcing that they were headed to Skaket Beach.

As expected, the party at the Millers' was quite over-the-top, but unexpectedly, no one there paid much attention to Liam and Esme. Mr. and Mrs. Miller were the hosts, and while they were happy to meet Liam's girlfriend from college, there were a lot of guests, and their conversation didn't get much past the standard niceties. Jed was busy chasing a girl, with Liam's encouragement, and the only other person who seemed to be interested in them was Jed's little sister, Morgan, an awkward teenager with braces and an obvious crush on her brother's best friend. She followed them around the whole night.

After taking in the view, the music, the lobster tails, and the oyster bar, Esme could see right through Liam's perpetual smile to the guilt that had been eating away at him.

"Want to get out of here and meet up with your other friends for the fireworks?"

"You wouldn't mind?"

"Of course not."

They drove up-Cape and pulled the car over by Skaket Beach, a bayside length of sand located on the shore of Orleans. The parking lot was already full, so Liam circled back and pulled off in the dunes. For Liam, both the parking lot and the beach were the scene of many a high school Saturday night. He was glad they had come. It made him feel nostalgic, and he was happy to be introducing Esme to his old gang, who were far more in tune with the real Liam than the crowd at the Millers'.

It was a dark night, and as they made their way from the sand to the pavement, Liam stopped to thank Esme for always seeming to know what was best for him. He gathered her in his arms and kissed her sweetly on the lips. As per usual, one kiss from Liam left Esme longing for more. Another kiss, followed by him nuzzling her neck and pulling down the strap of her dress with his teeth, and she was a goner. They found a secluded spot in the dunes and made love in the sand. They finished just as the fireworks began, their passionate oohs and aahs in sync with the distant crowd.

Half-naked and tired, they both drifted off in the warm sand. If it weren't for the mosquitoes, they might have slept there all night.

"Let's go home," Liam said, nudging Esme awake around 3:00 a.m. "We're getting eaten alive."

They shook off the sand and collected themselves, walking hand in hand to the car. Once inside, Liam looked at Esme and said, "I love you so much it squeezes my heart."

Esme smiled at his perfect description.

"I love you so much it squeezes my heart, too."

They drove home, holding hands the whole way, and Esme couldn't remember a more perfect night, until they pulled up to Liam's house and saw a police car parked in the driveway. Liam ran straight in. Esme collected herself for a second, noticing another officer and a group gathered at his neighbor's house. When she ran in, Liam's mom released her grip on Liam and hugged Esme as if she were seeing a ghost.

"What is it, what happened?" Esme asked.

Liam was now sitting on the couch crying. She had never seen him cry before. She felt scared and suddenly very far from home. His mother released her grip and explained that a dozen kids were in the hospital, and two, including the Murphy boy, Liam's oldest friend from next door, were in critical condition. They believed it was a drug overdose of some kind.

"I think it was Molly," Liam's younger brother piped in.

"What do you know from that?" his mother snapped back.

"That's what Timmy's sister told me, that some kid they didn't know well brought Molly. I don't even know Molly."

Though wrought with worry for his friends, his brother's innocence made Liam smile through his tears. "Molly is Ecstasy. It's a psychedelic drug that some college kids take."

His mother flashed him the look of death.

"Not us," Liam said, turning to his brother. "Obviously we would never do anything like that."

The conversation was cut short by guttural screams coming from the house next door. They rose to a deafening wail, and they all knew that Tim Murphy was gone.

Opioid and heroin overdoses at the Cape were often in the news, and there wasn't a local parent who didn't warn their child about it.

Apparently, when a kid from down-Cape pulled out a bag of what he claimed was Ecstasy, they thought it wasn't as bad and gave in to peer pressure. Until one kid's heart stopped and the one girl who was in her right mind administered CPR while her girlfriend called 911. After that, they started dropping like flies.

"I knew you were too smart to take that, but Daddy went out looking for you," his mother had cried.

Both Liam and Esme knew they weren't too smart to take it. Neither of them was very into drugs, but both had given in to peer pressure in the past and had even discussed trying Molly one day together. There was a good chance that this could have been the day.

"We weren't there. I'm sorry, I lied to you, we were at the Millers'."

Liam's father walked in just as he said it and engulfed his son in his arms. Through tears he cried, "*Thank God.*" And he promised to never complain about the Millers or Liam's chosen path again.

That night, Esme and Liam didn't retreat to their separate rooms but sat on the porch talking until the sun came up. Liam was not usually one to go too deep, but he spoke of his hopes and dreams and how he knew they included Esme. They would head to New York after graduation, where they would both climb their separate ladders to success. Liam had already been promised a spot in the Miller/Meyer training program alongside Jed. He knew he would succeed, as Mr. Miller had been filling his head with everything he knew on the golf course for years. Esme loved Liam's confidence, and the confidence he had in her was equal to that he had in himself. They decided that while their parents had lived small lives, they would live big lives. Together they would have what it took to make it in New York. To become a "power couple" with all the accoutrements.

Liam's dreams included buying a big house on the ocean on the Cape with a guesthouse for his parents to live in full-time. His biggest ambition was for them to never worry about the summer money lasting through the winter again—a problem that plagued many locals in seasonal businesses.

Neither Esme nor Liam had been so close to death before, and it bonded them deeply. It was as if they had gone to the Cape as two kids dating and left fully committed to a future together. They both understood and expressed the fact that they'd been spared that night by their love. They both promised to never forget it.

She wondered if Liam ever thought of that night.

SEVENTEEN

The New-and-Improved Fishnet Louboutins with Iridescent Jewels and One-Hundred-Millimeter Heels with Sole (Soul) Guards

Zach was due to arrive at six o'clock to pick Esme up for the ball. She had offered to meet him there; it seemed ridiculous for him to come all the way into the city only to go back to Brooklyn, but apparently Young George Clooney was all in. He insisted that fully immersing themselves in a boyfriend/girlfriend ruse would make the whole painfully boring event more fun.

Esme was game. Apologizing to Liam may have had top billing for the evening, but wiping that *Poor Esme* look from his eyes came a close second. She hoped that having a cute boyfriend on her arm and dressing the part of a girl who's got it going on would do the trick.

Sy had surveyed all the women at the dog park for the best places for hair and makeup, and it turned out that Bloomingdale's in SoHo had it all. He wanted to come along, which Esme found odd, until he explained that the best frozen yogurt in the city could be found there in a café called Forty Carrots tucked into the back corner of the second floor.

Of course it was about food.

After sampling each flavor of frozen yogurt, they both settled on a chocolate-peanut-butter combo with fresh strawberries and walnuts on top. Besides truly being the best frozen yogurt Esme had ever tasted, it brought her body temperature down about ten degrees, which was quite an accomplishment on a hot August day.

"Did you sell any sweets at Katz and Son?" she asked curiously.

"When we first opened we stayed clear of sweets, not wanting to step on the toes of Moishe the baker or Max the candymaker, but as time went on, and one by one most of the Jewish shops closed, we offered a couple: rugelach, babka, black-and-white cookies, and these."

He reached into his pocket and pulled out a square candy wrapped in black-and-white paper with the name *Hopjes* written in yellow.

"Here. It's a coffee caramel candy from Holland. The best!"

As she took it, she felt sad for Sy. So much to pass on and no one to pass it on to.

"Do they still sell these?" Esme asked.

"They do one better. At the café they give you a couple with the bill. The new owners are very good at keeping things the way they were. They pander to a hip new crowd, but they still appreciate the old-timers who are left. The same man whose grandfather brought him to the shop can bring his grandchild now. There aren't many places left that can cater to a hundred-year-old memory like that."

Esme unwrapped the candy and popped it in her mouth. It was indeed delectable.

"You like it?"

"Delish."

"I keep a few in my pocket when I need a little reminder of my past life. I'd keep a herring in there—but you know."

Esme laughed at the thought of it.

"You laugh, but I'm sure I smelled plenty fishy over the years—though I never minded it. It was the smell of my childhood. My pops would have probably said the same, and his, too. That's why it was so important to me to sell the shop. I failed to give an heir to the herring, but I fixed that by selling."

"I'm embarrassed to say I've never tried herring," Esme admitted. "It was a big deal when I studied in Vienna, they even had a festival for it, but it didn't appeal to me."

"The Heringsschmaus! I've never been, but customers always brought pictures into the shop to show me. The Viennese call herring the hangover cure. They say it purifies the body. Want to join me at the café for dinner next week and try it?"

"I would love that," she said, while disposing of their empty cups. It was nearly time for her hair appointment.

At the Drybar, the trendy salon attached to Bloomie's, Sy pulled down his glasses and looked over her shoulder while she flipped through the book of hairstyles with names like the Manhattan, the Cosmo, and the Mai Tai. They both agreed on the Dirty Martini, a tousled-and-textured look that said *I woke up like this*. Those were Sy's words, not Esme's. If she hadn't been head over heels for him before, this excursion certainly pushed her over the top.

She asked for the same sort of understated thing with her makeup—except for the smoky eyes that the perfectly-put-together makeup artist insisted would leave Liam staring into them like "reflections into his past and portals into his future."

Sy told everyone they came in contact with what Esme was up to that night. There may have been some Sy and Lena–Esme and Liam transference going on in his head. It was obvious that he was hoping she and Liam would get back together, while Esme's goal for the evening was to keep things platonic and slip in her apology.

If it took this much effort to feel as if she fit into Liam's world for one night, then how could she even consider fitting into it for a lifetime?

When all was said and done and she looked at her reflection in the makeup-counter mirror, Esme had to hold back tears—if it weren't for the smoky eyes, she may have considered outright weeping. Esme had not seen the girl looking back at her in the mirror in forever, and until that moment, she'd been pretty sure she never would again.

At six o'clock when the doorman buzzed, butterflies danced in her belly. She spun around in her dress and fishnet Louboutins.

"How do I look, Elvis?"

He barked a few times, as he always did when the intercom buzzed, but Esme took it as a compliment.

She could not believe she would be seeing Liam again, but when the door swung open and she got a good look at the very handsome tuxedo-clad Young George Clooney, she wondered if the butterflies were for him.

"Wow," Zach said, equally enamored. "You took my breath away."

She couldn't help but blush. Not just at the compliment, but because of the feeling being mutual. Zach dressed up in a tuxedo was something to behold. The square cut of the shoulders and the slim line of the pants did much more for him than the Che Guevara T-shirt and cargo shorts she had last seen him in. She quickly noticed that his costume for the evening and the role he was ready to play also included the removal of his wedding band.

He noticed her notice and responded, "It feels so weird to have taken it off. I feel like I'm cheating or something."

While he had just admitted that he was taken aback by how beautiful Esme looked when she answered the door, it was obvious that the absence of the ring on his finger had left him with a feeling of longing for his wife. Esme was glad he felt that way. She'd had just about enough of a complicated life.

Esme hugged him. "Thank you so much for doing this for me." Adding quite purposefully, "You are a great friend."

He smiled hugely on their release, clearly thankful that she had confirmed their relationship status.

EIGHTEEN

The Oscar de la Renta Feather-Strapped Spike-Heeled Sandals

Esme had never been to a benefit like the Bird Ball before but was thrilled that Zach had been brought up fancier than he cared to admit. She knew that he'd been raised in the Brooklyn brownstone he now shared with his mom, pre and post his parents' divorce, and attended selective private schools and summer camps. His grandparents, on his dad's side, were well-off—Park Avenue well-off. His own father, though minimally present, had always kept him and his mother quite comfortable, even by NYC standards. That was not to say that they were anywhere near the level of wealth of the Millers—they were far from it and not the type to be interested in that kind of lavishness anyway. Even though he rebelled against it, it was obvious that Zach would be able to handle himself quite well in an affluent crowd. He gave Esme the probable rundown of the night on the Uber ride there.

Entering the Brooklyn Botanic Garden, a fifty-two-acre oasis in the middle of the borough, was awe-inspiring on a regular day, but it was soon clear this was no regular day. They checked in and, as Zach had predicted, were given a table number and a paddle for the live auction. Esme slipped it into her bag, sure that it would remain there for the balance of the evening. Zach noticed her hands shaking a bit as she clasped her purse, and suggested they head straight for the bar.

A pride of peacocks—female acrobats adorned in turquoise feathers—directed them to the Lily Pool Terrace, where cocktails literally flowed like waterfalls. There were flowers as far as the eye could see: dahlias and roses and hibiscus covered the cocktail tables, the landscape, and the dresses of the female revelers. A roving band of "flamingos" played mariachi-style, and waiters flocked from the kitchen carrying trays of scrumptious-looking hors d'oeuvres.

"There's another bar at the far end of the pool," a passing waiter pointed out as they each snagged a coveted pig in a blanket from his tray.

Zach held it up to toast, proclaiming, "Any night that starts with a pig in a blanket has great potential."

Esme agreed before popping it into her mouth in one bite. Zach looked duly impressed. They headed to the less-crowded bar, where Zach took the liberty of ordering them two glasses of chardonnay.

Their second toast—"To putting the past behind you!"—felt like a premonition when she spotted her past approaching out of the corner of her eye.

"Oh my God, I see him," she somehow shouted without moving her lips.

"Where?"

"Behind you, three o'clock."

Zach casually spun around. "He's coming this way; *they* are coming this way."

Zach put his hand on her arm. "You ready?"

"Nope."

He took her hand in his and looked her in the eye. "Why are you shaking?"

"I don't know."

Her mind was running in a million directions, each one filling her with more insecurity. She landed on "I don't want to see pity in his eyes again. I saw it the other day, and I couldn't take it."

"Esme, take it from me, pity will not be what he'll be feeling when he looks at you."

"I want to run," she said, barely listening to his comforting words.

"We are not going to run. Look into my eyes and pretend there is no one here but you and me."

"Why?"

"Because unavailable and desirable go hand in hand."

"But I don't want to be desirable."

"The way you are shaking at the sight of him says otherwise."

She shook her head hopelessly.

Liam was getting closer. This wouldn't do. Zach drew her to him.

"Look at me," he said forcefully.

She did, and as she did the shaking subsided. He gazed into her eyes and leaned in with a gentle lingering kiss. Not in a way that would cause someone to shout "Get a room," but in a way that would cause a woman to melt beneath him. And Esme did.

As their lips separated, Liam Beck and his girlfriend, Morgan Miller, were suddenly right upon them. There was no need for Esme to wonder if they had seen; it was obvious from the look on their faces. Liam's eyes were not filled with pity; they were narrowed with envy. He reached for Morgan's hand and held it tight, in what felt more like a statement of ownership than affection, but it was Morgan who spoke first. Esme got the feeling that was usually the case.

"Hi, Esme, we're so happy you could join us!"

Morgan dropped Liam's hand and reached out for hers with a warmth that took Esme by surprise.

"Thank you for the lovely invitation," Esme responded in her best socialite drawl.

"Do you remember me? If you add braces and a little bump right here on my nose you may."

She said it in a self-deprecating way that only a pretty girl could pull off. Whatever it had taken to get her there, she was no longer Jed Miller's awkward-looking little sister.

Esme laughed. "Yes, Morgan, of course I do."

Morgan had trailed her and Liam all night at that July Fourth party on the Cape. It was obvious that she had a crazy crush on her future boyfriend at the time. Esme wondered if it had been unwavering. She wondered if Morgan had spent her entire adolescence pining over Liam Beck, writing his name in hearts on her school notebooks and trying to look old enough every time he visited to get him to notice her, until she finally was and he finally did. This girl had even more years invested in Liam than Esme had.

"Hello, Liam," Esme said, her voice sounding more like Marilyn Monroe's than her own. "Thanks so much for inviting us. This is my boyfriend, Zach, Zach Bennet."

Zach smiled and reached out his hand to Liam, who visibly checked him out from head to toe while responding as if it were a handshake competition. It got weird real quick. She wondered if Morgan noticed. She didn't have to ask if Zach did, because when the shakedown was over he placed his hand on her waist and gave it a little squeeze, as if to silently ask, *Did you see that? We made him jealous.* She reached her other hand around her waist and squeezed his in response: *I sure did.* The concept was fun, but really not what she was going for, or so she thought.

"Are you drinking the house wine?" Morgan speculated. "That won't do." She summoned a waiter for four glasses of Veuve Clicquot, and they arrived within minutes. It was obvious that Morgan Miller got whatever she wanted. She wore her privilege like an accessory—and not a subtle one. It incited something in Esme that she had not felt in years. That same competitive spirit that had led her to nail the best internship or win a hundred-yard dash reared its pretty head. Maybe she was lying to herself by insisting she didn't want Liam back. She pushed it out of her mind. He was obviously very entrenched in all things Morgan Miller, and she had no desire to set herself up for more heartbreak.

Morgan held up her glass to propose a toast, but Liam spoke first.

"To a fun night with old friends."

Esme wondered who he was clarifying his intentions for, her or Morgan.

"Old and new friends!" Morgan added, smiling kindly at Zach.

Esme resisted the urge to chug the entire glass in one swig for courage.

"I sat you next to us at dinner. The charity promised to keep the speeches to a minimum, so we should have time to chat," Morgan said.

Esme wondered if she was for real or subscribing to the "keep your enemies close" school of thought. Even the most confident girl may feel threatened by her boyfriend's first love. Esme would have to make it clear that she wasn't her enemy, just in case.

"Thanks, that sounds great."

"It's table three, right up front." Morgan motioned toward the ballroom, then redirected Liam. "Look, it's Harry and Diana— remember them from St. Barths last Christmas? They just got engaged; let's go congratulate them and get the details."

Liam's cheeks reddened, and he looked down at his Tom Ford tuxedo slippers, leaving Esme to wonder if he was really all in with Morgan's fancy feathered friends.

Morgan didn't seem to notice his discomposure. She pointed at Esme's feet, proclaiming, "Those shoes!" before smiling and running off.

Esme bowed her head in homage to Christian Louboutin. She was happy to have a moment to catch her breath. "Wow. She is something else, no?"

"That girl has nothing on you."

"Nothing but a zillion dollars."

"Well, she has nothing *else* on you."

"Please, Zach, she's perfect. She looks like a Christmas present that wasn't meant to be opened."

"What fun is that?"

Esme laughed on the outside, but inside she was determined to get herself together. She hoped she would have time to talk to Liam alone over dinner. She would offer her apology and never see him or Morgan Miller again until viewing their future engagement announcement in the *New York Times*. Hopefully by then she wouldn't care.

The revelers flocked to the ballroom, where floor-to-ceiling glass walls braced by white metal studs inspired the feeling of entering an enormous Victorian-style birdcage. It was certainly the perfect space for the event.

Esme was disappointed to find when they arrived at the table that she was not seated next to Liam. Neither she nor Zach had expected to be on the receiving end of the third degree, but there they were, seated in between the happy couple, with Liam interrogating Zach on the right, and Morgan interrogating Esme on the left.

"How long have you two been dating?" Morgan asked.

They hadn't thought to sync their story in advance, and when Esme came up empty, Zach took the lead. He took her hand in his and proclaimed, "It's only been a few weeks, but I think we may have a bit of that soul mate thing going on. We both knew right away."

Apparently, he hit a nerve, as Morgan said playfully, "Some people know; others have to be hit over the head with a golf club!"

They all laughed, Liam included, but Esme wondered how it had really gone down. Liam introduced himself to the man on his right while buttering two pieces of bread, keeping one for himself and handing one to Morgan, prompting a sincere "Thank you, baby."

Liam most definitely knew which side his bread was buttered on, thought Esme, but it didn't take long to see that he had true affection for Morgan. He had always been a wear-your-heart-on-your-sleeve type of guy, exceptionally loving to his mom and the little brother who looked up to him. Esme could tell by the way Liam looked at Morgan that he loved her, too. It was easy to recognize: he had looked at Esme that way for years.

Lucky for them all, the auctioneer interrupted the awkwardness with the start of the live auction. Zach asked Esme for the paddle in her purse. Esme shot him the stink eye, but he brushed it off, retrieving it himself.

The auctioneer announced, "The first lot up is very exciting for all the bird lovers in the room. Handwritten lyrics of the Beatles song 'Blackbird,' written and signed by none other than Sir Paul McCartney! Do I have one thousand dollars to start? I do. Do I have fifteen hundred—remember, folks, it's for the birds!"

Within seconds of the bidding starting, Zach was in the mix. With every rise of his paddle, Esme became more and more nervous, while their tablemates became more and more impressed by the handsome and generous bird lover in their flock. All but Liam, who just looked annoyed. Zach raised his paddle up and down and up and down for five nauseating minutes until he bowed out at ten thousand dollars. Esme didn't realize she was holding her breath the whole time until the auctioneer announced, "Going once, going twice, sold to the lovely lady at table twelve, in what I assume is a fake ostrich-feather boa!"

Esme whispered in Zach's ear, "What the hell was that all about? You nearly gave me a heart attack."

"Don't get your feathers all in a bunch; they only respect money," he whispered back.

Seconds later the previously disinterested man across from Zach asked, "What do you do, young man?" proving him right.

Esme wondered how Liam was surviving in this posh world. Did he feel like an impostor? Did he answer the story of how he and Morgan met with just "We grew up together on the Cape," leaving out that his lineage was funded by bloodworms and night crawlers, not bulls and bears?

When the auctioneer reached lot five, Morgan sat at the edge of her seat and announced to their table, "No one dare bid against me—I'm getting this for Liam's birthday!"

Her enthusiasm was contagious, and her love for Liam as obvious as it had been when she was a doe-eyed teenager. Liam's birthday, his thirtieth in fact, was coming up at the end of the month. Esme felt her cheeks redden—in an alternative universe it was very likely that she would have been married to Liam by thirty. She hoped no one noticed. She doubted they did, as all eyes were most definitely pivoting between Morgan and the auctioneer.

"Lot five is dinner for twelve in the infamous East Hampton barn of the Barefoot Contessa herself, chef Ina Garten! Let's start this once-in-a-lifetime opportunity out high at five thousand dollars. Do I have five?"

Morgan whipped her paddle in the air like it was a competition for enthusiasm. Zach placed a knowing hand on Esme's knee, and she tried to concentrate on the comfort she felt from his tender reaction as opposed to the frenetic bidding war that had begun around them for what felt like Liam's heart.

"OK, we have five. Do I see six—yes, six—thank you to the generous man in the plaid suit. Seven, do I have seven?"

The feeling of competition that Esme had felt before crept back in, and she pictured herself standing on her chair, holding up her paddle, and ending all this madness with a cry of, *He was mine first! I bid one million dollars!*

"Seven, right there, do I have eight? Eight—think of the birds— let's jump to ten. Do I have ten? Ten from the beautiful Morgan Miller, one of our cochairs. Twelve, do I have twelve? Twelve from the man in the plaid suit."

Esme remembered Liam's twenty-first birthday. They were both up at school early for student-athletes' week. It was their senior year, and she had never felt closer to another human being. She may not have been Ina Garten, but she made all his favorite things—chicken wings, meatball grinders, and red velvet cupcakes—and set up a picnic dinner right on the fifty-yard line.

"Twelve, I have twelve. Do I see fourteen, yes—sixteen, do I have sixteen?"

When he saw the location of the birthday feast she had prepared, his hunger quickly shifted from the banquet to completing the Dartmouth Seven challenge—which had nothing to do with academic or scholarly pursuits.

"Twenty, yes, twenty from our friend in the purple penguin suit!"

When participating in the Dartmouth Seven challenge, a couple must have sex in seven locations around campus, including

Dartmouth Hall, the top of the Hop, the stacks, and the fifty-yard line, the last being the only one standing between Esme and Liam, and success. Esme wondered how any birthday could be better than that one.

"Jumping by fives now, do I see thirty?"

Morgan turned her body around to the table next to theirs, where her father, Michael Miller, now sat with his second wife, who eerily looked like a much younger clone of his first. He glanced at his daughter and held up his hands, not to the auctioneer but to her. He spread all ten fingers wide and winked at her. She stood up, excitedly interrupting the auctioneer's cry.

"One hundred—I bid one hundred thousand dollars."

The room collectively gasped.

"I have one hundred, one hundred thousand dollars, do I dare ask for a hundred and one?"

Not a peep could be heard from the bird-loving crowd.

"OK, going once, going twice. Sold to the ever-generous Morgan Miller for one hundred thousand dollars!"

Morgan threw her arms around Liam's neck and kissed him all over his face. He blushed and laughed, and Esme tried to figure out if it was out of happiness or embarrassment. She wondered, *If he were asked which was his best birthday, would he choose twenty-one or thirty?* The Liam she knew would have zero interest in a fancy meal catered by a celebrity chef, even one as wonderful and charming as Ina Garten, but did she know him anymore?

Dinner was served—an inventive bird's nest made from noodles and filled with veggies. Morgan reached for Esme's hand and asked, "Will you still be in town on the thirtieth?"

"I'm leaving on the twenty-eighth, I'm afraid."

"You have to consider extending your stay and coming out to the Hamptons for Liam's birthday. Please, please! I know it would mean the world to him." She turned to Liam. "Wouldn't it, Boo Bear? They could stay with us at my mom's."

Apparently, Cassandra Miller had fled the Cape after the divorce and now summered out east in a twenty-thousand-square-foot beach shack on Lily Pond Lane. And also, apparently Liam was fine with being called Boo Bear in public. Esme waited for Liam's reaction before committing.

Liam smiled, adding, "It would be great if you both could come."

Boo Bear seemed sincere, Esme thought, and from what she now knew of Morgan, saying no in the moment may prove difficult.

Esme looked at Zach. "Could we?"

His eyes filled with confusion. He clearly had no clue what she wanted him to answer. She saw and helped him along. "It sounds like fun, right?"

"Anything you want." He rode one finger gently down her bare arm before linking it around her ring finger, resulting in a chill down her spine that both aroused and alarmed her.

Liam stood and told Morgan, "I'm meeting your dad and Jed for a Scotch at the bar." He turned to Zach, reluctantly. "Want to come?"

Zach looked at Esme for approval. She nodded and used the time to learn a bit more about Morgan. She discovered how long she and Liam had been together (two years, two months, six days—but who's counting?), what she did for a living (managed the Miller Family Charitable Foundation), and who designed the breathtaking spike-heeled sandals with feathered bands across her toes and ankles that ever so gracefully adorned her feet (Oscar). She didn't bother adding de la Renta, as if they had been on a first-name basis. Maybe they had.

By the time Esme and Morgan arrived at the bar, the room was emptying out. Liam was tolerating ribbing from the Miller men. Esme wondered if it was a common occurrence.

"Winner, winner, chicken dinner!" Morgan's dad exclaimed with a wink, still teasing him about Morgan's outrageous birthday gift.

The younger Miller added, jeeringly, "Very egg-citing, Liam. I bet Morgan will be *raven* about it for months!"

To which Liam chirped, "Oh, flock off, both of you," cracking them all up.

It was clearly time to say goodbye, and Esme hadn't had the opportunity to talk to Liam alone. She worried she had missed her chance until Liam quietly asked, "Will you answer if I call you tomorrow?"

"Of course," she said, grateful that she wouldn't have to navigate an apology in the middle of a rushed departure.

They both knew why Liam had worded it as he did. His asking "will you answer" was an obvious sign that the ever-confident Liam Beck was still harboring resentment about how they had broken up. He may not have hated her for it, but she had clearly done a number on him. Both in the way she broke up with him out of nowhere, and by subsequently ignoring the long string of phone calls that had followed. She ghosted him before it was even a catchphrase.

She felt bad about it but was relieved to step outside the gardens and be free of the evening's charade. Seeing Liam up close and personal definitely confused her. One minute he was buttering his girlfriend's bread, the next staring somewhat longingly at Esme across the table. She was very curious about what he would say when he called her, but right now she was just happy to have gone to the ball in her fancy shoes.

"Thank you! You were fantastic!" she gushed to Zach.

"You seem happy. I guess he accepted your apology."

She was happy, but mostly because it was over.

"I didn't get the chance to apologize, but he's calling me tomorrow."

"See, I told you, he's still into you. I caught him looking your way at least a dozen times."

"Nah, I don't think so. He was probably just comparing himself to you and feeling bad. I mean, you were amazing. I don't know what you would have done if you had won that bidding war, but wow!"

"I'm an old pro. I was my grandmother's date to the Lincoln Center benefit for many years. She taught me the art of driving up the bid."

"And that soul mates shtick. Perfect! It all felt so real I almost forgot it wasn't true."

Between the flowers and the moonlight and her shoes and the dimple that formed on his left cheek whenever he smiled, for a second she wished it were.

"Want to see the real Brooklyn?" he asked. "My college friends are at a club in Bushwick."

"Aren't we overdressed?" she worried.

"Nah—it's Brooklyn, they'll think we're being ironic."

NINETEEN

The I ♥ NY Flip-Flops

The blossoming beauty of the Brooklyn Botanic Garden did not spill out into the rest of the borough, yet there was still plenty of beauty to behold. Even at night, Bushwick felt brash and bold, brimming with reconfigured warehouses and art-worthy graffiti. It was a far cry from Esme's temporary home in Greenwich Village, but it also felt fun and hip, like Young George Clooney himself. It made her feel young again, or at least her actual age.

They met Zach's bearded bros from Brown on the roof of a four-story club called Elsewhere. To Esme, Brooklyn felt very far away from Manhattan and possibly the world. It was more like its own planet, one giant kingdom of hipsters who, when not participating in this sort of vice-induced merriment, were busy creatively collaborating, embarking on journeys of self-actualization, or just sitting in a corner quoting Nietzsche.

Ten minutes in, and Esme felt old and out of place. And it wasn't just because she was dressed like a socialite. The women were painstakingly original, and the men looked like they had spent hours grooming in order to look ungroomed. Esme flashed back to the scene in *Saturday Night Fever*, another nurses' favorite, when Tony Manero brought his brother, the priest, to the seventies version of a Brooklyn dance club.

I am the priest.

She thought it was funny but kept it to herself, thinking that this observation would be met with blank stares. Given the company she had been keeping for the last several years, even her references felt antiquated.

The revelers all seemed to be around her age, maybe a couple of years younger, and seemed not to have a care in the world. Was this what she had missed? In her parallel life, would her twenties have been spent thinking about the accuracy of her last tarot card reading or what color to dye her underarm hair? She knew it wouldn't. She knew if it were not for her personal apocalypse, Esme Nash would have adhered to her practice of succeeding at one thing after another until she reached her elusive goal—happiness.

She wondered where she fit in now. Certainly not with the elitist crowd at the benefit, who also seemed not to have a care in the world, beyond the birds. The "rosé all day" crowd, Zach had called them.

Where do I fit in?

She was desperate for the answer to be in Manhattan, working at a gallery. She had already checked off so many boxes toward that goal before all her hopes had fallen away.

I'll be happy when I get into an Ivy League school. (Check.)
I'll be happy when I find love. (Check.)
I'll be happy when I get a great job. (Check.)
When will I be happy? she thought.
If I get my old job back? If I get Liam back?

There was no real reason she couldn't pick those same boxes up again.

Zach approached, and she quickly tucked her thoughts away.

"I learned how to samba in Cuba. Want me to teach you?" he asked.

"It doesn't exactly go with this music."

"That's OK. Here." He pulled his headphones from his pocket and plugged one into each of their ears.

"It's a bit of a cliché, but all the Americans loved dancing to this one."

He held her close and overrode the techno music now blasting from the club's speakers with "The Girl from Ipanema." As they heel-toe-heeled around the hipsters, arm in arm, they seemed very connected, as if everyone in the room was from Earth and they were from Mars, orbiting in a direction all their own. If Zach were single, Esme thought, the scene would have probably marked the most romantic move of his life, and could have made for quite possibly the best first kiss ever—second, if she counted the stunt at the ball.

As the Latin legend João Gilberto crooned, Zach whispered the English translation into Esme's ear. When he got to the line "How can he tell her he loves her," his voice cracked. She wondered if it was a coincidence. When the song ended, they stopped and stared into each other's eyes. She blinked and came to her senses.

"I have to run to the loo," she said.

"What?" he said above the noise.

"The bathroom, I have to pee!"

Esme stared into the small part of the bathroom mirror that was free of stickers or graffiti—a space that barely revealed her lips in between a sticker that read *Free the Nipple* and another that read *Stay Infinite*. She thought so hard about what the second one meant that it gave her a headache.

When did I become an old lady? she wondered as she applied her lipstick.

She paused after exiting the bathroom and watched Zach with his friends at the bar. They were obviously grilling him—*Who's the girl? Where's your wedding ring?* And other obvious questions that seemed to have him on the defensive.

She saddled up, placing a hard stop on the inquisition.

"I'm famished," she blurted.

Zach agreed. "We literally ate like birds for dinner."

One of Zach's friends suggested they all head to a nearby place called Artichoke.

"I was hoping for pizza," Esme said, adding, "It's been a while since I had the kind of night that required a greasy slice to soak it up."

"You're in luck," Zach beamed. "Artichoke is a pizza place."

Brooklyn is even more confusing than the Village, Esme thought.

They all squeezed into a booth at the restaurant, where Esme happily kicked off her shoes under the table. Zach's friends told embarrassing stories about him in college, the kind of stories guys like to tell to mortify other guys in front of girls, even though they knew Esme and Zach were just friends. They all appeared to have been quite bummed that he dropped out their senior year. None of them seemed to approve of his wife. Esme didn't know if their reactions were legit or if it was just Yoko Ono syndrome, but clearly him staying in Cuba broke up their boy band.

From what she could put together, two of Zach's friends were attached and two were single. One of the girlfriends hadn't come because Mercury was retrograde, and the other seemed equally kooky. Upon hearing Esme proclaim, "I'm trying to figure out what to do with my life," she asked, "Personally or existentially?"

Zach and Esme both laughed, thinking it was a joke. It wasn't. And neither was her solution: "Make a vision board to figure out your life—I never do anything without first making a vision board?" She said it in this funny up-talking way that Esme had noticed earlier among the girls in the ladies' room. Like them, she ended every sentence in a higher octave than the rest, as if with a question mark—even when it wasn't a question. She could tell that Zach found this way of talking equally absurd. She knew he was an old soul, too, and didn't quite fit in there, either.

When it was time to go, Esme winced in pain, trying to put her shoes back on. It had been so long since she had danced the night away in heels that she forgot the cardinal rule of not taking them off until you arrive home.

"What's wrong?" Zach asked.

"My feet swelled up," she admitted, followed by a sad puppy dog face.

"I'll be right back, don't move."

He returned a few minutes later with a pair of I ♥ NY bodega store flip-flops and a big smile.

"My hero!" she cried. She slipped them on and followed him to the street, her Louboutins and purse dangling from one hand, the other gathering up the vintage Halston to prevent it from dragging on the ground.

Since she was handless, Zach did the honor of hailing her a cab.

"I'm gonna go home and make a vision board," she bragged.

"Maybe you should put a picture of Liam on it—take back what was yours."

"Nah, I don't want him back, and he's in love with her."

"Those are two very different things, Esme."

She knew what he meant, but she knew she had not come to New York for rejection and was not about to set herself up for it.

"Are you working tomorrow night?" she asked before getting in the cab.

"I am. Come by and keep me company?"

"Maybe I will." She smiled.

He kissed her sweetly on the top of the head and instructed the cabdriver to take her home in a way that made her feel cared for. It had been so long since anyone had done anything for Esme. Zach's small acts of kindness and concern stirred her emotions, and she spent the cab ride thinking about what it would be like to have a boyfriend again. Which led her back to thinking about Liam.

She pulled out her phone and googled Morgan Miller, intent on getting a better read of her possible rival. She was everywhere: rubbing designer-clad elbows at the Opening Night Gala for the Metropolitan Opera, stomping divots at the Hampton Classic, and sitting front row at many a fashion-week show. Morgan always seemed to be perfectly posed, arms angled back and right leg slightly bent and forward. It was clear that she had been told which was her best side and tilted her head at that angle for every snap, whether pictured alone or with Liam. It made Esme laugh.

Esme stared closely at Liam's face in the photos that included him, trying to assess his happiness level. It couldn't be easy to live his life feeling like he owed his success to someone else, especially when that someone else was his girlfriend's father. Still, even after just the one night together, she could tell his commitment to Morgan outweighed the circumstances.

As if on cue, her phone dinged.

It was Liam. Her heart jumped, but she acknowledged that it could have just been nerves.

Hi. Want to meet for a drink after work tomorrow and really catch up?

She didn't wait a second before responding.

Yes!

She did gather her senses enough to erase the exclamation point.

Yes.

And she pressed Send.

How about the Marlton at 7:00, for old time's sake?

Perfect, she responded.

The mention of their only shared NYC memory was a curious choice for a man in a serious relationship with his boss's daughter, but it would be as fine a place as any to apologize and bail on the Hamptons birthday weekend.

TWENTY

The Salvatore Ferragamo Patchwork Leather High-Heeled Sandals

As Esme slipped on a pair of hippie-chic Ferragamo sandals, she allowed herself to reminisce about meeting Liam for a drink in the lobby of the hundred-year-old Marlton Hotel that Miller/Meyer had put him up at in the spring of their senior year. It now felt like it was a hundred years ago.

At the time, they were both flying high and had sat down for a drink in the lobby to celebrate Esme's spanking-new job offer from the Hudson Payne Gallery. Staying at the newly chic Marlton, with its swanky tagline, "Honey, I Shrunk the Ritz," had them fluctuating between feeling way too cool and not cool enough. She remembered how they couldn't keep their hands off each other at the lobby bar long enough to finish the manhattans they had ordered, because, you know, they were in Manhattan. She wondered if Liam remembered it the same way, or if he had visited this or similar lobby bars so often over the past seven years that their tryst at the

Marlton was now indistinguishable from dozens of similar evenings.

As she stepped through the revolving door and found Liam sitting at "their" corner table flanked by two manhattans, she had her answer. She practiced her apology again in her head on the way to the table, but the sight of him, particularly him *there*, took her breath away and knocked her mission from her mind. He stood to greet her, a big mess of an interaction involving hands, cheeks, and lips never quite meeting at the same time. They laughed at the clumsy exchange and settled on a long hug before sinking into the cozy upholstered chairs.

She stared a little longer than was proper, but he did as well, rendering them equally awkward. At the ball, she had only taken him in in quick clips, scared to get caught looking for too long. She studied the familiar features of his face, the distinct sparkle of his eyes, and the new addition of the tiniest sprout of gray hair salting his temples. She wondered if he saw the way that time and circumstance had aged her, as she knew they had.

They set out on a back-and-forth of "remember whens" before moving on to more difficult conversations. They laughed about things like the time he swallowed a live goldfish to raise money for Dancers Against Cancer and threw it up in the toilet still alive—and how Esme had saved it, thrown it in a bowl, and named it Cat, in honor of its many lives. They compared memories of days spent at the Dartmouth Skiway, and both tried to recall the name of the kid from their first-year hall who always smelled like feta cheese. Liam admitted to looking everywhere for her the few times he'd gone back to Dartmouth for reunion weekends.

"I haven't been back since graduation—the day before, really, as you well know," she confirmed, stepping right into the sad conversation.

"I still feel awful about not being there for you that day."

"Don't. You had no idea."

She wasn't ready to sink into the hard stuff just yet, though it was the perfect jumping-off point for her apology. She changed gears instead.

"Morgan is awesome, by the way."

His eyes widened, and he smiled at the mention of her name. "She is!"

She wasn't sure what she was hoping for in response, but his enthusiastic reaction stung a little.

By the second round of manhattans, Liam was talking about his life—mostly reporting the trajectory of his career and how his family was doing. Esme mentioned that she was surprised he was still in their fourth-floor walk-up. His response deflated her a bit.

"I spend most nights sleeping at Morgan's at Fifteen CPW, but I like to keep my own place."

He said 15 CPW as if Esme should know it. She made a mental note to google it later but surmised it must be some high-end building on the corner of Central Park West and perfection. She guessed that he no longer concerned himself with the expense of keeping two places. It was obvious that some of Morgan's pretentiousness had rubbed off on him. She wasn't surprised; he'd always been something of a chameleon. In her heart she was hoping he would have said, *I stayed because I always wanted you to know where to find me.* Even though he had obviously moved on, it would have been a lovely sentiment. She had grown up next door to a family who had stayed in their tiny house long after they had outgrown it, so that their dog, who had run away years before, would be able to find them. About three years later, the little guy showed up at their front door, no worse for wear.

She eventually got around to talking about her dad and his

death, admitting, for the first time, how much guilt she'd been feeling.

"After my mom died, I woke up every morning feeling like I'd been punched in the gut. It was physically painful. But now, when I open my eyes and realize where I am, and that my dad is gone—I mostly feel relief. Relief followed quickly by guilt. It's awful, really."

Usually, that type of conversation was a room clearer. Not that anyone ever physically got up and left the room; it just always seemed like they wanted to run rather than confront such tragedy. The face they made, that pained face, left Esme wanting to yell "Fire!" just to put whomever she was talking to out of their misery. She hated that face. It left her feeling alone, self-conscious, and weirdly small. As if there was little to her beyond her tragic fate. She noted that it didn't feel that way with Liam. In fact, it felt the opposite. She felt seen for all that she was now, all that she had been, and all that she could possibly be. She was all set to apologize and say how happy she was for him that he had found true love again, but the feeling she got stopped her in her tracks. Suddenly, she began to seriously wonder, *Is it possible that we can pick up where we left off? Is that why he asked me here?*

She decided to let them both breathe a little before introducing her own agenda. Liam noticed her introspection and put his hands atop hers. She couldn't tell if it was anything more than residual sympathy from years before or an unyielding desire to touch her. Aside from taking sips of his manhattan, he kept them there for quite some time. The small act of intimacy definitely stirred something in her, and it became hard to concentrate on anything else. In the end, when they stood outside the hotel in the dense night air, the space between them felt electrically charged. She needed more time with him to assess everything, especially since her mind kept running to the hotel upstairs and how easy it would be to get a room and rip each other's clothes off. That scenario was right out of one of the hundred fantasies she had orchestrated in her head over the years during sleepless nights.

As if reading her mind, he said, "Oh boy . . . this is intense."

They both laughed, and it broke the spell a bit.

She chided herself, *Apologize now, Esme. Say what you rehearsed.*

Before she had the chance, Liam blurted, "I'm so glad we *both* have someone right now," cementing the boundary between them.

"Me, too," Esme wholeheartedly agreed. She was even beginning to confuse herself.

"I have to admit, I was ready to slug your boyfriend when I met him, but he seems like a nice guy."

"He is," she conceded, adding quite deliberately, "I don't know if you can call him my boyfriend, though. It's only been a few weeks."

"Really? Maybe you should tell *him* that."

She smirked. Zach had really fooled him.

It felt as if the moment to apologize had passed, or maybe she was looking for an excuse to see him again.

"Should we do this again?" she asked.

"I would like that. How about Tuesday night?"

"I'm having dinner with my friend Sy on Tuesday, and on Wednesday I'm seeing Shakespeare in the Park with Zach."

"Look at you, just a couple of weeks in New York and you've already captured two men's hearts."

"Not yours, though." She laughed to douse her honesty.

"You captured mine a long time ago."

His cheeks reddened as his words hung in the air between them.

What was Liam Beck thinking?

The Liam she knew was transparent about his feelings, and though a lot had changed about him over the past seven years, that trait seemed to have remained intact. He never hid his love for her or his family, and from the little she had seen of the happy couple at the ball, the same seemed true for Morgan. Maybe he was feeling conflicted from seeing her again; she certainly was. She needed more time with him alone to figure it all out. She brazenly suggested, "I could be free this weekend."

Well, not so brazenly; he did just admit to still loving her. *Didn't he?*

"I'm out east on most weekends, or on the Cape. It's summer."

Her sophisticated New Yorker facade felt like it ground to a halt. While Esme did know some things about the life of an NYC girl, she wasn't privy to the fact that everyone who was anyone high-tailed it out of town on summer weekends. She felt dumb.

"Are you still running?" he asked. "I do a six-mile loop over the Manhattan and Brooklyn Bridges every Monday morning, if you're up for it."

It had been years since she had jogged anywhere, and the idea of running six miles was intimidating. Maybe it was time to take it up again? The two of them had spent many a morning running together in Hanover. He wasn't her first male running companion. When she had initially joined the track team in junior high, her dad had made a real effort to run with her. They would get up early before school in the off-season and run the track at the high school. It would have been her fondest memory of him if not for the fact that his sweat always smelled like alcohol.

She had stopped running altogether soon after being told that her father would never walk again. The thought of saying the words *I'm going for a run* felt as if they would choke her upon exiting her mouth. She pushed it all out of her head.

"That sounds great," she answered.

"OK, let's meet outside your place. Text me the address. How's eight a.m.?"

"Perfect!"

On the way from the Marlton to the Mercer Kitchen to see Zach, Esme floated upstairs to her apartment to fetch Elvis for a quick walk. She was filled with the hope and excitement one feels after flirting with someone new, even though Liam wasn't new and it was more intense than flirting.

When she entered, Elvis greeted her as though she were returning from six months in the trenches.

"I had a nice time, Elvis, a really nice time!"

He smothered her with kisses.

Out of all the hearts she may or may not have captured during her visit to the city, his, she decided, might be her favorite—no head trips, no games, just pure unadulterated love.

Outside, in the stale August air, she began to come down from both the euphoria and the whiskey. It felt like the descent from a sugar high. Her steps became heavy, and her heart grew worried. How easy it was to open back up to Liam! She hoped her calves and quads had as good a muscle memory. She had no idea how she would run six miles on Monday.

Sitting and talking and touching hands with Liam had made Esme feel alive in a way that she hadn't in ages. She had always been known to have a strong spirit, but it had been a long time since she had felt one iota of what she had tonight. Any joie de vivre that hadn't died with her mother had certainly shorted out over the years of caring for her father. She barely recognized the old Esme anymore, and to feel her again, as she had tonight, made her mourn her own absence nearly as much as her parents'. She suddenly felt vulnerable. Vulnerable and tired. She just wanted to stay home, and texted Zach that she couldn't make it.

He responded, in all caps, **MISSION ACCOMPLISHED?**

She responded, **mission aborted 2 much 2 text Come by?**

It'll be late

Np I'll leave a key with the doorman in case I doze off

A true NY'er move!

His comment made her proud, and she thought of it as she peacefully drifted off to sleep. It didn't last long.

TWENTY-ONE

The Green Satin Gucci Mules with Bamboo Heels and Jewel-Encrusted Logos

That night, somewhere around three in the morning, Esme woke to Zach consoling her. Elvis was sprawled out between them in the marshmallow bed like a doggie divider. It was a good use for him, since he obviously failed epically as a watchdog. Zach's hand cradled her cheek. Apparently, she had been crying in her sleep.

He whispered sweetly, "Shhhh. Shhhh. Everything's OK."

Still half asleep, she instinctively leaned into his touch.

She had been dreaming of being caught in the middle of an argument between her parents. Her father laughing, her mother furious—about what, Esme didn't know. In the end it felt more like a memory than a dream. She was happy to see Zach.

"You came," she said, her pouting mouth turning up at the corners.

"I did. You looked so peaceful, I didn't want to wake you—I was too tired after my ten-hour shift to head home, and the couch was so uncomfortable the other night."

"It's fine," she said, resting her face against his chest.

"You OK?" he asked.

"Not really," she responded. "Bad dream."

His feet found hers.

"Esme, are you wearing shoes?"

"Yes. Green satin Gucci mules with bamboo heels and jewel-encrusted logos. I was so depressed." She smiled and wiped away remnants of her tears. "And you know what they say."

He didn't.

"So many shoes, so little time."

They both laughed quietly.

"What happened with Liam?"

"It was great, at first, but once I got home I felt awful. It's all so complicated—like one of those made-for-TV movies where the wife wakes up after a seven-year coma and the husband has a new family."

She sat up, reached for a tissue on the nightstand, and blew her nose.

"I had a similar conversation with Amara this morning. Well, maybe not a conversation, more like an argument. Just because something is complicated doesn't mean it's not worth it."

Esme was excited that he was finally talking about his wife with her. She couldn't remember him even mentioning her name before, though at this point she was pretty sure she existed. She perked up, kicked off her heels, and pushed herself back against the headboard. Elvis sat up next to her, making her chuckle.

"Tell us everything."

"It's three in the morning, I'll tell you tomorrow," he whined. She was sure that he would then come up with another excuse.

"Please, Zach, it will be like a bedtime story. I need to think about something other than my own troubles."

He folded his arms over his eyes to avoid seeing the two puppy dog faces staring him down.

"Amara is your wife, I assume?" she nudged.

"I guess. Apparently, she's having second thoughts about everything, losing confidence in us."

"Why?"

"Many reasons. I wouldn't know where to start."

"From the beginning, of course."

"OK, fine. I decided I wanted to study abroad for the fall of my junior year."

This really is the beginning, Esme thought. *I seem to bring this out in people. Maybe I should put* shrink *or* hairdresser *or even* priest *on my vision board.*

She got comfortable on her pillow and rolled to face him. He was still buried under his arms. It did feel more like a confessional than a conversation, but Esme didn't care.

"My father said I should 'beef up my résumé' and study economics in London or Copenhagen. 'A place that nurtures the minds of young capitalists' were his exact words. So I went right down to the study abroad office and I signed up to go to Cuba. It was definitely one of those decisions made for all the wrong reasons that turned out to be life-changing.

"By the time I landed in Havana, I was already bored with the dozen kids in my program. I was older than them to start with because I have a late birthday and took a gap year. Besides their immaturity, they seemed to be divided into two groups, neither of which I saw myself in. Half seemed more interested in creating a cool, *I studied in Cuba* persona than actually experiencing it, and the other half had suitcases filled with Charmin because they were overly concerned with wiping their American asses."

"Is there a toilet paper shortage there?" Esme interrupted, signaling that she would have been in the Charmin group. Zach uncovered his eyes and laughed. He rolled over to face her.

"Don't worry, it turns out that day-old copies of the *Granma*, the Communist newspaper, work nearly as well."

"Ew, please go on." She winced.

"So we all moved into this apartment building right in the heart of Havana, in a great neighborhood surrounded by a long seawall bordering a big promenade called El Malecón, where people fish, exercise, drink rum, and watch the sunset. There's a cool breeze off the ocean there at night. No AC, either."

Esme winced again.

"I studied at a place called Casa de las Américas. It's more like a cultural center where academics do research and publish books than a university, but it's renowned. It was pretty incredible. I really connected with my professors. They were brilliant and very open. I spent more time drinking Cuban coffee out of little tin cups and talking to them than with my suitemates. I may have been a bit of a dick at the time, but whatever.

"One night one of the teachers took me to this local nightclub, Café Teatro. Amara was performing there: singing and playing the guitar. She was beautiful, and her voice was so sexy. There was something about being far from home and doing it on my own terms that made me feel cocky enough to actually go up to her after she was done and ask if I could buy her a drink. I never would have had the nerve a month earlier. She agreed, but in a very nonchalant kind of way. I loved it. That's how she is, no games and very chill. Ironically, the thing I loved about her right from the start is the thing that is coming between us now.

"We spoke until the club closed down, and I asked if I could carry her guitar home for her. I'm sure she could tell I was harmless, so she agreed. She led us to El Malecón, which at that time of night was filled with couples hooking up. It was the perfect time for me to kiss her, but I was too chicken. I went back to that club every night after that to see if she was playing. When she was, I would buy her a drink after her set and again walk her home. After the third time she said in her imperfect English, 'Why is it you don't kiss me? Do you think I'm an ugly?'

"I laughed and told her how beautiful I thought she was, and I kissed her there and then."

"I love this story!" Esme couldn't help but chime in.

"Don't get your hopes up. That was the best part, I think."

By now they were both lying with their cheeks on their pillows, face-to-face, about a foot apart. He always seemed to have the perfect amount of stubble on his face. She wondered how that was even possible. She studied his dark brown eyes and the circle of green around his irises that she had never noticed before. If he wasn't telling her his big fat Cuban love story, she may have thought of kissing him. It had been a while since she had been kissed by anyone the way that Zach had kissed her at the Bird Ball. She wished he would do it again now, for real. She could initiate it but pushed the thought out of her mind and reminded herself that he was indeed married.

"Every day I fell for her more. She was like no one I'd ever met, beautiful on the outside, but on the inside—I don't even know how to describe her, just beyond. We're very different; sometimes you date someone who is so similar to you. If you were to put those people in any situation and draw little thought bubbles over each head, you would both be thinking the same things. Not Amara and me. We think differently. I didn't see this as a negative; she opened my eyes to so much. She has such a different perspective on life."

Esme put Liam and herself to the thought-bubble test. She decided that their thought bubbles were not the same when they were in college—also in a good way, like Zach seemed to think of his and Amara's. But now she wondered if they were different in a bad way. It confused her more.

"So the rest of the time I basically spent every minute that I could with her," Zach continued. "But as my semester was coming to an end, she started to pull away. She was upset with herself for getting too attached to me. You have to remember that at the base of everything, a dictator runs Cuba. It's a country whose people can't just pick up and leave. There's an amazing sense of tranquility there, because it's an island cut off from the rest of the world, but then you think about the other side of that: it's an island cut off from the rest of the world."

"I never considered the implications. That is intense."

"It is. Everyone saw Obama shake Castro's hand and thought it all changed, but it's not true."

She nodded in understanding as he looked at the clock.

"Should I keep going?"

"Of course."

"So when I left, we decided it would be a clean break. We wouldn't even speak. There was no point—somewhat like you did with Liam."

"It stunk, right?"

"Yes. It stunk. I was wrecked when I got home. Miserable at school; my friends had to drag me out at night. Finally I reached her on the phone and poured my heart out. I promised that if she would have me, I would find a way to get back there that summer. I got a job teaching English to Cuban dance instructors at a dance school in Havana through an old professor. That's how I learned to mambo and samba."

Esme did a little samba move with her head, and Zach smiled

at her. She noticed his cute dimple again and fought the urge to "boop" it with her index finger.

He went on to explain that the minute he saw Amara on his return, he knew that he wasn't going back to Providence in the fall. When his job was over, he reached out to his old professors for work, but they had nothing. If he stayed after his visa was up, he'd be thrown out quickly. The week that he was supposed to leave, Amara met an American translator for a media company who had to go home before his job was done because his mother became ill. Zach took over that job and was granted temporary residence for as long as the job lasted. He dropped out of Brown, and his dad completely cut him off, which only made him feel more Cuban, really, and they were happy. A few months later, out of nowhere, the company he was working for closed, and his job ended. He had one week to leave.

"The day I got my notice I came home and found Amara crying her eyes out. She is a bit psychic, but there was no way she could have known. Before I could say a word, she blurted out that she was pregnant. I knew with the way her old-fashioned father was that we had to get married immediately. I actually felt relief, like it was meant to be. A legal wedding of the state wasn't possible, so we got married on the beach by a Santería priest. It's an unofficial Caribbean religion, but to them, in the eyes of God, we were married. We decided that the best life for our family would be in America and that I would leave and prepare for her to come and give birth in America. About two months after I got home, Amara miscarried."

"Oh my, I'm so sorry," Esme said as she rubbed his arm in sympathy.

"She was devastated and grieving, and I was a thousand miles away. It was awful. After a while she started acting very laid-back about coming here, like it will happen when it happens, but she mixed up the English idiom and mistakenly said, 'It won't happen when it happens.' The mistake felt more truthful. There is this expression that Cubans use all the time, *resolvemos*, which translates roughly to 'we'll figure it out.' It's like their answer for everything that doesn't have a clear answer. She kept muttering it, but I could tell she didn't really mean it.

"As the shock of it all wore off, she decided that we only married for the baby, and the whole thing was a big mistake and not meant to be. She told me this morning that she doesn't want to leave her family and that she was considering taking a job with the Ministry of Health."

"What does that mean?" Esme asked.

"If you take a government job, you have to sign up with the Communist Party. Once you become a member of the Communist Party, you're basically disqualified from immigrating to America. I know if I could go back and see her again, I could convince her to believe in us and not to do such a permanent thing, but school starts on the third."

His eyes filled with sadness. Esme noticed and put her hands on his face.

"Resolvemos," she said with an encouraging smile.

"You really think so?"

"I'm not sure, but I think you have to get back there. Face-to-face, she will remember what she is giving up. Believe me, I know."

She kissed him sweetly on the forehead. He responded by doing the same.

"Let's sleep," he said quietly. She rolled over on her stomach, and within seconds he gathered her up and pulled her toward him. She melded right in, confident that she would sleep peacefully, his embrace shielding her from further nightmares. She was happy for the physical comfort and did her best to ignore the stirring it brought about. She wondered if he felt it, too. They woke up the next morning in that same position. It was the first time in her life that someone had held her for the entire night.

TWENTY-TWO

The Dior J'Adior Kitten-Heeled Ribboned Slingback Pumps

Between sleeping in and general laziness, Zach and Esme barely left the house that rainy weekend except to walk the dog. Zach promised her they weren't missing anything good.

"New Yorkers generally have each other's backs," he said, "until it rains, and then they act like selfish assholes."

She pictured herself losing an eye to some umbrella-wielding, post-blowout blonde running for a cab and happily changed into her coziest sweats.

They were both thankful for the weather, as it gave them an excuse to lounge around. They played cards (spit and gin), ordered in brunch (pancakes from Bubby's in Tribeca), and read the *New York Times* and the *Post* from cover to cover.

Zach taught Esme an entire dance routine that he'd picked up at the Cuban dance school to Louis Prima crooning "Pennies from Heaven." By the sixth time Esme heard the line "If you want the thing you love, you must have a pizzioli baby," she insisted on Italian for dinner. They ordered in from Little Italy, followed by a God-father marathon and a very late Sunday wake-up.

Young George Clooney left for work around three, but not before marveling at the gift that was their "lost weekend."

"Before I go," he inquired, "are we really going to this birthday thing in the Hamptons? I have to put in for days off now if we are."

She wasn't sure.

"I'm supposed to run with Liam in the morning. Maybe I will come right out and ask him if he really wants us to come or was just being nice. Can you wait till tomorrow?"

"Sure, good idea."

He gave her a great big bear hug and proclaimed, "Esme Nash—this was the best slumber party I have ever attended."

She beamed with pride.

Within minutes of unavailable man number one's departure, unavailable man number two texted with a welcome request.

> **Can't make our running date in the morning. Any chance you're free for dinner tonight?**

Esme was filled with relief regarding the run and confusion that he thought it qualified as a date.

> **Sure, where and when?**

> **I'll call the Beatrice Inn and see if they can squeeze us in—best fried chicken south of Harlem—more to come . . .**

Esme had no way of knowing the pull one must have to get squeezed into the Beatrice Inn at the drop of a hat. A reservation was usually attained one month in advance, to the day, and, after the telephone lines opened at eleven thirty, slots were commonly filled up by noon. If she had, she would have questioned Liam's motives: Did he want Esme to experience the tiered silver trays of crispy crunch-covered chicken glazed with spicy honey, or did he want to impress her with his ability to move mountains and maître d's at the drop of his name?

As she looked at herself in the full-length mirror, from her Glossier-covered lips to the ribboned Dior works of art that adorned her feet, she decided the evening would be somewhat of a fact-finding mission. Liam's answer to the birthday-weekend-invitation question would go a long way to help her understand his intentions without coming right out and asking. She ran through her apology again in her head.

Liam—I'm so sorry for the way I ended things. I didn't know what else to do at the time, but in retrospect I know I hurt you, and that wasn't my intention. I just couldn't see any other way.

At this point she knew it as well as she knew her name. She left the apartment with a renewed sense of confidence, determined to expunge the explanation from her head and to never think of it again.

When they arrived at the Beatrice Inn, Liam asked the maître d', who called him Mr. Miller (to which he offered no correction), to be seated at the bar. Her hope dimmed. Sitting elbow to elbow with strangers on each side breathing down their necks was no place for intimate conversation.

"I thought you weren't around on the weekends," she said instead.

"We're usually not, but that rain! We were bored out of our minds and came back early this morning."

She thought about her time with Zach and how easily and happily they had filled it. She considered bragging about it, planting a seed of doubt in him regarding Morgan, but the night wasn't about flaunting her "relationship" as much as deconstructing his. If she were to open up her heart to Liam again, she wanted to know that it wouldn't get broken. First up, why did he want to sit side by side at the bar as opposed to face-to-face at one of the cozy tables that dotted the room? She had to know.

"Not that I mind, but why the bar?"

"Good question. They only serve the fried chicken at the bar. I once read that the chef fears that serving it at her tables would turn her renowned subterranean hideaway into a basement chicken joint."

She liked that answer, channeling her joy into her response. "Wow. I can't wait to taste it."

After perusing the menu, she was doubly happy to let Liam order. She loved fried chicken, and many of the other dishes she was interested in were curiously marked MP, which she would never have the guts to either order or inquire about. The whole place made her feel like a fish out of water, especially in contrast to Liam, who was getting on swimmingly.

He went through the wine list with the sommelier, comparing the bouquet of a '96 Louis Latour to a '94 Far Niente chardonnay. At that point, Esme's inner turmoil turned to amusement—she laughed to herself, looking at the guy whose beverage of choice used to be a two-dollar Pabst Blue Ribbon tall boy.

He chose the Far Niente, stating how it went perfectly with the appetizer of choice, Le Grand Coquillage, which he pronounced as easily as Esme would a tuna melt. She questioned whether she had it in her to catch up to Liam, or whether to just let him go on his merry one-percenter way.

As if reading her mind, he said, "So, Esme. What's next? Are you thinking of staying in town? Have you kept up with the art market?"

The Esme Liam knew lived and breathed two things—Liam and art, and not always in that order. But it had been a long time since those parts of her were aroused. Since she had come to New York, it had all come bubbling back to the surface, and while the jury was still out on Liam, there was no denying that art made Esme happy—happy and fulfilled.

"I really let that whole part of me slip away back home, for obvious reasons, but as soon as I got to New York I caught the bug again. I've been scouring the museums and galleries and even attended a lecture at NYU on career options in the art world."

"Well, that seems like a waste. Just go back to the Hudson Payne and get your old job back."

Esme laughed, thinking it a joke.

"I'm not joking, Esme. What are you going to do? Teach, or show people around a museum like you did in college? There's no money in that. You should walk into that gallery with your résumé and tell them who you are."

"What do you even mean?" she asked. "Who am I?"

A girl who has spent the past seven years sponge-bathing her father.

She only thought that last part. She had no desire to ruin the forthcoming Le Grand Coquillage—whatever the hell it was.

"You're the woman who graduated at the top of her class from an Ivy, interned for Robert Longo, and scored a top job in the art market, beating out dozens of other applicants right out of college. Did you forget?"

"Yes. I forgot." She laughed.

"Walk in there with your résumé—"

"I did just update it," she interrupted.

"Good. Walk in there with your résumé, tell them that you were meant to work there and what happened."

"No, thank you. I don't need a sympathy hire."

"It doesn't matter how you get in the door in this city, only what you do when you get inside. Morgan and I can feed you customers. You could make bank!"

She wondered if he had used that same rationale for himself, wondered if it bothered him that the maître d' called him Mr. Miller instead of Mr. Beck, but she didn't ask. It did give her food for thought until the arrival of the actual food—a giant seafood platter (they could have just called it that), followed by what was most definitely the most delicious fried chicken she had ever tasted. There was no fried chicken like this in Rochester, she thought, though she noted that New York City hot dogs had nothing on the famous Rochester red hots. She tried to envision him visiting her there when she got back, showing off her town's more simple gastronomic delights. She watched him devour a drumstick and wondered if that were even a possibility. She doubted it. If she wanted to be with him, and vice versa, it would have to be in New York City.

Could she see herself really taking back the life she never got the chance to live? She wasn't sure that she could and still wasn't sure she was capable of walking away from her childhood home. Every inch of it, covered in memories of her parents—it was all that was left of them and the only place she had ever called home.

Liam was eating quietly because he could hardly wait to swallow one bite before taking another, but he stopped to question Esme's silence.

"What is it, Esme? I'm sorry—was I too tough?"

"No, it's not your fault. I can't think so far in advance. I ran out on everything, you know?"

"How about my birthday weekend? Can you think that far in advance?"

"I'm glad you brought that up. Do you really want us to come, or were you and Morgan just being polite? Please be truthful. I know it's a small group."

"I really want you to come! I love Morgan's friends, but they really are her friends, not mine. If we were to break up, I doubt they would even speak to me again."

Esme's head spun from the words *break up.*

Why would he even think that way unless it were a possibility?

"Not that that's likely," he added, quickly bursting her bubble. She was more confused than ever. Did he want her around because he was interested in seeing where this could go or was she now completely in the friend zone?

"You know Morgan's office is only a floor below mine? We are together day and night."

Not tonight, though, she thought, wondering if Morgan knew where he was right now.

She contemplated asking him about his mixed signals, but his answer could very well stop this in its tracks, whatever this was. She decided to bite the bullet and apologize to him, even though they were sitting at a bar, surrounded by fancy chicken-lickin' New Yorkers.

"Liam, there is something I have wanted to say since bumping into you, but it never seemed to be the right time."

She took a deep breath to calm her nerves.

"I'm beginning to realize there is no right time, so I am just going to say it."

He recognized her seriousness, placed down his drumstick, and turned to her. When they were eye to eye, the other diners seemed to fade away, and it felt as if they were alone.

"I'm so sorry for the way I ended things. I didn't know what else to do at the time, but in retrospect I know I hurt you, and that wasn't my intention. At the time, I couldn't see any other way."

Tears formed in her eyes, both surprising and embarrassing her. Liam was quick to wipe them away.

"It's OK, Esme. I'm really happy with my life now. It took time, I'd honestly never been rejected like that before, but eventually I saw that it was for the best."

Esme nodded and did her best to collect herself. She was relieved to have gotten it out, but not sure it had gone as she expected, though she had never really anticipated his response when planning her apology. He was still facing her, staring into her eyes. She couldn't take it anymore. She grabbed the menu and asked, "Do you have room for dessert after all of that?"

"Of course. The bone marrow–bourbon crème brûlée is out of this world."

She thought about the time they shared a box of frozen Yodels for dinner and wondered who the real Liam was. She wondered if he even knew.

"Sounds good. I prefer my crème brûlée with bourbon and bone marrow."

"Who doesn't?" he joked back.

At least she thought it was a joke.

TWENTY-THREE

The ASICS Kelly-Green Running Shoes

The next morning, Esme awoke with a familiar feeling of melancholy, but instead of leaning into it she leaned out. She rummaged through her suitcase and pulled out her old ASICS running shoes. The fact that she had packed them was evidence that running again had been on her mind even before Liam had brought it up. Running had always cleared her head, and she needed to clear her head now more than ever. If she could start with a fresh slate, then maybe she could figure out what was next for her.

There was no way she could run six miles in her current shape, so she mapped out a nice course from the apartment across the Brooklyn Bridge that came in at about three.

From the first stride she felt good, so good that she spent the next half mile beating herself up for letting it go for so long. When the anger passed, she embraced the clarity that had always come when it was just her and the pavement.

She continued in a slow stride as she reviewed her dinner with

Liam in her head. If she were to be with Liam, she decided, she should start first on Esme. The old Esme's dreams and wants would have to be analyzed and possibly reenacted. She was sure of one thing: there was no way the guy sitting next to her at the Beatrice Inn would have any interest in trading in that fried chicken for Honeoye Falls KFC. That ship had long sailed. And while she still wasn't sure she wanted to be on board, she was sure she wanted options. In the end, she concluded that in order to figure it all out, she needed to see him and Morgan together and spend more time with him alone. The Hamptons weekend would definitely serve its purpose.

Of course, that would mean being alone with Zach, too. The more time they spent together, the harder it was to deny her attraction to him. She didn't want to feel that way, but it was out of her control.

At the Bird Ball, seeing Liam and Zach standing by the bar together, she couldn't help but let her mind wander to a side-by-side analysis. Even in their tuxedos, the difference between the two men was obvious. She could picture them as the models for a *New York* magazine article titled "Generation Y: Who Is Mr. Right?" They were both poster children for stereotypical men of their age. One, a finance type, brought up modestly, arriving in the big city to work his ass off on "the street," spending long hours hedging and leveraging and liquifying. The other, equally attractive in a purposefully unkept way, who was brought up comfortably but rebelled against it due to his desire to save the world.

Both handsome, both taken, Esme concluded as she arrived at the foot of the Brooklyn Bridge. It was just the kind of frustrating thought that used to push her into a sprint—challenging herself to outrun it. She picked up her pace and flew across the East River.

Even with the incline and the wind going against her, she clocked it at under eight minutes.

I'm back, she thought, vowing to never give up running again.

The Dumbo neighborhood, where the bridge lets out, was actually named for the Manhattan Bridge (down under the Manhattan Bridge overpass). It was a trendy part of Brooklyn known for its cobblestone streets lined with contemporary restaurants and galleries, one of those up-and-coming New York neighborhoods where tourists coexist with locals. Esme was done running for the day but thought about walking back home over the Manhattan Bridge until a cramp in her calf benched her right in front of the landmark Jane's Carousel. She sat and massaged it as gleeful children with names like Flannery and Zelda jumped on and off the glass-enclosed structure and into the arms of their waiting parents.

Families.

The melancholy she had felt that morning reared its ugly head again, but this time she decided to mentally squash it. She took out her phone and made a list. Three new very specific boxes to check off would go far toward her feeling in control again.

1. Put any thoughts of romance with Zach out of your mind.

He loves Amara and you care about him too much to mess with his head like that.

2. Go to the Hamptons and see where things stand with you and Liam.

If you leave NYC still wondering about him, you'll have failed epically.

3. Drop your résumé off at Hudson Payne Gallery TODAY with
a cover letter asking for an interview.

If you fix your own life, everything else will fall into place.

She zipped her phone back into its pouch and strolled over to
the dock adjacent to the bridge. Within a few minutes she was
seated on top of a sleek ferryboat crossing back over the East River
to Manhattan, the theme from *Working Girl* playing in her head.
Her heart swelled at the site of the approaching skyscraper-filled
horizon. It felt as if she were heading home. She noted the feeling
and pulled her phone back out, adding, for her consideration:

4. Call the Honeoye Falls Realtor.

Still waffling about that, and needing to be honest with herself,
she made a minor adjustment—*4. Call the Honeoye Falls Realtor???*—before putting it away and taking a deep cleansing breath
of the sea air. It invigorated her. There was something magical
about arriving to Manhattan by boat, even if the ride was only a few
minutes long. She stepped off the ferry ready to face whatever came
her way.

TWENTY-FOUR

The Nine West Wraparound Sandals

The next night, Esme met Sy under the arch of Washington Square Park at dusk to walk over to the restaurant for their dinner date. With all the soul-searching she'd been doing over the past twenty-four hours, she decided to wear her own Nine West sandals in an effort to remain grounded in reality. Just as she and Sy met up, the lights in the park came on.

"Time for dinner," Sy proclaimed, pointing to the streetlights. She took his arm, and they began walking.

"When I was a kid we would hold on to the light of day as long as we could. The streetlights were like our dinner gong. When they came on, all the kids would collect their marbles and head home."

Esme could relate: not to the marbles, but to the dinner-gong reference.

"In my neighborhood it was the sound of Mrs. Cartucci down the street. She would yell, 'Anthony! Dinner!' And we would all tease him before heading home as if it were our own moms calling us. It was the source of my father's biggest dad joke. For years after I stopped playing in the streets with the neighborhood kids, he would call for me upstairs with 'Anthony! Dinner!'"

"Was he a funny guy, your dad?"

He didn't know it, but it was a loaded question.

"My dad always played to the room—you know, the life-of-the-party type. When I was young I thought his antics were hysterical, but as I got older I found his humor kind of sophomoric and embarrassing. Though that may have been my mother's influence. I remember when I first realized that my mom wasn't laughing, too; after that I was always kind of torn."

And just like that, honest memories of her parents, more so of her dad, soured her mood again. The truth was, in the years before the accident, Esme had little to do with her father. He worked all day, and most nights at dinner during high school, he was nowhere to be found. Her mother would say either that he was out with clients or upstairs nursing a headache. If Esme had given it more thought at the time, she might have concluded that her mother was covering something up, that it was more probable that he was nursing a glass of whiskey than a headache. But high schoolers are notorious for being self-absorbed, and Esme was no different. Track, AP classes, ACT prep; she wasn't very present during high school, and then she was off to college.

A male voice yelled, "Sy! Esme!" as loudly as Mrs. Cartucci, interrupting the unpleasant thoughts that had been bubbling to the surface lately regarding life before the accident.

They both turned around to see the rock star running toward them with his neighbor's dog.

"Hey," Kurt said as he reached them, a bit out of breath.

"Hey," Sy replied, making Esme giggle.

"I was wondering if you've heard from Catherine recently? I've texted her a few times, but no reply."

Esme nudged Sy, who mumbled "Yenta" under his breath. She took matters into her own hands.

"I have. She's fine."

"Did you happen to mention I've been asking about her?"

Esme had brought up Kurt when Catherine called to check in again, but Catherine had quickly changed the subject.

"I did."

"Oh."

Sy butted in. "You know, Kurt, did you ever hear the saying, 'closed mouths don't get fed'?"

Kurt looked confused. Sy spelled it out.

"If you miss this woman so much, maybe you should ask her out on a date when she gets back. A date without the dogs."

"I don't think she dates."

"Well, if you ask her and she says no, then you'll have your answer, won't you?"

Esme stepped in.

"She's back August twenty-ninth. And she loves gerbera daisies, if you want to drop some off at her place to welcome her home."

"You think I should do that?"

"She wasn't telling me!" Sy laughed.

"OK. Thanks. I will."

With that, Sy took Esme's arm and announced rather abruptly, "Well, then, that's settled. So long for now," before escorting her away, his hand resting in the crook of her elbow.

"A little hangry?" she ventured.

"I guess I am," he admitted.

In the short time Esme had known him, she had already surmised that nothing came between Sy Katz and his next meal.

"How do you know she likes daisies?" he asked as they headed toward the café.

"I figured everyone does, and it would be nice for her to come home to flowers. She seems so lonely."

"You sure you're not Jewish—a yenta and a shadchan!"

"A shadchan?"

"A matchmaker!"

Esme smiled, proud of her new title.

Stepping into the café at Katz & Son felt like stepping into all the stories that Sy had told Esme about his shop. For starters, the place was beautiful, somehow managing to be hip and modern while still reflecting old-world charm—a lot like Sy himself, actually. The picture he had shown her of his father pushing his herring cart filled an entire wall at the entrance. On the other side, a mural of famous patrons over the years: Derek Jeter, Larry David, and even the Honorable Justice Ruth Bader Ginsburg caught Esme's eye. Not one to brag, Sy hadn't even mentioned them when they were sitting at Berger's perusing her collection of famous customer Polaroids.

"Is that Pavarotti?" Esme asked, pointing to a realistic likeness of the tenor.

"Yes. He once did a beautiful rendition of 'Hava Nagila'—right there. He would literally sing for his supper."

"Come on."

"Emmes," Sy insisted.

"Emmes?"

"Truth!"

As soon as they were noticed, Sy was greeted like a king, and not just the Sturgeon King: he may as well have been the king of England. The customers and workers stopped just short of bowing.

Esme whispered in his ear, "You ride the subway when you're

lonely instead of visiting this place? You could come here for lunch and company every day."

"Nah. I don't like to make a nuisance of myself."

The workers stepped back to welcome Sy and Esme behind the counter so that he could show her what was what while giving them all attaboys and attagirls, whichever the case may be, for their herring handiwork. First he gave her a tour of the appetizing counter, stopping at each case and rattling off their contents. Esme had never seen so many types of cream cheese in her life. The fish selection was even more exciting and unfamiliar—by the time they got to the actual herring, Esme's head was spinning and her stomach rumbling. She was glad that Sy would be doing the ordering.

He put on a plastic glove and reached deep into the pickling barrel to select a good herring—no bruises, bright scales, and firm but plump to the touch.

"Here, give it a squeeze!" he instructed Esme.

She did.

"Feels good! I think it's a keeper."

Sy held the fish to Esme's face as if introducing them. "Esme Nash, meet your dinner! One shayna punim to another?"

Esme flashed the confused expression she often exhibited when Sy spoke Yiddish.

A Dominican man who had been working there since 1972 easily translated it for her. "One pretty face to another!"

She took it as a compliment. That herring, and a few of its comrades, were sent to the kitchen to be hand-filleted for their dinner, every piece of bone and skin removed by a team of experts in the back before being offered in traditional cream sauce with onions, mustard dill sauce, and wine sauce. Esme was thankful she had skipped lunch.

In between courses of pickled herring and smoked sable, as well as bowls of borscht, Esme took the opportunity to ask for some advice—words of wisdom from a childless old man to a parentless young woman regarding her future. Sy was thrilled to be needed in that way. From the warm reception he got from his old employees at the café, she could tell that she wasn't alone in her feelings for him. It was a shame he had never had children.

"How did you manage such a big comeback after everything you went through, Sy?"

He guessed that she was really referring to herself.

"Esme, one day when you're as old as I am, you will tell your grandchildren how you spent a few years when you were young taking care of your father. As awful as it was, by then it will be just one of the many things that happened in a lifetime of many things."

Sy pointed to a photograph on the wall of himself standing in front of the stall at the Essex Market, wearing an apron and a proud grin.

"That's me at your age. There's plenty of time left in your life."

"I guess. I'm hoping to interview with the gallery I was supposed to work at—I sent them my résumé and they promised to be in touch. Maybe I just need to get back on track."

"Maybe, or maybe you don't. You don't necessarily have to stick to the life plan you started out with. Look at cauliflower!"

"Cauliflower?"

"Yes, for centuries it was just a vegetable. Now it's rice, pretzels, even pizza. If cauliflower can be pizza, you could be just about anything!"

She found the analogy weirdly inspiring.

"Thank you, Sy."

"Thank you, Esme."

"For what?"

"For making an old man feel useful."

They were interrupted from going any deeper by a sweet-looking older woman named Mrs. Madelbaum, who must not have known that Sy no longer worked there, or more likely knew but didn't care. She asked him questions anyone at the counter could have answered.

"Excuse me, Sy?" she said, completely ignoring Esme.

"Hello, Mrs. Madelbaum. Nice to see you. How is your granddaughter's scoliosis?"

"Maddie? She's all straightened out now, thank God. She got engaged last month—to a cardiologist."

"Very nice."

"Let me ask you, I'm having six for brunch tomorrow. How much lox should I order?"

Something told Esme that Mrs. Madelbaum knew exactly how much lox to order, but that this was all part of the show. A trip to Katz & Son on the day that Sy Katz was there would no doubt be prime table talk at her brunch.

"A pound should do," he answered knowingly.

"I want to just do?"

Sy laughed. "Then a bisl more."

"Perfect. Zei gezunt, Sy."

"You, too, Mrs. Madelbaum, be well."

As Mrs. Madelbaum walked away, Esme marveled at how little had changed.

"I can't believe that you've been serving the same customers your entire life."

"Yes and no, look around."

She read the room. The shop was closer to the United Nations than an Eastern European shtetl.

"These are the faces of people who love herring now—it's beautiful!" Sy beamed.

Esme smiled. It really was.

They finished the night off with a piece of babka and a chocolate egg cream. Both were out of this world.

Before hugging her goodbye, Sy asked, "We're still on for sailing on Friday, right?"

"Yes! Wait till you see my shoes!"

Sy laughed, adding, "Bring one of your boyfriends with you, too, OK?"

"You know they're not my boyfriends."

"I'll be the judge of that," he said, adding his classic sign-off, "So long for now."

Later that night, Esme's cell rang, interrupting Elvis's nighttime walk. Esme hoped it was Zach but was not unhappy to see that it was Catherine for one of her now weekly phone calls.

"Hi, Catherine! Elvis and I are out for a stroll—want to say hello?"

Esme held the phone up to Elvis's ear while Catherine said loving things to him, with zero response.

"Did he react?" Catherine asked Esme when she got back on the phone.

"Yes! He definitely knew it was you," she lied. She could tell Catherine needed it.

"I miss him so," Catherine said in confirmation. "It was a hard day for me here."

"I'm sorry" was all Esme could think of to say. A few seconds of silence sat between them, and Catherine found a welcome solution.

"So, have you seen the old boyfriend again?"

Esme had spilled her whole dilemma during a lull in their last conversation, and Catherine, clearly bored, was instantly caught up in the drama.

"I did! He invited me to a benefit, and I got all glammed up, including arm candy—my very cute friend Zach. It was perfect, and I must thank you—I broke into your stash again, and it gave me just the boost of courage that I needed! I probably shouldn't tell you that, since you're trying to break that habit, but it worked well."

"It does, until it doesn't."

"I'm sure," Esme said, regretting that she had brought up the shoes.

"So, did you feel any of the old sparks?" Catherine rebounded.

"A little, but I think he thinks of me as an old friend."

"Well, there's still time to right that wrong if you want to. I'm all about righting wrongs lately—especially with old friends."

"Talking about old friends." Esme took a shot. "I know I asked before, but what's the real deal with you and Kurt Vaughn?"

"There's no real deal, I told you. We're just dog park friends."

"I don't know about that. He is very concerned about you. When you get your phone back, I think you will have a lot of texts from him."

"I was helping him with some copyright infringement thing. It's probably about that."

"It didn't seem that way. It felt much more personal."

"You have it all wrong, believe me. I'm ten years too old and twenty pounds too heavy for that man. He only dates models. Google him."

"I think you're underestimating yourself—and maybe him. Don't be surprised if he asks you out when you get home."

"I'm telling you, there's no way. I'm sure of it. I have to go."

Esme sensed that the sudden stop was again based on her inquiry about Kurt and not the time.

"OK," Esme conceded, worrying she may have misled the rock star. "Hang in there—only a week to go," she said, encouragingly.

"But who's counting?" they said in unison, both laughing as they hung up.

TWENTY-FIVE

The SJP Metallic Mid-Heel Mary Janes

Esme and Elvis met Zach bright and early on Wednesday morning on the corner of Eighty-First Street and Central Park West to partake in the great New York City ritual of waiting in line for tickets to Shakespeare in the Park. He warned Esme that she should be prepared to wait between four and six hours and they both filled their backpacks accordingly. Zach knew of many ways to beat the system, but the adopted Cuban in him insisted they wait with the masses.

They unfurled a small blanket, spread out an assortment of magazines, snacks, and drinks, and before long made friends with the people around them. On one side sat a young couple, Caroline and Fletcher Graham visiting from Iowa City, and on the other, Ruthie and Jack Greenfield—Upper West Siders who hadn't missed a production in sixty years.

"Even when Ruthie was nine months pregnant," Jack said.

"And even when Jack's hemorrhoids were so bad he had to lie on his stomach in line the whole time," Ruthie added.

"You're like a magnet for old Jews," Zach teased Esme.

"Are you allowed to say that, Mr. Politically Correct?"

"I am, because I'm half Jewish."

"Really, what's the other half?"

"Episcopalian. We ate brisket on Friday nights and ham on Sundays. What about you?"

"No religion, really. My father basically prayed to a bottle of Jack Daniel's, and my mother prayed he wouldn't finish it." She laughed, even though it wasn't funny.

Before long, everyone nearby was sharing food, planning the rest of the visit for the couple from Iowa, and shouting out the answers to the *New York Times* daily crossword that Jack claimed to have not missed since returning home from the Korean War. Esme was sure that the fun they had in line could not be topped by the performance, but when returning for the eight o'clock show that night in the most fun shoes in Catherine's entire closet, she was quickly proven wrong. The experience of sitting in the Delacorte Theater in the magical metallic Mary Janes floored her. It was perfectly situated in the middle of Manhattan, with Belvedere Castle peeking out from behind as if it were part of the set. When the play was over, she felt as if she had been holding her breath the entire time. It was truly spellbinding.

As they exited among the hordes of theatergoers into the park, under the night sky, Zach placed both his hands on Esme's shoulders, ceremoniously knighting her.

"I deem you, Esme Nash, a true New Yorker."

Between her new title and the lingering high from the experience, Esme couldn't help but skip along the winding path. There was a real thrill to being in Central Park at night, a hint of danger from watching too many episodes of *Law & Order*, that felt palpable. The sound of the ominous *chung-chung* played in her head.

"It feels especially cool to be in the park after dark," Esme expressed rather joyfully.

"It does," Zach agreed. "It's breaking every New York City parent's number one rule—don't go into the park after dark. I could probably count the occasions on one hand that warranted it."

"Please do," Esme encouraged him. She loved hearing about NYC childhoods. Zach held out his hand as a prop and counted.

"OK, well, when I was young, my grandparents would babysit me on New Year's Eve, and we would meet their cronies by Tavern on the Green to watch the fireworks at midnight. Plus there were a bunch of nights like this, and others when I would go night-skating at Wollman Rink."

"I want to do that one day!" she exclaimed, while pulling out her lipstick to reapply. As she did so, she wondered about the hard stop of their friendship. Would they keep in touch after this inseparable month they were having? Would they ever do winter things together, like skate at Wollman Rink?

Zach watched her intently as she placed her lipstick at the center of her lips and slid it toward one corner of her mouth and then the other. She pretended not to notice until her eyes caught his. He quickly turned away.

"Wait! I forgot about my most monumental foray into the park after dark," he rebounded.

Esme took a dramatic step back. "Are you sure you want to share this with me?"

"Good instincts, Esme Nash—it is a very sordid tale!"

She grabbed hold of his arm and pulled him close as they continued down the path toward Fifth Avenue.

"Do tell!" she said, in her best Shakespearean accent.

"A few blocks down from here is a rock with the initials *ZB +
LM* scrawled on it. That's where I had my first kiss, after dark in the
park, at age twelve."

"You went into the park with a girl at night at twelve? Weren't
you scared?"

"Yes, but mostly of my mother, who would have killed me if
she'd known."

On the walk to the subway, Zach spilled the details of his adventures with a very brave girl named Linda Malino, who convinced him to repeatedly cut out of Barclay dance school on East
Sixty-First Street and spend the hour making out on a rock, before
running back in time for their parents to pick them up.

"Dance class?" Esme inquired, a bit amazed.

"Yup. It was a real throwback to old New York society—it's still
around, I think—boys in blue blazers and girls in white gloves and
Tory Burch flats. My grandmother insisted on it, and my parents
just went along, as they sometimes did, to appease her. She said it
would give me confidence on and off the dance floor. She was actually right. We would meet the first Saturday night of the month to
learn the waltz, the cha-cha, the foxtrot, and a shitload of etiquette.
Not described that way in the brochure, of course."

"Wait—so the dance school in Cuba was not your first foray?"

"Well, it actually was, because Linda Malino and I never learned
a single dance step, though I used the moves I acquired on those
Saturday nights for the rest of my life. We would sit on that rock
every month and get better and better at kissing. It wasn't easy,
because I had a full mouth of braces, and she had a palette expander
right here." He pointed to the roof of his mouth.

"No way."

"It was quite a challenge, but I believe it made me the expert kisser I am today. What about you?" he added as they bounded down the subway stairs.

"Me what?" she responded, thinking more about what would lead one to qualify as an expert kisser than his question.

"Your first real kiss?"

Esme went to sit down on the wooden bench on the subway platform, but Zach stopped her. Between the possibility of bedbugs and who knew what else that had gone down on that bench, it was a real rookie move. Esme had already broken two of the cardinal rules of subway travel during earlier descents underground. The first was when she'd stopped on the stairs to check her phone, causing an unfortunate domino effect behind her, and the second when she'd entered an empty subway car—a lesson, and smell, she would not soon forget. She was not about to cop to either.

"Ugh, you're not going to demote me now, are you?" Esme asked as she stood up.

He laughed. "Nah, you can't develop twenty-eight years of NYC skills like mine in twenty-eight days!"

"It's not twenty-eight yet," she said. "I still have more to go!"

"OK, then, I won't demote you if you tell me about your first kiss."

"My first real kiss, like the kind you're talking about, was behind my bunk at summer camp with a boy named Leon Gordon. He had shaggy brown hair, lots of freckles, and a really big mouth."

Esme got lost in it, just like Zach had. She hadn't thought about it in ages.

"I honestly don't remember kissing like that since; the newness of it and the uncertainty, the way our tongues first felt searching around each other's mouths, how I never even worried that he would try and feel me up or something, and how we could just kiss and kiss and kiss until curfew."

The train arrived, and all the seats were taken. Esme followed
Zach's lead, gripping the center pole with as few fingers as possible.
When they reached Times Square, throngs of *Playbill*-carrying
theatergoers entered, abuzz with conversation. Esme ate up the the-
atrical excitement. It reminded her of that first time she had sushi
in the Village with her parents. Like then, the car was filled with
real New Yorkers, vibrantly analyzing whatever play or musical they
had seen as if they were actual critics. Some were even humming
show tunes. She eavesdropped as they compared shows and actors
and theaters. It was far more interesting than eavesdropping in line
at her local Wegmans back home. As they all claimed their personal
space, Zach pulled her closer to him to allow room for the others.
Her thoughts refocused, landing on the feeling of his warm breath
against her neck. She tingled inside.

Somewhere between Twenty-Eighth and Twenty-Third Streets,
the train came to a jolting stop, and within seconds the AC shut off,
followed by the lights, followed in turn by a collective groan from
all the passengers. Zach pulled her even closer, and his touch sucked
the air from her lungs. He told her quietly not to worry.

Worry was not the emotion consuming her. They were pushed
smack up against each other in the dark with little room to move.
She could feel his heart beating in his chest against hers—*ba-bum,
ba-bum, ba-bum*. It pulled her into a trance until he wiggled out one
of his arms and touched her face, pushing a few errant strands of
hair away from her eyes. She followed what she thought was his
lead, the back of her hand finding his jawline and gently brushing
over his perpetually perfect stubble. It felt soft. She wondered if it
would feel scratchier if she kissed him. Without much thought of
cause, consequence, or the first item on the list that she had composed just the day before—*put any thoughts of romance with Zach out
of your mind*—she did. Not full on, as she had with Leon Gordon,

just lightly placing her lips on his and pulling them away a few times in a playful, teasing way. She thought about reining it back in, ignoring the stirring inside of her, but it felt too good. Reckless desire often does. Zach must have felt the same, as he took the bait and kissed her back, first gently as well, but soon with a pent-up passion fueled by weeks of sleepovers and tequila and honest intimacies. It eased into a slow and sensuous pace, in the true fashion of two twelve-year-old kids, exploring something new. They kissed like that for what seemed like both forever and just a minute. It was transcendent, almost otherworldly, and it felt as though neither of them wanted it to end. But when the lights came back on, they abruptly stepped away from each other, hit by the stark reality of what they had just done.

The train stopped at Fourteenth Street and Esme said goodbye. Zach barely responded, his face marked with her lipstick. She wondered if, when he got home and looked in the mirror, he would hate himself. She had a horrible feeling he would.

TWENTY-SIX

The Shiny Black Prada Loafers

The subway kiss radio silence lasted nearly twenty-four hours— the longest that Esme and Zach had gone without at least a check-in since they'd met. Esme broke it with an invitation to sail. She sent a text, choosing her words carefully.

Sy said I could bring a friend, and you are the best friend I have in this city.

She crossed her fingers—hopeful that he would agree to come but fearful that he would say something serious about what had transpired between them.

She watched the dots on her phone appear and disappear and appear and disappear again and again until she lost her patience and called him out on it.

Zach, I see you deciding what to say.

Her phone rang.

"We have to talk about the other night before we see each other again, and especially before we go to the Hamptons."

She was happy he was still considering coming that weekend. She could never go it alone. She had to make him completely comfortable, and the only way to do that was to fall on her sword. He continued with "I'm feeling—"

And she immediately cut him off. She didn't want to know what he was feeling, her fear of abandonment taking precedence over all else. She said every single thing she could think of.

"Please, Zach, stop! It was all my fault. It was just a fun night, and between the drama on the stage and all of that talk of kissing, I got carried away. I am so sorry that I kissed you; it will never happen again."

He was quiet for a beat, and she filled it.

"Please don't let it ruin what we have."

She held her breath until he said, "I've never sailed on the Hudson, you know."

Esme breathed a deep sigh of relief.

"Meet me at the Seventy-Ninth Street Boat Basin at noon?"

"Aye aye, mate."

Esme was very excited for the day, mostly because it was the first time that she was the one showing Zach something new. She searched the Temple of Sole for boat shoes and settled on a chunky rubber-soled Prada loafer. *Settled* may have been the wrong word; after pairing them with white anklets and her new blue-and-white-striped marinière, she felt beyond seaworthy.

They met Sy and his friend Captain Andrew, a bearded old-salt-type straight out of central casting, on board his thirty-two-foot

Beneteau. The captain seemed very serious, tapping his watch and announcing it was time to shove off. They rode the engine to the middle of the Hudson, where he began setting the sails. Everyone was given jobs to do. Esme and Zach were instructed to raise the mainsail as the captain brought the boat into the wind, which there wasn't much of. They took a selfie as they did so, causing the captain to grimace. He had no way of knowing he was actually with the *least* millennial millennials on the planet.

"Look how cute!" Esme showed Zach, beaming.

It was a great picture, and she was so happy that things weren't weird between them after the kiss.

"Looks to me like a picture of a girl who's ready to go back on social media."

"You think I should?"

"Well, you went off because you had no life, right? And from what I can see in that picture—life's looking pretty good."

Esme stared at it a bit, contemplating unlocking her Instagram account, while Sy put out the lunch he'd prepared.

"I made us a little nosh," he said, grinning as he spread out his feast. There was sliced pumpernickel and sourdough bread and spreads of egg salad, baked salmon, and his famous whitefish salad. He had even made a noodle kugel. If Esme was contemplating adopting him before, she was now sure she should. From the look on Zach's face when he bit into the kugel, she was going to have to fight him for the privilege. For a moment it felt as if the three of them were family, and Esme found herself wishing they really were. The wind was still dead, so they decided to sunbathe and digest before heading back in.

Zach nudged Esme. He had come up with this big idea that it may not be too late for Sy and Lena and had been nudging her about it every five minutes on line for Shakespeare in the Park. She had entertained the idea then, more for killing time than having any real interest in it. She was wary because she thought the whole concept could very well break Sy's heart all over again. If the state of her own heart since seeing Liam was anything to go by, the crack in the wall she had built around it was widening every time the two of them met. Eventually Sy brought up Lena, and this time Zach nearly nudged Esme overboard. She gave him the stink eye but plunged in anyway.

"Sy, we were wondering if you ever heard about Lena's whereabouts since sending that Dear Jane letter from England."

Even the antisocial captain's ears perked up at the mention of Lena's name. It seemed Sy was more open about his history than he had led Esme to believe.

"Well yes, when I got back from the war, I went to her house to propose."

"You did? What? You left off the end of the story?"

"I didn't want to discourage you. And what difference does it make? The end is the same."

The three of them looked at him with pleading eyes. He gave up.

"Fine, stop hocking my chinik," he mumbled in Yiddish. No one asked for a translation.

It turned out that Sy received excellent care in England, mental and physical, and arrived home during the summer of 1945 feeling more like his old self than he ever thought possible. What he didn't know was that while he was overseas, Sheldon Schusterman's aircraft was shot down over the Pacific. Lena, as Sheldon's fiancée, was included in the mourning rituals and became a great comfort to Sheldon's family, especially his brother, Lenny.

As time went on, sometime after receiving Sy's letter, Lena and Lenny began spending more and more time together. His family was so happy to have her around. Sy assumed that she gave up on the big love that she had felt for him and even for Sheldon, and just settled in with Lenny. Of course he had no idea about any of this until way after the fact, when his friend Mel filled in all the holes for him. He told it to them as it had happened.

"Within a day of returning home, I went to Lena's house with a small diamond ring that I'd bought for her in London. I finally met her father when he answered the door. He invited me in, happy to see a man returning home in uniform, I thought, but equally happy to tell me that his daughter, Lena, was off to Bermuda on her honeymoon.

"She had married their neighbor, Len Schusterman, a week earlier in a small ceremony at city hall. I thought I would die right there in her living room," Sy said. "I asked him not to tell her that I came to visit. I have no idea whether or not he did."

"Oh my God. That's awful." The stoic captain was the first to speak. Esme could swear she saw a tear in his eye when he added, "Did you ever tell her the truth?"

"How could I? She was married. Mel said she was happy and that both families were very healed by the marriage. They would soon have a baby boy and name him for Lenny's brother. After that happened, I asked Mel not to tell me about her ever again."

"So you have no idea what happened to her?"

"About ten years ago, Mel got lung cancer. I went to visit him out in Jersey somewhere, and it was pretty clear that he didn't have long to go. I asked him whatever became of Lena. He said she had lived her life in New Rochelle and had two children, a boy, Sheldon, and a girl, Susan. That's all I know of her. I'm sure she's heard of me. I think that's the real reason I did that taxi message and agreed to life-size billboards with my image on them. I was always half hoping she would see one and march into my store asking for a pound of nova and my heart. But that never happened."

"Do you know if she's still alive? And her husband?" Zach asked to Esme's obvious annoyance.

"I don't."

"Do you want to know?"

He got real quiet before saying, "I don't want to rock the boat."

Esme shot Zach an *I told you so* death look while the captain got him to change course.

"A boat that doesn't rock doesn't move, Sy."

Sy seemed to take in the nautical advice before saying, "I guess it would be interesting to know if Lena was on the market."

They all cracked up, even the stoic captain.

"Want me to google them?" Zach asked.

"Sure, Lena and Leonard Schusterman, S-c-h-u-s-t-e-r-m-a-n." He spelled the last name as quickly as if it were his own.

"Ah, S-*c*-h, I was spelling it wrong."

Zach had already googled Lena Shusterman to no avail. He got to work with the proper spelling. The first thing that showed up was Leonard's obituary. He read it out loud.

"Leonard Schusterman died three years ago," Zach pronounced, adding a bit tackily, "Bad news for him, but possible good news for you and Lena."

Esme whispered nervously in his ear. "You'd better read the 'survived by' part before you say that."

"'Survived by his wife, Lena; their children, Sheldon and Joy Schusterman and Susan and Jay Goldenberg; and four grandchildren, Jasper, Sawyer, Bo, and Willow.' Looks like your girl is back on the market."

"Do the google on her, too," Sy said.

Zach and Esme both went at it.

"She's a Democrat," Esme announced. "She donated to Biden's campaign and Obama's."

"She always liked handsome men," Sy said proudly.

"She was president of the Sisterhood of the New Rochelle Jewish Center in the nineties."

"That's nice."

"We can call the temple and ask about her," Zach added.

"I don't think they would just give out her whereabouts to strangers," Esme argued.

"Hold on, are you saying we should find her in person, after all this time? That's meshugana!"

"Meshugana?" Esme asked, struggling with the pronunciation.

"Crazy!" Sy translated, clearly not on board.

"It's not that crazy," Zach said. "I bet it would be easy to find her."

Esme quickly countered his enthusiasm.

"Sy, before you say yes, you have to think about it. You may be opening yourself up to all kinds of new heartache. We may not actually find her, or we may find her and she may not want to see you. Or worse, she could be in a bad way. Then all of your memories of your beautiful Lena may be replaced by sad ones. Your memories of Lena seem very important to you."

"But there's also a chance you could find her and make new memories." Zach swooped back in with his optimistic logic.

"You know, I go to sleep every night thinking about seeing her again."

Zach and Esme realigned with their matching thought bubbles.

Over seventy years of missing the same person. It wasn't lost on either of them.

"If you re-up your Instagram, we can check out her kids. Maybe get some clues," Zach suggested.

It was just the push Esme needed, and quite easy to do. She

logged back in with her old password and voilà—she was back in business.

"What are her kids' names again?" she asked, ignoring the parade of old friends on her re-upped feed.

Zach went back to the obit. "Susan Goldenberg and Sheldon Schusterman."

She tried Sheldon Schusterman.

"No luck."

"Try Shelly. Sheldon isn't such a modern name," Sy said.

"Nothing. Wait, let's try the grandchildren."

"Yup. Willow Goldenberg, there's only one. Look, so cute!"

She held out her phone for all to see.

"She looks like her grandma," Sy said with a hint of melancholy.

Esme read her profile.

"Willow goes to Columbia, right about there," she said, pointing to the shoreline around Morningside Heights.

"Let's sail over and ask her where her grandma lives," Sy said— kidding, they thought.

Esme scrolled through her posts until she hit the jackpot.

"No need. Look right here."

Under a photo of Willow with her arms wrapped around a pretty white-haired woman with lilac eyes was the caption:

Me and My Bubby
Location: Hebrew Home at Riverdale

She handed Sy her phone, and he sat back to look at Lena. It felt like an hour until he spoke, but it was really just a few minutes. His eyes were watery as he held the phone for Esme to see the photo again.

"Look," he said. "She's still a beauty."

He pulled the compass out of his pocket and held it up to the sea. There she was, due north up the Hudson River from where they were right then. They thought he was going to start yelling Coast Guard phrases like "Damn the torpedoes, full speed ahead!" but he did no such thing.

"You still carry around the compass she gave you?" Captain Andy asked, in awe.

"For all these years, even when I was married."

Esme laughed. "It's no wonder the marriage didn't last."

"Yes, well, it's hard to be married to one person when you are in love with someone else."

His words hung in the air between them.

As they motored back to the marina, the sun was starting to set. Zach patted the deck between his legs for Esme to slide in and rest her back on his chest. She was filled with relief at his offer, so thankful that kissing him hadn't poisoned the intimacy of their friendship. She tried to ignore the lustful sensation traveling down her body and concentrated on how at home she felt lying against him like that, as if she had been there all her life. She vowed to never risk what they had together again. Then she pulled her phone back out, posted the selfie on Instagram, and wrote what felt like the obvious caption—*Life is good*.

For the first time in a long time, it felt genuinely true.

TWENTY-SEVEN

The Inaugural Scuffs on the Red-Bottomed Shoes

That night, after scrolling through the Instagram feeds of nearly everyone she had ever met, Esme decided to check her email. She screeched with joy at the sight of one from Vivian Rococo of the Hudson Payne Gallery. Esme remembered her name from her first go-around. She had laughed that the manager of a modern art gallery shared a surname with an eighteenth-century baroque art movement. She wondered if her name predestined her for a career in the arts. She once knew a woman named Rita Book who said she never questioned her life's calling to become a librarian.

The email said that Vivian had received her résumé and would like to offer her an interview for an associate position. She had just received a cancelation for the next day at eleven. She asked if Esme would like it. Esme responded yes right away before giving herself a chance to chicken out. She spent the rest of the night studying recent art developments and woke up feeling confident, doubly so after deciding to wear the graduation shoes from her mom for the very first time.

She skipped the morning visit to the park and just walked Elvis around the block.

"I have to do this on my own, buddy," she said in response to the guilt-inducing look he gave her when she went back out without him. She was really going to miss this little guy when August was over.

Esme walked over to Berger's carrying her own red-bottomed shoes that had yet to be worn out of the house. Upon seeing her, Mrs. Berger motioned for her to come around back, skipping the line. Esme felt like Greenwich Village royalty. She gave Mrs. Berger back the Halston dress and pulled out the red cloth bag with her prized Louboutins.

"My mother gave these to me seven years ago, and I've never worn them out of the house, but I have a big interview today." Her eyes welled up, intimating her loss and threatening to ruin her makeup. Mrs. Berger handed her a tissue.

"Sit, sit, bubbala."

It was obvious that she had made her way to Mrs. Berger's soft side. She was honored—she knew it was a very small space. Mrs. Berger fetched the magic shoe savers while giving Esme the third degree about everything that transpired since the Bird Ball. She didn't seem to care that there were customers waiting, while Esme could think only of the dirty looks she would receive as she exited.

"Now, you do honor to these shoes and your mama on this interview," she just about ordered her.

Esme didn't dare to disappoint. She tossed her flip-flops in her bag, donned the cherished gift from her mama, and paraded past the ordinary subjects and out the store as if she had been walking in Louboutins all her life. From there she marched herself over to the Hudson Payne Gallery and confidently stepped inside.

A young woman near the entrance looked her over from head to toe. It was clearly the toe part that garnered her approval.

Oh, what a silly world I want into, Esme thought.

"Can I help you?" she asked Esme.

"I'm here for an interview with Vivian Rococo," Esme replied with the doggedness of a woman in seven-hundred-dollar shoes.

"And who can I say is here to see her?"

"Esme Nash."

Vivian came out quickly, and with a certain degree of warmth—well, warmth may have been an exaggeration; more like not cold. She said, "Your name was very familiar to me when I saw your résumé, but I can't place your face."

Esme's nerves began to flare; she wiggled her toes in her shoes, hoping to resurrect her mojo.

"We met years ago. I had to give up my internship here due to the sudden family obligation that I mentioned on my résumé. You were kind enough to say that I was welcome to reapply anytime. So here I am." She smiled earnestly.

She received nothing in return but "I remember. Follow me."

They sat across from each other at a round table in the back, where Vivian studied her résumé again. From where Esme sat, she could see one of John Giorno's more famous works. The $45,000 words painted in bold black letters on a gold acrylic background seemed to be beckoning for her attention:

PREFER CRYING IN A LIMO TO LAUGHING ON A BUS

She imagined the woman asking that as her first question: *Esme, do you prefer crying in a limo or laughing on a bus?*

If you choose the first, this is the job for you; if you choose the second, it is not.

Vivian Rococo interrupted her imaginary interview with the real one.

"Were you able to keep up with the art world?"

It was clear that she wasn't playing to the tragedy—for which Esme was mostly grateful.

"I have," Esme replied, also grateful for the crash course she had given herself over the past month.

The woman didn't take her word for it and put her on the spot. "Have you noticed any rising stars?"

"Well, Hans Op de Beeck killed it at Art Basel," Esme answered boldly, before worrying that her answer was too obvious. She wiggled her toes again in *her Louboutins*, reminding herself she was a grown woman with knowledge and skills and style.

"How about under the hammer?"

Esme knew that was a tricky way to ask about secondary-market sales. She had just read an article about a Harlem-based artist named Jordan Casteel, whose prices were skyrocketing on the secondary market.

"Jordan Casteel?"

"Yes, but everyone has heard of her. If you want to wow Mr. Payne at your virtual second interview, you need to do better."

"Second interview? Thank you!" Esme blurted, before quickly reeling back in her excitement. It wasn't really necessary, as Vivian Rococo was right there ready to put a damper on it anyway.

"Don't get too excited. It really is an entry-level position; most of the other candidates will be right out of college."

"I'm willing to start anywhere," she promised.

"OK, Esme. We will be in touch." She said it rather stoically, but then added in a whisper, "Think about attracting the next generation of wealth, the 'woke' generation—what will attract *them* and what will turn *them* off?"

Visions of carbon footprints danced through Esme's head.

"I will—thank you!" Esme gushed, immediately reining it back in again.

She waited till she was out of view to skip home in her one-hundred-millimeter heels, not an easy feat. About halfway there she reached down and pulled off her sole savers. She wanted the day to leave its mark. It was time she stopped shielding herself from whatever lay ahead, and she may as well start with her feet.

Once back at Catherine's, she thought about calling Zach or Liam with her promising news, but both options felt complicated to her. She didn't want to hear Liam's "I told you so" or Zach's "Are you sure selling art to the one percent will fulfill you now?" It was a thought that had slipped into her own mind on more than a few occasions over the month, but hearing it from him would just annoy her. She settled on spilling all the details of her afternoon to Elvis, who reacted with his trademark kisses and enthusiasm. She opened up her phone and pulled out her sacred to-do list, bravely adding:

5. Adopt a dog!

TWENTY-EIGHT

The Jessica Rich Princess Flats

About seven minutes after leaving the boat basin, Sy had called and proclaimed that he wanted to see Lena.

"That was quick!" Esme remarked, noting that it took her longer than that to pick out her shoes.

He was adamant that he didn't want to just show up there, so with her interview behind her, Esme rang the Hebrew Home and made an appointment for Sy to see the place as a possible residence. It wasn't an odd thing at all for a ninety-year-old man living alone to be doing. Esme invited Zach to come along.

And so it was, on a bright sunny August morning, some seventy years since he had last seen her, that Sy Katz, along with his "great-niece and nephew," Esme and Zach, set out for the Hebrew Home in Riverdale to find Lena Schusterman.

Sy was visibly nervous. He must have asked them six times how he looked, and he refused to buckle up in the Uber for fear he would wrinkle his shirt.

Zach tried to distract him with fish talk.

"You know, Sy, my grandmother would travel from the Upper East Side to buy sturgeon from you. She always claimed that sturgeon was the best fish, better than sable."

It worked.

"Better—what means better? Everyone's a maven. Yes, sturgeon is special—caviar comes from it, you know—but I'm partial to sable."

Just as expected, he spent the rest of the time giving them a smoked-fish primer, detailing the qualities of white fish and nova, Scottish salmon, gravlax, and kippered salmon. By the time he got to peppered mackerel—"the steak au poivre of the appetizing counter"— they were there.

Their appointment was with a woman named Mrs. Green, and Sy made them promise not to ask her straight up about Lena. He listened to all the info about the place as if he were really interested in living there. He asked pointed questions, especially when it came to the food and having his own refrigerator in his room to keep some noshes of his own, and if they allowed dogs. It was then that Zach and Esme looked at each other with their now increasingly frequent matching thought bubbles. *Lena or not, this may be an excellent place for Sy, a place not to be lonely.* It seemed as though Sy was realizing it as well.

Soon it was time to take the tour, and all three of them took a deep cleansing breath to calm their nerves as they exited Mrs. Green's office. Esme took Sy's hand in hers, and he seemed grateful. His hand felt cold and fragile, his vulnerability tangible. He suddenly seemed his age.

The first stop on the tour was the light-filled dining room. It was lovely but empty. Mrs. Green appeared disappointed that Sy didn't want to spend more time there, since eating seemed to be his primary interest. Next, the art room, where residents were crocheting tissue box covers. No Lena. The screening room, Spencer Tracy and Katharine Hepburn, but no Lena. The card room, no Lena, and so on and so on. The tour was nearly over when Sy asked if they could see the outside grounds.

"Thirty-two acres for scenic strolls," he said, quoting the brochure. It was a really hot day, but Sy insisted.

"The brochure says waterfront views. Where are the waterfront views?"

Mrs. Green was not thrilled to leave the air-conditioned building, but Sy was adamant. She took them out back to a promenade overlooking the Hudson, where wrought iron benches lined the panorama. They were empty, except for one a few feet away where a woman was sitting alone watching the sailboats passing by. The irony wasn't lost on any of them. Sy practically ran to her. Mrs. Green was quick to follow, but Esme gently held her arm.

"Please, wait. I think he knows her."

She agreed, but only because they were in the shade. Zach and Esme stood glued to the scene unfolding in front of them. As he approached the bench, Sy called out hopefully, "Lena?" She responded with the greatest look of awe they'd ever seen on a person's face. Her violet eyes immediately filled with tears that quickly escaped down her cheeks. He reached her and searched his pockets to offer her a handkerchief to dry her tears. By the time he sat down, she was using it to dry his. Zach and Esme began to cry as well. It was the most beautiful thing either of them had ever seen.

Lena and Sy sat on that bench and spoke for more than two hours. Zach and Esme found a shady spot under a big maple tree, keeping a close but discreet eye. Though they both worried that they should interrupt the reunion and offer them water or shade, they just let them be—as if interrupting them would burst the dream they were watching unfold. They fell into their own thoughts, until Esme at last broke the long silence.

"Do you feel the kind of love for Amara that they feel for each other? Like you could never be whole without her?"

"I don't know. When I first got back from Cuba I felt as if I could barely breathe without her. But now, looking at them . . ." He paused, then added, "What about you?"

"I don't think I've ever loved like that. Maybe I was too young. And now I don't feel brave enough to give of myself so fully."

She didn't feel brave at all. In fact, she felt weak.

"You are most definitely brave enough."

He pulled her into him and she kicked off her Jessica Rich Princess Flats. Objectively the gold-stud-embellished, bowed thong straps were a bit grand for the occasion, but subjectively the perfect match. She sank into Zach's chest once again, noting that the cowardly feeling immediately subsided. It was hot, really too hot to touch another human being, but the comfort of it outweighed the discomfort. They went back to watching Sy and Lena.

At times they seemed to argue. They imagined Lena berating Sy for not being honest with her after the war, or Sy berating Lena for not believing their short time together was enough to bank a life on. At times it looked as if they were just catching up on what they had missed, telling stories of a comfortable marriage with children on Lena's part, and building a notable company on Sy's. And at times they were just looking into each other's eyes, searching for two kids who had met in Brooklyn over seven decades ago. In the end, Esme and Zach agreed that sitting in the shade watching two people reunite after all that time may have been the most extraordinary afternoon they'd ever spent. It definitely did a number on them both, regarding their first loves.

Finally, Sy walked over to them with Lena.

"You two kids didn't have to wait," he said.

They laughed, realizing he had no idea how much time had passed.

"No problem, Sy," Zach said, patting him on the shoulder.

He introduced them to Lena.

"This is Lena, my girl," he said with wide-eyed pride.

"Hello, Lena. So nice to meet you."

They both gushed all over her.

"Did you recognize this guy right away?" Zach asked, placing his arm around Sy's shoulder.

"I recognized the bounce in his step. It was the same bounce he had as a kid. He's as beautiful to me today as that young man in uniform who I never stopped loving."

"Where is that Green lady?" Sy barked. "I have to tell her I'm staying."

They held in their laughter. Zach broke it to him gently.

"I don't think you can just stay, Sy. I think you need to see what's available, fill out paperwork. Bring your furniture, your clothing, Scout!"

"That room she showed us had everything I need. I'll take that place and run home later to fetch a few incidentals and Scout. After that, I'm not letting Lena out of my sight ever again."

"But . . ." Esme was ready to reel him in a bit.

"No buts. There are only so many days left, even fewer good ones, I imagine. To be excited to wake up in the morning again, to feel lucky to be alive!" He shook his head in disbelief.

Zach took a deep breath before releasing it with a "Wow!"

"Wow what?" Sy asked.

"Wow everything. Your story makes me feel like I shouldn't let distance come between myself and true love."

Sy mumbled under his breath, loud enough for them both to hear him. "Especially when that distance is just a few feet."

Zach blushed while Esme ignored him, exclaiming, "I'll go and fetch Mrs. Green!"

Sy pulled Mrs. Green aside to speak to her and, lo and behold, convinced her to let him have the model apartment. He explained it to them afterward with just two words—"Money talks"—before pulling Esme aside to have a word with her in private. She could see from his expression that he was suddenly very serious.

"To me, the worst thing about getting old was not that my friends have all but disintegrated. Though that has been very painful, I was prepared for it. I know we all come with an expiration date. And it's not that I can't hear so well, or keep up, though I do a pretty good job."

"You do," Esme interrupted.

"The worst thing, to me, was being overlooked. Tossed aside as if I had nothing left to contribute to the world."

Esme began to protest, but Sy stopped her, placing the back of his hand against her cheek.

"But you looked at me. You looked at me and didn't just see an old man. You are a very special person, Esme Nash."

He reached into his pocket and pulled out the compass.

"I don't need this anymore, but I have a feeling you do."

He squeezed it tightly in her hand as if it had the power to lead her in the right direction.

She was touched that he wanted her to have his most prized possession, and that was expressed by the tears that now flowed from her eyes.

"Thank you," she said, hugging him tightly.

"You've already walked through the fire, Esme. Don't spend the rest of your life sitting in its ashes. Don't waste your life."

"I won't, I promise. I hope you don't feel like you wasted yours. I think you've had a great life."

"I have. I just hope I saved enough room for dessert." He laughed, and she laughed with him. He was so happy, it was truly something to behold.

Sy gave her and Zach a warm hug each, thanking them both for the extraordinary gift they had given him and Lena, before proclaiming, "So long for now!"

"So long for now," they both responded as they walked off in the August heat in introspective silence.

Esme and Zach parted ways after the reunion, both still lost in their own thoughts. She had no idea what his thought bubble was saying and decided not to ask. She was drawn to him more and more every time she saw him and had to constantly remind herself of the promise she had made not to act on her attraction again, not to mention the little fact that he was in love with someone else. No matter what Sy perceived to be true, Esme was sure that she knew better.

Both her old job and her old boyfriend may be within reach. Surely picking back up where she left off would be the smartest course of action.

At home she cuddled up on the couch to read a mindless magazine with Elvis, who was mischievously eyeing the ridiculously decadent pair of baroque Versace slippers at her feet.

"Don't even think about it, Elvis. I'm not spending my last day in the city at the shoemaker!" she warned. Seemingly understanding her, he buried his face in his paws.

She heard the faint buzz of her cell phone and reached into her purse to retrieve it, her hand first grazing the smooth face of the compass. She squeezed it and rubbed her thumb across the words inscribed on the back before grabbing the vibrating phone.

It was a text from Liam.

Look out your window!

Eight floors below was Liam Beck, jogging in place in gym shorts and a Dartmouth tee. She opened the window and waved. She could see his smile as he bellowed, "Good night, Esme Nash!"

Her heart filled with joy at the mention of their first inside joke, the night that she had escaped out the back door of his frat house. She shouted back, "Good night, Liam Beck!" and watched in awe as he jogged away.

She squeezed the compass and whispered into the dark night, "Are you my north?"

TWENTY-NINE

The Saint Laurent Tribute Platforms

On her last full day in the city, Esme did all of the usual stuff, but with a little less enjoyment. Sy's absence at the dog park definitely put a damper on things there, though she supposed it was better than a long, sad goodbye. She would save the long, sad goodbyes for Elvis.

Back at the apartment, she got down to the business of packing, straightening, and cleaning. She did her laundry in a pair of Chanel two-tone slingbacks, vacuumed in Aminah Abdul Jillil Tuxedo sandals, and cleaned out the fridge in a pair of Dior combat boots. She ordered in her favorites from Momofuku Noodle Bar for dinner, and when Ralph, the previously cranky doorman, buzzed it up, he added, "Enjoy your dinner, Ms. Nash."

She had won him over by day three.

While the delivery person was on the way up, Esme donned the high-heeled stiletto Tribute sandals with beveled heels and intertwining straps. She had been ogling the iconic patent Yves Saint

Laurents since day one, always second-guessing whether the occasion that presented itself was Tribute-worthy. With nowhere left to go, she decided that the "last supper" would have to fit the bill. She invited Elvis to join her for dinner—a ritual she had started a few weeks back that had now, she was afraid, instilled bad habits in her canine friend. She imagined him jumping up on a chair the first time Catherine sat down to eat upon her return. At least Esme would have made her mark on more than just her employer's shoes. As she savored the last bite of her roast pork bun, her cell phone rang. She hoped it was Zach, which gave her pause, but it was Catherine Wallace.

Esme had enjoyed their chats and was happy to say a proper goodbye, plus she wanted to push the envelope a bit more regarding the rock star from the dog run. While she didn't really know Catherine, their honest phone conversations and the fact of living in her world for a month left Esme feeling like she did. Catherine seemed to be even more alone than she was. It may have been one of the only reasons that Esme didn't construct a plan to kidnap Elvis and flee the country. She hoped that Catherine's time away would lead to healthier relationships, not least the one she had with her shoes. As far as Esme could tell, most were barely worn at all.

Catherine had her own agenda for the call.

"First things first," she said. "About my stash."

Esme was about to thank her for the opportunity like no other when Catherine added, "Some people come home and ceremoniously pour all their alcohol down the drain"—Esme's heart thudded to a halt—"but I don't think I'm that type. I want my one-day-at-a-time practice to make it past day one. If you don't mind, could you please pour every last drop left of my stash down the sink and dispose of the evidence?"

My stash!

Esme kicked the thousand-dollar YSLs off her feet and sprang from her chair. How could she have gotten that wrong? Her mind raced back to their first conversations—my stash—had Catherine used those same words? Oh God. Esme had thought she meant her shoes—not her tequila!

Maybe Mrs. Berger makes house calls?

Esme was flipping out but quickly regrouped. She had to do something to return the favor. She knew just what it was.

"Of course. I will do it when we hang up." She picked up the shoes from the floor and inspected them.

"Can I ask you something personal, Catherine?"

"Sure—I feel like we know each other by now."

"Do you? Because I'm not so sure I know you. Nosy Miguel told me you have lived here for fifteen years, but your apartment, and, well, your shoes—they don't really seem lived in. I'm not saying it to hurt your feelings. . . . I'm sorry, but I'm curious—"

Catherine cut her off.

"You're right. I haven't been living my life as much as I've been hiding my addiction. It's taken every effort and left me with little time for anyone else—beyond Elvis, really. That's why I'm here. Because I almost lost him, and if I had"—she choked up and continued through her tears—"if I had, I don't know what I would have done."

"What do you mean?"

"I was drunk, and we went for a long walk one night. I ended up by that big liquor store on Broadway, and I went in. Someone said 'No dogs,' and instead of turning around and heading home, where I had plenty of alcohol, I tied him up outside. I risked his life because I couldn't wait ten minutes for another drink. When I got out, a man was running off with him. I screamed and ran after him but fell and cut up my knee. A group of kids from NYU saw the whole thing and went after the guy for me. They saved Elvis and helped us home. The next day I checked myself in here."

Esme was taken aback by her honesty.

"Wow, I had no idea. I assumed it was an intervention."

"That's just it. There is really no one to intervene. Just Elvis, who looked at me so shaken and scared that night that I finally asked for help."

"You're wrong about that. There is someone else who really cares about you: Kurt Vaughn. Every time Elvis shows up at the park, the look of disappointment on his face that it's me walking him, not you, is evident."

"That's just your imagination. I told you. He's just a dog park friend."

"Kurt Vaughn doesn't even own a dog. He brings his neighbor's dog to the park every day just to talk to you."

"That can't be true."

"It is. I'm sure of it," Esme said, although after the shoe mix-up she was not sure of much.

"If it were true—do you feel the same?" she added hopefully.

"I actually brought it up in group, since you mentioned him last time. You know, you're not supposed to change anything or date someone new for a year after you're sober, and Kurt knows that—he's sober, too. But I kind of feel like he doesn't count, because it's really not new."

"How so?"

"Well, if I'm being honest with myself, it wasn't just for Elvis that I got sober. Being with Kurt every day at the park always left me wanting more. Sometimes when we walked together, we would get so caught up in conversation that he ended up walking me home. But I could never invite him in."

"But I bet you could tell that he wanted you to, right?"

"I would never have thought that way. My self-worth was really in the toilet. It's more like it left me thinking about the lack of intimacy in my life. There was never enough room for alcohol, my job, and a relationship. I couldn't maintain the ruse of being a functioning adult and become intimate with him, or anyone else for that matter."

"I get it. You were only intimate with Don Julio."

"Exactly." Catherine laughed. "Though I sometimes two-timed Don with Johnnie Walker."

"He's a smooth one, that Johnnie Walker—I can't blame you."

They laughed some more, until Esme grew serious.

"Well, it sounds to me like you've made room for Kurt now. And since you say he's sober, he could even be a helpful ally in sobriety."

"I still doubt that you're right—but I am ready to have a life."

"And a reason to wear all those shoes. I have to say—I've never seen anything like it!"

Catherine, thankfully, laughed, too. "I make a lot of money—can't spend it all on booze! Plus, my weight goes up and down; sometimes my shoe size is all I can depend on."

Esme pictured poor Catherine spending drunken nights online shoe shopping. She wanted to push her to go deeper. Her collection was way beyond folly or fetish, but talking more about it would require Esme to come clean, and there was no easy way to admit she had been wearing her shoes all month. She hoped Catherine would have reasons to wear them now.

"Will I see you tomorrow before you leave? It would be nice to meet in person."

"It really would, but after I walk Elvis in the morning I'm heading to the Hamptons. Believe it or not, Zach and I are staying with Liam and his girlfriend for the weekend."

"Wow, that's a little crazy, no?"

Esme laughed. "It is. But I'm determined to put the relationship either behind me or in front of me. We shall see!"

"Hey, if you don't want to schlep everything to the Hamptons, you can leave stuff at my place and pick it up after the weekend."

The thought of walking into Morgan's house with all her stuff from the month had actually been bothering Esme. It seemed very déclassé, plus her luggage game did not compare to her shoe game.

"Thank you! That's so sweet of you."

"I actually have an ulterior motive. I will be dying to know what happened with you and the old boyfriend."

The guilt of not being honest suddenly outweighed Esme's nerves; plus, how could she face Catherine in person after the weekend? Although Esme treated her employer's shoes like the fine art that they were, Catherine would likely notice they were worn.

"Catherine, I have to tell you something. I thought you were at rehab for a shopping addiction. When you said I could break into your stash, I thought you meant your shoes."

Catherine laughed, probably thinking it a joke, Esme imagined.

"I'm serious. I've been wearing your shoes all month."

Her laughter was replaced with silence. Esme's stomach churned, and her cheeks reddened. She was mortified.

"I'm so sorry. I took great care of them, but I can double-check each pair tonight and bring any problems to Berger's in the morning."

Catherine's silence flipped back again to laughter, flooding Esme with relief.

"Don't worry about it. It's about time they went to good use. You must know, it's not exactly normal for me to have bought all those shoes."

Esme knew it wasn't normal. It was pretty obvious that Catherine had an addictive personality.

"Feel free to borrow anything for the weekend. There's a pair of

Valentino slingbacks in there that have a night in the Hamptons written all over them."

Esme was about to decline the invitation, but—those Valentino slingbacks!

"Thank you, Catherine! I will do them proud, I promise."

The thought of bringing all the right shoes for the weekend gave Esme a much-needed boost of confidence. As shallow as she knew it was, she would definitely feel less out of her league if she was on equal footing with her hostess. And she had yet to wear the infamous pale-pink satin, jewel-encrusted Manolo Hangisis, which she was determined to dress down with her favorite cropped jeans and a white flowy blouse.

Now she was excited to pack.

Esme went to sleep that night snuggled up with Elvis for the last time, dreaming of neither Liam nor Zach. She dreamed of Esme. Esme in her own life-worn, shiny black Louboutins sashaying across the floor of the Hudson Payne Gallery.

THIRTY

The Hermès Calfskin Oran Sandals

When Zach picked up Esme for the drive to the Hamptons in his aunt's fancy Range Rover, she immediately thought of Sy collecting Lena for their big night on the town. She started to blurt out the comparison but reined it back in. It was clearly not a friend-zone observation, and she was well aware that for Zach, the friend zone and his comfort zone were one and the same. If she had any doubts about it, his feelings were confirmed by his first sentence after hello.

"I'm thinking on the way out we should make a plan and sync our stories. If you want to stick with this boyfriend-girlfriend ruse, we shouldn't just wing it—like we did at the Bird Ball."

She laughed at his pun but didn't think it was a necessary exercise.

"We know each other pretty well by now. It's not like we're being interviewed for a green card."

"I know, but it would be kind of embarrassing for you if they found out the truth."

"All right, I wouldn't want to look like a psychopath. I'm game."

Zach imitated Morgan: "Esme, where did you two meet?"

"At the Mercer Kitchen. Zach is bartending there before starting law school."

"Going with the truth—good idea—we can't mess up, then."

"Exactly." She jumped on the imitation bandwagon with "So, Zach, do you want children?"

"Well, that's jumping ahead, no?"

"I don't know. Morgan's definitely the type that already has the names picked out."

"OK, we want a boy and a girl. I don't know what we will name the girl, but we are definitely naming the boy Sy for this incredible man we met who has no one to keep his memory alive in that way."

"Oh my God. That's the sweetest thing I've ever heard, although we'll have to talk about that when the time comes. I love my name, but having an unusual name is not always easy."

"Look at you, method acting—bravo!"

Esme laughed, pretending that was her intention. It was alarmingly easy to get caught up imagining a real future with Zach.

The banter continued, as was always the case when they were together, and soon all nerves regarding the upcoming weekend's interactions dissipated.

Time, and the miles between NYC and East Hampton, flew by. Esme had never been to the Hamptons before. She was amazed by the different Main Streets that popped up between mansions and cottages and farm stands along the way. It was certainly understandable that well-heeled Manhattanites headed out east at the first hint of summer.

They stopped for clam chowder at a yummy place called Bostwick's about a half hour before reaching their destination. Esme spent some time at the bathroom mirror freshening up her effortless look in advance of their arrival chez Miller. But when she checked out her outfit, a wispy sundress that was sexy in all the right places, it was Zach's face that ran through her mind.

Snap out of it! she admonished herself, in the spirit of Cher's famous line from *Moonstruck*.

"How do I look?" she asked Zach, clearly in violation of item number one on her current to-do list—keep Zach in the friend zone.

"Nice," he said, blandly and in obvious contrast with the *wow* expressed in his eyes. He sometimes confused her more than she confused herself.

The last part of the ride was marked by exquisite landscapes and more silent introspection.

They stopped at a local farm stand where Esme bought Morgan a beautiful bouquet of sunflowers, which Zach found hysterical.

"Esme, you are aware that you can't be liked by Morgan *and* steal her boyfriend, right?"

"Very funny—I'm not going there to steal her boyfriend. This is a fact-finding mission!"

"OK, but to be clear—what facts are we trying to find?"

"I just want to see how serious they are—and spend more time with him, out of the city."

The second-to-last turn, a left on Lily Pond Lane, left both Zach (who, like most private-school kids, had been to many a house in the Hamptons) and Esme (who had never been to a single one) equally gobsmacked. Gated houses that looked as though they'd been plucked from the English countryside or the French Riviera peeked out from centurion oak trees and perfectly coiffed hedges. Esme and Zach each proclaimed, "Look at that house!" over and over as they turned their heads from one side to the other as though they were in the stands at Wimbledon—and these homes weren't even the pièces de résistance. That title belonged to the houses that sat at the end of clandestine, hedge-flanked gravel lanes leading to oceanfront estates. As they approached the sign for one such passage, TIDES TURN LANE, the GPS startled them, shouting, "Your destination is on the right."

Mouths agape, they rode down in silence apart from the sound of the tires crunching the gravel. Zach took a beat before pressing the intercom at the gate.

"Wow. Cassandra Miller must have had some divorce attorney!"

"You ain't kidding. I wonder what size shoe she wears," Esme joked.

Zach laughed before squeezing her knee, his touch sending an unsettling zing to her heart. "You ready?"

"Ready as I'll ever be."

As they rounded the circular driveway, Liam came out to meet them. As she stepped out of the car, it was evident that her look had the same effect on Liam as it had had on Zach, though it was hard for Esme to believe that anything or anyone compared to the beauty of their present surroundings.

"Wow, you look beautiful, Esme."

Liam gave her a big hug and broke away, leaving his hands on her waist a little too long. As always, his touch brought back memories of their intimacies. She often wondered if he had grown as a lover over the years. Their college lovemaking was usually on the quick side. Between his youthful libido and the fact that there was always the risk of someone's roommate walking in, there was never much time for languid afternoons in bed. That's what she'd dreamed of: the chance to reacquaint herself with every inch of his body and mind, before deciding what was or wasn't meant to be.

Zach put down the bags and reached for Liam's hand, obviously intent on separating the two of them in the process. It was the perfect jealous boyfriend move, and Esme winked at him in gratitude as they entered the house. Though neither of them would have thought it possible, the inside of the house was even more stunning than the outside. It was classic and elegant, yet modern and sexy. Esme thought, *If it were a shoe, it would most definitely be a Louboutin.*

"Welcome to our beach house!" Morgan bellowed as she came sweeping down the grand staircase like Scarlett O'Hara on Prozac. Her embrace was so warm and sincere it almost made Esme feel guilty for the racy thoughts she'd just had about Morgan's boyfriend.

"I'm so happy you could make it! We have the place to ourselves all weekend, except for our house couple, who are both delightful, really. Come on, I'll show you to your room."

Zach took the duffel from Esme's shoulder and followed them upstairs to the guest wing. They settled into a spacious room with a four-poster bed and French doors that opened up to a balcony with breathtaking views of the Atlantic.

As if that weren't enough, above the fireplace hung an oil painting of a mother and baby with an indecipherable signature that Esme strongly suspected was Mary Cassatt.

She looked out the window in awe, until she realized that the insane view was a part of her competition. If she were to want Liam back, then the view, the house, the painting, the delightful house couple—whatever that meant—all stood in one column, while Esme stood alone in the other.

Morgan was talking nonstop. Esme wondered if it was nerves or if this unreal person was truly happy that they were there. She pondered whether her geniality was fueled by confidence, naïveté, or just a lifetime of getting her own way.

"I figured cocktails on the beach this afternoon, then dinner at eight at the Palm. It's casual, and delish."

Esme chuckled inside, thinking of what Morgan's definition of casual would be. Liam peeked his head in, apologizing for having to jump on a conference call. While he was dressed like the old Liam, in shorts and a sports tee, she could see that past his boyish charm a more serious man now existed. Or pretended to exist. Esme was not quite sure, especially after his run-by the other night.

"Bloody Marys when I'm off my call? With extra horseradish—just how you like it," he said, accompanied, no doubt, by a fresh stalk of celery and an *I know her best* air.

Esme smiled in return, masking the fact that she despised horseradish and that was actually the way *he* had liked his Bloody Marys.

"I'll leave you to unpack." Morgan smiled before fluttering off.

As soon as the door closed, Esme inquired, "What's a house couple?"

She was amazed by how much she didn't know.

"Never heard that one before, either, but I guess if you marry a maid and a butler you get a house couple."

"That's convenient. I wonder what you get if you marry a Manhattan socialite and a working-class boy from Cape Cod?" Esme joked.

"A rock-solid prenup?"

Esme laughed and messed with his hair. "Zach Bennet for the win!"

She reminded herself not to touch him again, for her own sake. They stared out at the view for a long minute, breathing in the sea air before quickly unpacking and throwing on suits.

Even though it had been wonderful to be in Manhattan for the entire month of August, it felt great to exchange the stillness of the city heat for the breezy beach. Zach took out paddleboards and taught Esme how to ride the waves. She had paddleboarded before, on Lake Ontario and Irondequoit Bay, but the swells of the Atlantic posed a whole different challenge. Once she proved that she could do it, she quit while she was ahead and settled into a lounge chair next to Morgan, armed with the book she had brought, aptly titled *The Beach House.* She hoped that opening it would discourage conversation. It didn't work.

Morgan took the opportunity to grill Esme.

"Zach's so cute, are you two in love?" she asked.

"Does it show?" Esme nonanswered.

"It really does. I can tell by the way that you look at each other that you're in the honeymoon phase of your relationship."

What phase are you in? Esme wanted to ask but refrained. That was not an answer she needed from Morgan's perspective.

In the end, Morgan definitely spilled more dirt than she received. Esme learned that Morgan Miller was born and raised on the Upper East Side, where she graduated from Hewitt before heading just across the park to Barnard. She spent time on the Cape until her parents' shocking and tumultuous divorce, after which she began splitting her summers between the Cape and the Hamptons. And, although Esme knew it was a tacky question, yes, that was an actual Cassatt over the fireplace in the guest room.

Esme looked back at the stately house and wondered what other priceless works of art lived there. She discreetly googled *Is it proper to ask your hostess for a house tour?* which the internet answered with a resounding no.

Damn.

She'd have to sneak around on her own.

They headed back indoors as the tide was coming in, and Zach presented Esme with a beautiful piece of turquoise-blue beach glass.

"Nice," Morgan said. "Turquoise is the rarest kind."

"So is Esme," he sweetly proclaimed while playfully nuzzling the side of her neck.

Liam joined them just in time to insert his great-son-of-Cape-Cod wisdom.

"It's actually not the rarest. Turquoise usually comes from vintage seltzer bottles. Orange is the rarest because there was so little orange glass made."

Both Esme and Morgan seemed impressed by his beachcomber knowledge, while Zach rolled his eyes.

"Just enough time to shower before dinner," Morgan announced happily. "Come on, Boo." She winked at Liam, leading them to imagine that they would be showering together. Esme felt bothered by it and wondered if it were jealousy or just some part of her that still laid claim to him.

THIRTY-ONE

The Manolo Blahnik Hangisis with Ninety-Millimeter Heels

Liam drove them to the restaurant that night in the family's Aston Martin convertible—another huge check mark in Morgan's column.

Good thing that Liam wasn't a list man, Esme rationalized.

Apparently, they were taking Morgan's mother's standing Friday night reservation. Liam explained the familiar scene they were about to encounter on the way over.

"The Palm is like the old-school dining mecca of the Hamptons. This car practically drives itself there."

Morgan added, "My mom goes every Friday night. She's probably consumed more lump crab meat and jumbo shrimp cocktail there than everyone north of the highway combined."

She and Liam laughed. Zach rolled his eyes again. Esme kicked him. It bothered her that he was judging them, judging Liam, really. She wondered why she cared what he thought of her ex, why she wanted Zach to like Liam. She had no intention of asking him if he did.

They entered the Palm to a scene that made the Mercer Kitchen look mellow. It was packed, and Esme could swear the entire crowd looked up in unison to check them out when they walked into the dining room.

"What are they looking at?" she whispered to Liam, still thinking of him as her fish-out-of-water ally.

"They just want to see if you're a Seinfeld, or a Baldwin, or possibly someone more unusual for the Hamptons."

Esme clicked her perfectly dressed-down ninety-millimeter pale-pink heels together and joked, "I guess we're not in Kansas anymore."

"Most definitely not," Liam responded while slipping his hand around her waist for the second time that day to guide her to "their" table. For a split second it felt as though he were hers. It felt like this was as it should be.

Between the overwhelming volume of the dining room chatter and the food—the aforementioned shellfish appetizers, followed by steak, creamed spinach, mashed potatoes, and an order of chicken Parmesan for the table because "You just must!"—the conversation at dinner was thankfully sparse and benign.

Esme noticed again that Liam buttered Morgan's roll and sadly determined it must be their thing. Zach noticed, too, and one-upped them by feeding Esme lump crab meat dipped in cocktail sauce from his fork. It made Esme laugh and brightened her mood.

By the end of the meal they were all overserved, so Liam phoned the delightful house couple to pick them up. While Esme was happy that he wouldn't be driving drunk, she was constantly surprised at how entrenched and comfortable Liam seemed in Morgan's moneyed world. Though when he asked the waiter to wrap up the rest of the chicken Parm to go, it was clear that Morgan wasn't digging the uncouth move.

They waited outside in the garden, both couples snuggled up on wooden benches in the suddenly crisp August air.

"It was smart to call for backup; I hope they weren't sleeping," Morgan worried.

"Better safe than sorry," Liam preached, followed by "Esme, remember how your dad used to play around with the headlights on dark nights driving home?"

She hadn't thought about it in years, but sometimes on the winding roads upstate at night, her dad would think it funny to turn off his headlights and drive "blind." Neither Esme nor her mother were amused by it. In fact, the opposite was true, but apparently the one time that Liam experienced it, he was tickled by the performance. Either way, she found it odd that he would bring up her father driving at all after what had happened. Zach got that and wrapped his arms around her in comfort. It felt an awful lot like love, as opposed to acting, and it poked at her heart.

Liam similarly put his arm around Morgan and asked Esme, "Can you believe this is the little kid who followed us around all night at that Fourth of July party?"

She was surprised he'd brought that up, too. And even more surprised that that was what he remembered of that weekend. Esme was quiet and seemed in need of saving, so Zach stepped in.

"When did you finally notice she wasn't a little kid?" he asked.

"At a company conference in the Bahamas about five years ago."

Zach and Esme had both seen Morgan in her bikini that afternoon. There was no need to ask what caught his eye in the Bahamas.

"How did you two meet?" Morgan asked.

Zach told them how he first met Esme at the Mercer Kitchen. Morgan dug deeper.

"What made you fall for her?"

With everything Zach and Esme went over in the car, that question had never come up.

"Too many things to pick just one," he improvised.

Morgan didn't let it go. "Try!"

Zach got very intense, reeling them all in.

"If I'm being honest, it was love at first sight. She had finished her mojito and was fishing with her straw in the glass to pull out a piece of mint. She had such a determined look on her face until she looked up at me and smiled. There was a big piece of mint caught in her teeth. I pointed it out and referenced the location on my own mouth, and we went back and forth like people do, but with no luck. After the third attempt she laughed and buried her head in her hands, embarrassed. She made a funny face, exposing all her teeth and leaned across the bar for me to remove it. That was it for me."

Morgan was clearly enamored by the story, while Liam looked like someone had punched him in the gut.

"How about you?" Morgan asked Esme, to no reply.

Esme was equally enamored.

"Esme, how about you?" she asked, a bit louder.

"Oh, me?" She snapped out of it.

Morgan laughed. "When did you fall for Zach? Like, when did you know for sure?"

She looked into Zach's eyes and took a telling breath. "Just now."

There was a pause so long she could hang the moon on it, until Liam blurted out, "Car's here, let's go."

Morgan chatted the whole way home, pointing out who lived where and which shop carried what Hampton must-have. This time Esme was happy for her chattiness. The air between her and Zach in the wayback of the car was saturated with desire—so much so that

Esme thought she may explode. When the delightful houseman made a sharp right, causing Zach to fly into her space and his leg to press up against hers, she nearly did. All she wanted to do was kiss him like she had that night on the subway, though this time she doubted that she would be able to keep it PG. She wondered if their thought bubbles matched. It was just as likely that he was still acting and she was falling for it. Someone had mentioned playing pool after dinner. She prayed that Liam and Morgan wouldn't bail and go to their room when they got back. She recommitted to her "just friends" promise to Zach. His was not the home she was contemplating wrecking. As if reading her mind, he bellowed, "I'm psyched to play pool when we get home," flooding her with relief, relief laced with disappointment.

When did I become so fickle?

The billiard room was in the basement of the house, along with its shabby neighbors: the three-thousand-bottle wine cellar, the state-of-the-art gym, and the Ziegfeldesque screening room. Esme thought back to Liam mentioning how bored he and Morgan were over that rainy August weekend. She and Zach could have "made do" in this place for a good six months without getting bored, seven if they had the delightful house couple.

Zach helped himself to a brandy and suggested that they mix things up.

"How about Morgan and I against you and Liam?"

His proposal felt like an insult to Esme, and that insult registered on her face, which embarrassed her. Luckily for all, Morgan bailed. Which seemed suspect, because she was the one who had initially suggested playing back at the Palm.

Maybe she's not so self-assured after all.

"I'm sorry, guys, but I'm not feeling up to it. I'm gonna head upstairs."

She put her hand on Liam's arm.

"Are you coming, Boo? You want to be fresh for the party to-morrow."

"Morgan's right. Rain check?"

"No problem. Would it be too noisy if Esme and I play?" Zach inquired ridiculously. It felt like the bedrooms were a mile away.

"Not at all. Have fun, guys. Good night."

"Good night."

"And thank you for dinner," they said in unison.

Somehow a check had never arrived at the table. Of course Zach asked Liam, "What do I owe you?" Liam's response—"Nothing, we have a tab here"—made Esme's stomach knot. She added an endless supply of lump crab meat and shrimp cocktail to Morgan's column in her side-by-side analysis.

Zach lined up the balls while Esme wondered if he really did want to play or really didn't want to go upstairs alone with her. He looked exhausted.

"You sure you don't want to go to sleep? It's been such a long day."

"No, I'm good. Do you want to break?"

"All right."

He lifted the triangle, and she broke with a misdirected ven-geance, sinking nearly half the balls.

"What's up, Esme?"

"Nothing—I'm stripes. Nine ball in the corner pocket."

"Really, 'cause you look like you want to poke my eye out with that stick."

"Well, what do you think is up?"

"I don't know—that's why I asked."

"Why did you suggest switching partners for the game?"

"Because I figured it would be good for you and Liam, you know, to be partners. Pool can be very—sexy."

"I agree. Eleven ball in the side pocket. So why would my boy-friend suggest such a thing?"

"I thought it would help to move things forward for you."

"Well, you thought wrong. Fourteen in the corner pocket."

"What are you, a pool shark?"

"Don't change the subject. I like things in order. I will get to the intimate part of the Liam plan if and when *I'm* ready, not *you*. It's like you went right for the eight ball."

The fourteen ball went in, followed by the white ball.

"Scratch!" Zach said, in a tone better suited for telling her off.

Esme retreated to the couch. She picked up a small bronze sculpture of a reclining figure on the end table and turned it over.

"Jeez, of course it's a Henry Moore. It's like we're staying in a museum. You know, that really was a Mary Cassatt in the bedroom."

"That's insane."

"I know, right? It's pretty amazing."

"I meant it's insane that only guests of Morgan's and her mother's, the ones who choose that particular bedroom out of the four in the guest wing, would have the great privilege and honor of seeing that painting—three ball in the side pocket."

"You realize you just shat all over my dream job, right?"

"You still think that selling art to the überwealthy patrons of the Hudson Payne Gallery to hang in their powder rooms is your life's calling? Six ball in the corner pocket."

It was the exact thought that had been plaguing her since her interview at the gallery. Yet she fought hard against it with Zach, almost as if she were arguing with herself.

"I know I'd be lucky to get that job back, and to get the life back that I lost."

"There's no guarantee that you would still have had that life, Esme, or want it."

"Zach, why don't you just say what you want to say? You don't like Liam."

"I don't dislike Liam. I just wonder why he let you go in the first place."

"He didn't. You know I pushed him away."

"Well, I never would have let you go. And if you really meant that much to him, he would have fought for you. You're setting yourself up for more heartbreak."

"Thank you for putting it so delicately."

"I thought you would have figured it out for yourself this weekend. There's no chance that guy is giving all this up."

"You know nothing about him. If there is no chance, then why did he yell up to my apartment the other night like Romeo to Juliet?"

"I have no idea. Maybe he's a two-timer."

"Takes one to know one, doesn't it?"

She felt badly as soon as she said it. She knew that *she* had kissed Zach first on the subway, and she could see how guilty and conflicted he'd been feeling ever since.

He came back with both guns blazing.

"You're setting out in your life like nothing has happened to you. Like you have been living in a vacuum for seven years—when you haven't. You met a guy and created a plan at twenty-one, and you think your life has no meaning unless you follow that plan. He's not even right for you anymore, Esme. Neither is that job."

"You're just jealous because I'm going about getting what I want, while you're just letting what you want slip away—and doing nothing about it!"

"I am doing something about it."

"You're here with me, in the Hamptons, and your wife's in Cuba. What are you doing? You think you're going to become a big immigration lawyer and change the world in time to change your life? Is that your plan?"

He took his tone down a notch.

"Actually, that's only a part of my plan. I spoke to Amara last night. She's not going to take the government job, and I am going to spend a month there over winter break so that we can figure things out."

His words stung like a slap, and the pain it left confused her. *If I came here to test the waters with Liam, then why do I care if Zach is going back to work things out with his wife?* She took a minute to let it all sink in: Zach was not hers, and Liam was not hers. The wall that had been faltering around her heart slammed back up.

Esme shouted angrily, "Good. Then we both know who we are and where we want to be."

"Eight ball in the corner pocket," he said.

He sank it and put down his stick.

"I'm done. I'm going to sleep."

He took a deep breath and added calmly, "Even I know there's a different girl standing in those Louboutins than there was seven years ago, Esme! And until you figure out who she is, you're not going to be happy."

She wasn't having it but couldn't think of anything to say except, "You don't know anything! They're not even Louboutins—they're Manolos!"

He walked out, and she let him go.

She sat on the couch for a bit and thought about what he said, dissecting his words and wondering if they came from a place of anger or truth. Her eyes started to shut, but she fought it off. Sleeping on the couch would definitely blow their soul mates cover. By the time she made it upstairs, Zach was sound asleep in the four-poster bed.

She washed up and changed before sliding under the covers, getting as close to the edge of the bed as possible without falling off. Watching Zach sleep as if nothing had happened may have infuriated her more than his words. She was tired, too, but her thoughts overrode her exhaustion. Her mind was running in more directions than that damn pool game.

Anger in the right corner pocket, confusion in the left, lust in the side. She gave up and headed downstairs for a midnight house tour.

Cassandra Miller's taste in art was beyond eclectic. A Koons Balloon Dog sat on a pedestal in front of a nineteenth-century Italian still life. A Rosenquist hung next to a Hudson Valley landscape, and an O'Keeffe shared a wall with a Warhol. It was thrilling to explore, even though Zach's opinion on private collectors had already gotten under her skin. She heard noise coming from the kitchen and followed it. Liam's handsome face lit up when she entered. *One more beautiful piece of art obtained by the Millers,* Esme thought cynically. Zach had really put her in a mood.

"Chicken Parmesan?" he asked, standing next to the sink, happily scarfing it down. She had seen this midnight-snacking Liam on many occasions before. His teenage-boy appetite seemed to have survived his yuppie transformation.

"Sure." She boosted herself up onto the counter next to him and opened wide for a bite. He cut one with the perfect ratio of cheese and chicken and popped it in her mouth.

"It's cold." She laughed.

"I like it cold." He smiled at her. "Remember when we ordered that pizza, fell asleep, and ate it cold for breakfast?"

Esme laughed again. "I do."

"You couldn't sleep?" he asked.

She weighed her response. Maybe it was a good time to infuse some doubt in her relationship status.

"Zach and I had an argument."

"What about?"

She wasn't about to rehash it.

"It's not important." She changed the subject. "So, the big three-oh tomorrow—pretty crazy, huh?"

"It is," he agreed before taking a huge bite.

"Well, I'm happy for you. You seem like you are exactly where you wanted to be."

His chewing slowed, as if he was thinking about his response. In the end he swallowed and smiled earnestly. "Well, if you remember, I wanted to be married to you by thirty."

She was taken aback by his candor but rebounded nicely. "Well, all of this really seems to suit you," she stated purposefully.

"I think so. It's the big life that you and I had always talked about."

"That's an understatement." Esme laughed.

"I haven't forgotten where I came from, Esme, believe me. You know, I paid off my parents' entire mortgage with my first real Christmas bonus. My father would have worked for the rest of his life to do that."

"Wow, Liam, good for you. That's amazing!" And an absurd example of the imbalance of wealth in this country, she thought. Zach's liberal rhetoric was really rubbing off on her.

"I told my mom you were here; she was so happy to hear you're doing well. She always loved you."

"My mom was crazy about you, too—remember?"

It was one of the first things that ran through her mind when she thought about the possibility of getting back with Liam. She knew she would never have her mother's approval of a man ever again. There was no denying it, that part of Liam was literally irreplaceable. Her thoughts were all over the place again, and she had the overwhelming desire to step out to make a quick pro and con list.

Liam cut her another bite, but this time he wedged himself between her legs and fed it to her. He rested his hands on her thighs, just watching her chew. His eyes fixed on hers. Her overwhelming desire quickly shifted. Dreaming of this moment had gotten her through many hard nights. And here it was, within her reach.

Zach's know-it-all line—*there's no chance that guy is giving all this up*—entered her mind for the umpteenth time since he'd said it. But now it felt like a challenge. A challenge she could take right now if she wanted to. She was sure that if she leaned in and gently kissed Liam on the lips, he would respond in kind. But to what end? Would Liam regret kissing her, like Zach had? Was it right to upend his life again, to satisfy her curiosity—or worse, to prove a point to Zach?

She looked down at her dangling feet, bare except for two coats of Berry Naughty polish on her toes. She wondered if selecting that color was the nail polish equivalent of choosing Louboutin Pigalles—they both held the promise of the unexpected. The funny thing was, Esme now strongly desired the opposite. Her definition of happiness had most definitely changed. It didn't seem that Liam's had.

"Are you happy, Liam?"

"Very," he answered, obviously in the moment.

He reached for a strand of her hair, twirling it around his index finger before dropping it and running it across her shoulder and down her arm. He wrapped his hands around her waist and pulled her into him, overriding her sensibility and replacing it with lust. She had meant to start a discussion about his life, about his life with Morgan, but she had started something entirely different. She paused to enjoy the feeling of desire, as reckless as it was, and nuzzled into his neck, longingly soaking in his familiar scent. His hands slipped under the back of her shirt, causing her breath to stop and her heart to drop in anticipation of his next touch. She thought about tracing her fingers down the line of his abs, and possibly further, but when their gaze met again, the raw honesty and uncertainty reflected in each other's eyes broke the spell. Liam took a step back. He ran his hands over his hair—over his brain. Even with his abs within reach, she wasn't unhappy that he had backed away. It felt as if they both needed to get that close for it all to become clear.

"What are you thinking?" she whispered, hoping they would meet on the same page.

"That I never stopped loving you, which is very confusing to me because I am wholeheartedly in love with Morgan." This time it didn't feel like a slap. This time it felt right.

"Maybe what we are feeling now is nostalgia for our youth—or just plain old lust."

"Maybe," he agreed.

The stairway light flicked on and they heard the distinct sound of footsteps overhead. Esme jumped off the counter and hurried over to the other side of the island, while Liam got to work scraping off his plate in the sink. She barely had time to get her breath back when Morgan entered the kitchen. Liam turned to face his girlfriend, and Esme saw shame fill his eyes—just for thinking about being unfaithful to her, she imagined. It made Esme feel awful for her part in it. She worried that Morgan had noticed it as well. It was soon clear that she hadn't.

"I'm sorry I gave you a hard time about taking home the leftovers. Are there any more?"

She slid her arms around Liam's waist, and he hugged her in return, looking at Esme sheepishly over his shoulder.

Esme yawned purposefully.

"I'm gonna get some sleep. Thanks for the midnight snack, Liam."

"Of course, anytime."

"Sweet dreams," Morgan added.

Not a chance, Esme thought. *Not a chance.*

THIRTY-TWO

No Shoes Allowed

Esme slept in the next morning. More like she faked sleeping in. She had no desire to see Zach, or Liam, or even Morgan. Eventually Zach came in to see if she was breathing. He was holding a fresh cup of coffee, and a fresh-picked daisy was stuck behind his ear.

"Wake up, sleepyhead."

His voice didn't sound angry anymore. Esme was relieved. She needed her ally back to survive the next twenty-four hours. She opened one eye. Then both.

He placed the cup on her nightstand.

"You made me coffee. So sweet."

"The delightful house couple made it. It's actually a double shot mochaccino made from freshly ground beans imported from Somalia." He handed her the daisy.

"And a peace offering. I'm sorry about last night," he said sincerely. "I shouldn't have said the things I did. It's your life, and obviously you know it better than I do."

She had tossed and turned for hours thinking about what happened—or didn't happen—with Liam and thinking about her fight with Zach, but mostly thinking about herself. Her future, her happiness, her life. She felt more confused than ever. She wished she hadn't come to the Hamptons and wanted more than anything to disappear.

"Things got pretty intense with Liam last night," she admitted.

"Really? Do we have to pack our bags and run for the hills?"

"No. But I could use some time away from here, that's for sure."

"I know the perfect place. Get dressed!"

"Tell me where."

"Nope. It's a surprise."

"I hate surprises, and I have to know what shoes to wear!"

"I'm pretty sure you have to take your shoes off."

"Hmmm. Should I wear a bathing suit?"

"No need."

"Intriguing. Are we bowling?"

"No. We are not bowling. Stop asking, you will never guess. Just get dressed and meet me downstairs, where I will do you the huge favor of telling our hosts that we are skipping the day's activities."

Esme handed him back the flower and said casually, "I may love you."

"You should." He laid it back in her lap and left her to get ready.

She pulled off its petals and said out loud, *He loves me, he loves me not*, not completely certain whom she was referring to.

———

The drive to the surprise destination was filled with as many twists and turns as the weekend had held so far. Esme was clueless and had no idea where they were headed but tried her best to figure it out.

"How far is it from here?"

"Close, about twelve miles."

She grabbed for his phone to see the GPS, but he playfully pushed her hand away. "Why do you have to know everything that's going to happen? Life's more fun when you don't."

"Your life, maybe. Is it a natural or man-made surprise?"

"Man-made. And that's my only hint!"

"The Jimmy Choo store in East Hampton?"

"Absolutely not—meshugana."

She laughed and gave up, settling into her seat to enjoy the scenery: Ralph Lauren, Vilebrequin, Citarella, an old cemetery, a windmill, a horse farm, another windmill, a charming general store, and then a sign that made her jump from her seat.

"The Pollock-Krasner House?"

Zach's smile met Esme's exuberance.

"We have a noon tour. I wasn't sure if you knew all there was to know about Jackson Pollock and Lee Krasner, but—"

Esme interrupted him. "I don't know all there is to know—but I love both their work so much! I'm so excited, thank you!"

They soon arrived at the former home and studios of the infamous artists Jackson Pollock and his wife, Lee Krasner, which were set back on five acres in Springs, bordering Accabonac Creek.

The twelve o'clock tour group met under the shade of a sprawling silver maple to hear general info about the property that the newlywed artists had acquired back in 1945. The first stop was the barn studio, where a sign explained Zach's cryptic comment about shoes.

"Aaah, no shoes allowed!"

Esme couldn't help but kiss Zach on the cheek at the first sight of the paint-splattered floor with the remnants of Pollock's groundbreaking technique spilled onto it. It amazed her how well he had come to know her in such a short span of time. That, and the obvious happiness he felt upon witnessing her happiness, gave Esme pause. She didn't get much further than thinking, *That Amara is one lucky girl!*

They each removed their shoes and donned the special slipper socks provided. Stepping into Jackson Pollock's studio, which looked as if he had left it just a few minutes before, was the most beautiful surprise. The docent explained the discovery of the original wooden floor, one that Pollock and Krasner had subsequently covered with Masonite, while Esme took in every inch of its surface. Walking on the actual floorboards where Jackson Pollock had created his most famous works felt like an out-of-body experience. She needn't have taken off her shoes, because her feet barely touched the ground.

The tour continued to the main house, a small cottage with modest furnishings, and concluded with the whole group stuffed into the upstairs bedroom that Lee had originally used as her studio. There, the docent narrated over film about some of Krasner's important works and concluded with a detailed account of Pollock's death, details that Esme had once known—but had long since forgotten.

She began with the story of the last work Krasner created in the cottage studio: an abstract life-size portrait in oil that she had painted in 1956 of a bloated man with a large gash on his head. The painting was titled *Prophecy*, and when the docent said it, the hair on Esme's neck stood on end. It was all coming back to her.

At the time *Prophecy* was painted, Jackson was having an affair with a much younger woman named Ruth Kligman. Lee gave Jackson a "her or me" ultimatum before escaping to Europe without him for a break.

The docent went on to tell the story of the night that Jackson, a notorious alcoholic, drove his girlfriend, Ruth, and her companion

Edith to visit a friend in a nearby town. Minutes into the journey, he fell asleep at the wheel of his 1950 Oldsmobile convertible, so they turned around and headed back home. She continued in great detail.

"For no good reason, since he was only going home, he stepped on the gas and sped back down the winding road. He missed the curve on the left and veered off to the right, where the convertible shot forth into the woods. Jackson was thrown from the vehicle, fracturing his skull and killing him. The car flipped over on Edith, instantly breaking her neck, while the girlfriend, Ruth, was thrown clear and survived to tell the story."

Esme's hands shook. Images of her parents' accident, of her mother's similar demise, raced through her mind. It wasn't as though she'd never been faced with triggers over the years, when watching a car wreck on television or seeing people rubbernecking on the highway, but this felt epically different.

A chaotic feeling of shock choked her as the docent continued.

"In Paris, Lee was devastated by the news and filled with guilt. I don't know how much you know about alcoholism or alcoholics and their dependents," she continued, "but people who have alcoholic spouses often feel like it is their job to protect the alcoholic. They can't."

Esme thought of her mother and the possible load that she had been carrying on her own. Evidence of it filled her mind as the walls in the small room closed in around her. The docent explained that Lee was Jackson's guardian, always calling his friends, asking where he was. "Is he out at the bar? Is he out with you?"

Strikingly similar conversations came flooding back to Esme. Hushed words spoken over the telephone from her mother to God knows who. She once went as far as waking up a young Esme and throwing her in the car in the middle of the night to search for him.

The fight in the front seat on the way home, after she'd finally found him at a local bar, was the basis for one of Esme's earliest memories: a fuzzy picture of her mother shouting and her father laughing on a cold winter night. Her mother kept it better hidden after that.

The docent spoke her final sentence. "If Lee Krasner hadn't found the courage to leave Jackson Pollock, she would likely have been the one to die in that crash by his side."

That was it, there wasn't enough air left in the room for Esme. A strange sound escaped her throat before she ran off in tears. She kept running until she reached the marshy banks of the creek, where she collapsed on the ground and sobbed.

Zach ran after her, disappointment, confusion, and guilt written all over his face. Esme felt awful when she saw him.

"It's not your fault, Zach, this was so nice of you, really."

"I'm so sorry," he sat down beside her. "I had no idea."

He stroked her hair and coaxed her to talk.

"Esme, was your father an alcoholic?"

Esme laid her head in Zach's lap and took a beat before admitting, "I've never said it out loud. And it was never discussed, but yes, I'm pretty sure that my father was an alcoholic. It's very possible that he was drunk at the time of their accident."

These were thoughts Esme had never allowed herself to process over the years, let alone verbalize. As soon as they formed in her brain, she would do everything in her power to replace them with excuses. She would think about all the times her dad was funny, cutting off her memories right before things got out of hand. It was suddenly obvious that being in denial was not serving her anymore.

"I don't understand why she stayed with him. If she'd left like Lee—she would still be alive," she cried.

"I don't know. She probably loved him. I mean, look what you gave up for him over the past seven years. And you know that alcoholism is a disease as much as cancer."

Esme was in no mood to hear that sermon, true or not. She blamed her father—not any disease—and her mother, too, for not leaving him, for leaving her all alone in the world. She thought back again to the time her mom visited her in Europe without him and how she had signed just her own name on Esme's graduation gift. Maybe she was planning on leaving him after all. Esme would never know.

They sat there in silence for a long while, staring out at the marshy creek where carefree kayakers were enjoying their carefree lives, Esme imagined. Her nerves again sat raw and exposed, after she had tucked them away for the month. She hadn't felt this sorry for herself in a while. Zach must have sensed it, because he insisted they get up and move on.

"Let's get out of here, go get lunch."

"I'm not hungry," Esme whined.

"You can just pick. You haven't eaten all day."

They stopped at Springs General Store, a charming old shop complete with retro gas pumps outside that one could imagine Jackson Pollock himself frequenting back in the day. They picked up egg salad sandwiches, sodas, and penny candies and sat at a picnic table outside to eat.

Esme further explained how she knew her dad drank but did not know the extent of it. As far as blaming him for her mother's death, it was much easier for her to live in denial while caring for him than to break down what really could have occurred on the night of the accident.

"By the time my mother's funeral was over, the story that they must have swerved to avoid a deer was repeated so many times it became my reality."

"You have no way of knowing that it wasn't, without a witness or a toxicology report," Zach reminded her. "The deer scenario could very well be true. He could have been perfectly sober that night. Was his blood alcohol level even taken?"

"I honestly don't know; it may have been but just as easily may not. There were police at the hospital asking about him, but he had been rushed right to surgery."

When she had finally come out of her mother's room on that awful night, one of the cops from the highway department who was sent from the scene of the accident was still waiting there to question her.

"Was your dad drinking tonight?" he had asked, somewhat gingerly.

His words had snapped her to attention.

"I was at school. You'll have to ask him."

"We have been waiting to do that, but we can't because of his condition."

"Well, my mother is dead, and my father is in surgery. Do you think *I* am in any condition to deal with this now?"

She took a deep breath and said emphatically, "I can tell you that my dad is not a big drinker at all. I have to go talk to the doctors now."

She had held her own hands, trying to stop them from visibly shaking, and walked away signaling she had nothing else to say. She never heard from the police again.

Esme had no interest in repeating the conversation to Zach or anyone else. She indicated that she was done talking by popping a Tootsie Roll in her mouth, standing, and heading to the car. Zach dutifully followed.

THIRTY-THREE

The Valentino Rockstud Sandals

Eyes still puffy and swollen, Esme hoped to get back in the house and up to her room unnoticed, but of course Morgan chose this occasion to answer her own front door.

"What happened?" she asked upon viewing Esme's face and adding in a whisper, "Did you and Zach have a fight?"

"No, it's nothing," she insisted.

"I have just the thing. Go upstairs and take a hot shower, then meet me in my dressing room."

For some reason, Esme took solace in Morgan's empathy and did as she said.

Even after the hot shower, she could still tell she'd been crying. She wrapped herself in the luxurious terry bathrobe that hung behind the bathroom door and contemplated whether it would be wrong to consider it swag as she made the long trek to Morgan's dressing room. It was a sight that made the Temple of Sole look like a glorified gym locker.

Morgan held up two dresses. "Which one?"

They were both stunning.

"I can't decide. I guess the colorful one is more festive," Esme said.

"I think so, too. Here, want to wear the other one?"

Obviously Esme had a dress in her room, but the classic Max Hammer little black one that Morgan was now swinging in front of her looked too good to pass up.

"I brought a dress, but it can't hurt to try it, I guess."

Once it was on, there was no way it was coming off. Esme spun around in the mirror, and her mood improved tenfold.

The doorbell rang, and soon a pit crew consisting of a hairstylist and makeup artist were escorted into the room.

"Hair or makeup first?" Morgan asked.

Esme chose hair, and the two sat side by side getting powdered and coiffed like two debutantes before their cotillion.

"I'm so glad that you're feeling better. Was it an argument with Zach? I can't even function when Liam and I fight."

"No, not at all."

She was unusually honest.

"Zach took me to the Pollock-Krasner House and, well, hearing how he died kind of triggered me."

"Oh no, he died in that awful car accident. Of course it did, you poor thing!"

The fact that no further explanation was needed was not much of a surprise. Obviously Liam had told Morgan her whole sob story. She imagined that a whispered explanation of her parents' demise often preceded her introduction. How could she have thought otherwise? She wondered whether that was why Morgan had been so nice to her. *You poor thing* was Esme's least favorite refrain, but for some reason, hearing this exceptionally spoiled girl recognize the hard luck Esme had suffered and the sacrifices she had made felt satisfying. Satisfying followed by guilt-inducing—for having shown up with two-faced intentions.

"I'm so nervous for tonight! I have a big surprise for Liam!" Morgan gushed. She really adored him. She'd probably been in love with him even longer than Esme had. She thought about asking what the surprise was, but the stylist turned on the blow-dryer, and Esme was happy to just sit and veg below the whir.

When she got back to her room, she locked herself in the bathroom and composed a long, formal text to Liam. Her second apology since seeing him again. She had avoided him all day and knew it wasn't fair to go to the party with their awkward interaction hanging between them. She worried that whatever it was he was feeling (guilt, confusion, regret) could spoil his birthday and Morgan's big surprise. She wanted to make her feelings clear. They felt clear to her.

> **Don't feel bad about what happened last night, the more I've thought about it the more I know that it was just pent-up lust and longing. Morgan is perfect for you and I am falling hard for Zach. I really think we're both where we should be. Let's just celebrate tonight with no weirdness between us. Happy birthday!!!!**

It was one of those texts that she would usually let breathe a little, like the fancy wine at dinner the night before—putting a little space between her and it before having another look and sending it off.

Zach knocked on the bathroom door, startling her. "Esme, come on! They left ten minutes ago!"

But not today. She pressed Send and hoped for the best.

———

Esme checked her phone for a response from Liam about every two minutes on the ride to the party. Zach noticed her nervousness.

"What's up?"

"Nothing." She changed the subject. "Did you know that Ina Garten was the White House nuclear policy analyst for Presidents Ford and Carter?"

"I did not—it's pretty cool that you can be so many different things in one lifetime."

"Like cauliflower," she responded, stealing a joke from Sy.

Zach laughed, needing no further explanation.

Thought bubbles.

She also knew the coincidental fact that Ina had met her husband, Jeffrey, at Dartmouth, an interesting tidbit that Esme would have once considered a sign of some kind but now chose to keep to herself. She went back to obsessing over the unanswered text still suspended out there in the universe.

They pulled up to the barn, situated next to the Gartens' stately shingled "farmhouse," and parked the car. Zach valiantly opened her door and confessed.

"I didn't get the chance to tell you with all the rushing, but you look absolutely stunning tonight."

His words were all for her, as there was no one else around to hear them. They filled her with confidence and warmth.

The grounds of Ina Garten's home and barn somehow succeeded in being both immense and quaint at the same time. Her television show, *Barefoot Contessa*, was a night-nurse favorite. Esme was quite familiar with the "barn" it was filmed in, and more than a little starstruck by the Barefoot Contessa herself—even though her moniker was anti-shoe!

The barn door opened to a sultry woman in a sparkling pair of Dolce & Gabbana high-heeled, cross-strapped sandals holding a large satin sack, who announced, "Phones, please!"

Relief flooded Esme's face; Liam hadn't been ignoring her.

They both assumed Ina Garten didn't want her place photographed as they dropped their phones in the bag.

"Maybe she's scared we'll capture secret recipes," Zach surmised.

"Very Willy Wonka of her!" Esme agreed.

Zach and Esme spent the cocktail hour in close proximity to each other, sipping pomegranate gimlets and munching on tidbits of meatballs and baked fontina. Zach was easygoing in his introductions and conversation, while Esme was not as fluent in mingling with Manhattan's transplanted elite. She silently thanked Catherine for her rock star shoes and her mother for the small advantage of her highbrow name. Esme Nash had never really sounded like a girl from outside of Rochester.

Morgan's crowd was like a throwback to the eighties, when one's social footprint was calculated by things more far-reaching than Instagram followers. It was obvious that these people had bonded at the right schools and summer camps and rehabs, mostly before the tender age of sixteen. It was a very exclusive and well-to-do world made up of a limited selection of socially prominent bloodlines that had been mixing it up in Manhattan and the Hamptons for decades. One could only gain later-in-life access to this privileged lot through marriage—though that type of entrée seemed to come with an unspoken B-level status.

Or sometimes, spoken.

A man wearing an ascot walked right past a waiter and asked Liam, "Is there any Pellegrino or just Perrier? I prefer Italian water to French."

"I'll ask," Liam said, confirming that his status was most definitely B.

The tidbits of conversation they picked up throughout the room were endlessly entertaining:

"Mykonos is so last year."

"I know, everyone is honeymooning in Dubai."

"I love your sweater."

"Thank you, after Fido passed I had it spun from his fur."

"You did all that cocaine back in high school and now you're worried about the legality of consuming raw Amish milk?"

Zach happily excused himself to interrogate the bartender making the gimlets while Esme tried her future on for the few guests who inquired, elevating her status as she went along.

"I'm trying to find myself."

"I had a great interview at a gallery last week."

"I'm considering an offer from Hudson Payne."

The last was met with a plea from a woman no older than Esme to help cover the walls of the ten-thousand-square-foot château she was building on Georgica Pond.

Esme looked around the room at all of the asses she would need to kiss if she wanted to make good on such offers and wondered how Liam managed. From the look of him, he was doing just fine, effortlessly schmoozing, as Sy would say. He may even have been thriving.

Zach returned and again read her mind, whispering, "This has to be exhausting for Liam. I bet that perpetual smile is masking perpetual self-doubt."

Esme wasn't so sure.

At eight o'clock sharp, Ina Garten appeared, not barefoot, but in her signature denim button-down shirt. She welcomed the group and wished Liam a happy birthday. She was just as Esme had imagined, lovely and warm and the kind of person who immediately seemed like an old friend. Esme could see a big jar of homemade vanilla up on the shelf and was already dreaming of dessert as Mrs. Garten announced the Mediterranean-style menu.

She smiled genuinely and proclaimed, "Dinner is served!"

As the dozen partygoers mopped up tzatziki and imported Greek feta with warm wedges of fresh-baked pita bread, the woman in the Dolce & Gabbana sandals, who had greeted them when they arrived, announced, "Let the games begin," while ceremoniously emptying the bag of phones onto the center of the table.

All eyes went from her to Morgan as she stood to explain the rules of the party game she claimed to have invented for the occasion. She called it Cell Phone Truth or Dare.

"And I'm in charge," she added, "because, you know, it's Liam's birthday!"

This caused a round of laughter, with Liam bravely making a joke at her expense.

"What's your reasoning the other three hundred and sixty-four days of the year?"

Which of course spawned more laughter from everyone, except for Morgan. She took back the room and continued. "When I point to you, you take your phone from the pile, and without looking at it, choose truth or dare. For truth, you have to read your last text message out loud. For dare—I'll give you a phone-related task."

Remain calm, Esme nearly said out loud, trying to remember every word of her text to Liam. Had she written *Don't feel bad about what happened last night?* or *Don't feel bad about what almost happened last night*? And would that slight difference even make a difference? No amount of comfort food would mitigate this debacle. And aside from what her words would do to Liam's party and his life, she had also admitted her true feelings for Zach. She was seriously considering escaping out the bathroom window.

The guy seated next to dead Fido's mom stopped petting her sweater and announced, "I'm game. Truth." He waded through the pile and picked out his phone.

"OK, read your last text out loud," Morgan demanded. She seemed really turned on by the power of it all. Even amid the insanity of her own situation, Esme found it unnerving.

Contestant number one read a benign text from his mother.

"'Come for dinner Sunday, and bring that shirt you were wearing last time, it had a stain,'" which yielded a bit of ribbing that he took like a champ.

Morgan chose the next victim, who held his phone in the air and bravely announced dare, prompting Esme to begin praying to every god imaginable that Liam would do the same.

Morgan declared, "Marco, please read the last five searches in your history."

"Oh my God! Truth—please, truth," he begged.

"Nope, no turning back."

Marco pulled up his history, covered his face dramatically, and handed his phone to the woman to his left.

"You do it."

Happy to oblige, the woman stood up and did her best imitation of an abridged David Letterman top ten list:

Number 5: *Adult coloring books.* (Prompting Marco to bury his head.)

Number 4: *Sexy grandmas.* (At which he picked up his head and smirked, his cheeks now the color of tomatoes.)

Number 3: *Is it OK to date your second cousin twice removed?* (Met with a resounding *NO!* and causing a woman at the end of the table, who one could only assume was a relation of Marco's, to bury her own head.)

Number 2: *The lyrics to* The Fresh Prince of Bel-Air. (Which prompted the whole table to break out in song.)

Now, this is a story all about how
My life got flip-turned upside down
And I'd like to take a minute
Just sit right there
I'll tell you how I became the prince of a town called Bel-Air.

Completely, and thankfully for Marco, drowning out number one, which was quite simply: *Porn.*

The next victim looked so torn between choosing truth or dare that her pain distracted Esme from her own. She finally chose dare, and Morgan instructed her to "like" the tenth picture on her ex-boyfriend's Instagram feed. It yielded gasps from those in the know, which made Esme think the breakup must have been a bad one, which led her to wonder if sweet, perfect Morgan was a big phony, which made her feel less awful about the possibility of what may soon unfold but still left her frantically searching for a way to stop it.

That was how many directions her brain was running in.

As the girl pressed Like on a photo of her ex-boyfriend dancing with the girl he dumped her for at Pacha in Ibiza, Esme realized she needed backup, regardless of the incriminating "I'm falling hard for Zach" sentiment her text revealed.

As the main course was served, Greek lamb with yogurt mint sauce and orzo with roasted vegetables, she covered her face with her napkin and whispered in Zach's ear, "I texted something very bad to Liam. We have to stop him from picking truth."

Zach put his napkin to his mouth and whispered back, "How bad?"

"I don't know? How bad is 'don't worry about what happened between us last night'?"

Zach's eyes nearly popped out of his head; Esme eyed the exits.

As the plates were cleared, Morgan started up the game again, announcing, "OK, now, my love, Liam Patrick Beck, are you up to the challenge?"

"Of course I am." Liam stood and retrieved his phone. Zach, grasping at straws, tried to incite a group cheer by shouting, "Dare! Dare! Dare!" with only Esme desperately joining in with the passion of Henry VIII at a beheading. With Liam's natural inclination to think of Zach as his mortal enemy, it had the opposite effect.

He yelled, "Truth!" He held up his cell like King Arthur's sword while Esme again eyed the exits.

Liam dramatically unlocked his phone.

"My last text?" he asked Morgan, who was grinning like the Cheshire Cat. Esme stood, too, with the intention of getting Liam's attention and warning him, but when she opened her mouth, no words came out. At least she was in a better position to run. Zach instinctively stood behind her for support. They both watched as Liam read his text.

His eyes widened, and his bottom lip faintly quivered before he read the words out loud. "'Liam, will you marry me?'"

Esme didn't even realize that she was holding her breath until she released it with an abundance of relief. Liam got himself together, smiled, and joked to the crowd, "Who could this be from?"

He lovingly touched Morgan's face while everyone else but her jumped to their feet.

He got down on one knee and faced his bride-to-be.

"Of course I will marry you, Morgan Miller!" Liam shouted with full exuberance. She dove into his arms, and they kissed.

Zach placed a comforting hand on the small of Esme's back, and it sent an ache right to her heart. An ache for him. Liam caught Esme's eye for a brief second. She smiled sweetly at him before pointedly wrapping her arms behind her and around Zach, clearly indicating that all was right with the world. She wished it were. She had come to New York dreaming of Liam and would leave dreaming of Zach. She felt discouraged and more than a little ridiculous.

The cheering and celebrating that happened from that point on were truly something to behold. Happy tears flowed from both Liam's and Morgan's eyes, along with multiple magnums of champagne. Ina Garten's perfect chocolate cake was wheeled out covered in sparklers and inscribed with the Instagrammable announcement *He said yes!* Esme wondered if there was an alternative version of it out back and what it would say. She imagined there wasn't—imagined that no one had ever said no to Morgan before. As much as Esme wanted a piece of the perfect chocolate cake, she really wanted out of there.

Zach took notice. "French exit?"

"Please!" Esme begged.

They slipped out unnoticed.

A mile or two down the road, Esme began to sulk.

"I'm sorry—that must have been awful for you."

"Yes. The one chance in life I had to taste Ina Garten's perfect chocolate cake blown by my old boyfriend being proposed to!"

Zach laughed.

"What's so perfect about it?" he asked while placing a consoling hand on her knee. His tender touch filled her with a yearning for more than chocolate. She fought through it.

"She adds a cup of hot coffee into the mix, that and the good vanilla."

"Oh—the good vanilla," he laughed. He pulled over in front of the local ice cream parlor to fetch her a soft-serve cone as a consolation prize for both missing the perfect cake and attending the imperfect engagement. They sat in the front seat, eating in silence.

It had been a very strange twenty-four hours, Esme thought when they eventually turned back up Tide Turns Road.

"Wasn't that sign facing the other way when we left?" Zach joked.

Esme appreciated the humor, but it was obviously true—the tide had most definitely turned.

THIRTY-FOUR

Just Berry Naughty Polished Toes

The awkwardness of going to sleep in the house the night that Liam and Morgan got engaged was too much for Esme to bear, so she convinced Zach to take a walk on the beach. She kicked off her shoes while he grabbed a colorful Pendleton striped blanket that reminded her of a coat she had as a child and made her question what he had in mind.

"Grab two," she said.

The thought of snuggling with him under a blanket and making it out of the Hamptons without living up to her Berry Naughty polished toes seemed unlikely in the one-blanket scenario.

"You still OK?" he asked. "I didn't see that coming!"

"Me neither."

"Why would Morgan do that? Invite Liam's old girlfriend to her popping-the-question soirée?" Zach asked.

She also questioned why Morgan was so keen on inviting her. She wondered if Liam had any friends of his own at this point whose last names weren't Miller. The funny thing was, she didn't really care. She knew she'd rather be eating ice cream with Zach in the front seat of his aunt's car than be entrenched in the world of perfect chocolate cake.

The tides had most definitely turned.

"I agree. It's kind of bizarre," she said, dismissing her thoughts on the subject. She was tired of thinking about Liam and Morgan and thought she may never, or at least hardly ever, again.

It was a cold night, so they didn't walk very far. The moon was full, and its reflection on the still ocean was mesmerizing.

"If we stood on our heads, it would be hard to know which way was up," Zach commented.

Esme had no idea which way was up while standing perfectly straight. The month was over. She was headed home the next day and possibly felt more confused about her future than she had when she arrived.

They sat down in the sand, each cuddled in their own blanket, taking it all in. Esme wondered what Zach was thinking about. She assumed it was Amara and thought of asking him but chickened out.

Instead, he did the honors. "Whatcha thinking about?"

"Nothing," she fibbed. "You?"

"Nothing."

They both knew it was BS.

"My butt is cold."

"Mine, too."

"Should we go back?"

"No way. I can't face them tonight. I'm sorry. We can't go back till we're sure they're asleep."

"OK. Stand up, then," Zach ordered before spreading out his blanket on the ground. They both sat down on it and wrapped the other blanket around them. At first Esme just concentrated on the warmth that the sandwiched blankets provided, but she was still cold, and a shiver ran up her spine. Zach felt it and slid his arms up and down her back until she melted into him. The warmth of his breath on her neck made her yearn for his lips to be on hers. His breathing got heavier, as did her desire, like a chain reaction that would never be satisfied. She couldn't remember longing for anyone to hold her as she did for Zach at that moment. She noticed that it was so much harder to control herself than it had been the night before with Liam. Now it felt impossible. And it wasn't just a longing for his touch. It felt more like a longing for him to never let go. At first it was so intense she could think of nothing else, but then she did, and her thoughts doused her desire.

How did I go from the arms of one unavailable man into the arms of another?

He wrapped his unavailable arms around her, squeezing her tightly in his embrace before sliding them down her torso, grazing the sides of her breasts and silencing her objections. She couldn't take it any longer. She flipped over and lay prone on top of him. Their hands ran over each other's bodies under the false pretense of keeping each other warm. She would not be the one to kiss him first. Not again.

She was suddenly completely aware of her entire body. Each touch left her wanting more. She wanted so badly to lose all control, just for this one night. She could tell he felt the same. His breathing grew even heavier, and his strong body pressed against hers ushered in waves of both warmth and hunger. She felt dizzy with desire, but her mind took over again, pushing her thoughts ahead—ahead to the morning, to the long drive back to the city, where she was sure he would be filled with guilt and remorse if this were to go any further. His words from the previous night ran through her head—

not the angry ones, the ones referring to fixing things with Amara. He had seemed so sure of himself, so sure of them. She got control of her mind and her body, rolled off him, and tucked her head into the crook of his arm. She couldn't face him or the loneliness that the light of day would inevitably bring.

"Zach. We have to stop. I can't be the one who comes between you and Amara. You'll resent me for it."

"I would never resent you." He shuddered, and not from the cold.

"You say that now, but you will."

She could tell that he knew she was right.

He took a few breaths in and out and in and out before looking up at the house. The lights were now off.

"It looks like they're home and asleep. Should we go back?"

"Yes, and let's leave first thing in the morning."

Back at the house, they left the shades open and awoke with the sunrise.

"Is this an early enough start?" Zach teased.

It was.

Esme left a note of thanks and congratulations for Liam and Morgan. It may have seemed rude to slip out after the hospitality they were shown, but she knew that Liam would probably prefer it. At best, it was a strange situation.

They escaped unnoticed, except, of course, by the delightful house couple, who appeared out of nowhere and handed them two take-out cups of Somalian coffee and hand-rolled apple cider doughnuts for the ride.

"I'm beginning to think they're androids," Esme joked.

"Honestly, if you removed those two from the equation, you may have won."

She laughed. "I did win. I'll never have to wonder about the one that got away again," she said.

Not that one, at least.

Esme tried to stay awake on the ride home, but even with the delightful coffee, she was out by the time they reached the highway.

Zach ruffled her hair a couple of hours later as they approached the Williamsburg Bridge.

"Hey, sleepyhead. Want to reach out to Catherine and tell her you're almost there?"

As she opened her heavy eyes, she drank in the sight of the city and the way it appeared out of nowhere, as majestically as Oz had for Dorothy. Though she had lived there for only a month, she felt as if she were heading home. There was truly no place like it.

"I'm so sorry," she said. "I slept the whole way."

"It's fine. You have a long haul ahead of you."

She did. She couldn't believe that she was heading back to Honeoye Falls. It felt like both an eternity and just one minute since she had left. She was happy about one thing: she had closure with Liam. She hoped that closure would open her up to new things and not a repeat of those same mistakes. Now she worried she would spend the next seventy years thinking of Zach. Giving up her story with Liam was hard enough, and she was now quite aware that chasing the unavailable didn't suit her. She vowed, right then and there, not to put herself in that position again.

When they got to 250 Mercer, Esme's throat constricted and her eyes became damp. She suddenly wished she had gone straight to the bus stop. It would have been easier to say goodbye there, though there was always the remote possibility that the bus stop version would catapult them into rom-com territory. She pictured the bus driver honking that it was time to go, Esme stepping aboard reluctantly, Zach running alongside the moving bus as it left the terminal, Esme staring straight on, not seeing his romantic gesture and proving once again that her life would never provide a Hallmark movie ending.

Once she left the city, she knew she could cage up all her feelings for him under lock and key and enter her favorite state—denial—but now that she was faced with saying goodbye in the middle of Mercer Street, she was worried her tears would flow. She wished she had woken from her nap earlier, giving her time to rehearse her farewell. She took a deep breath and got ready to tell him how much he meant to her, how much August had meant to her. All that came out was "Thank you, Zach, for everything. This month wouldn't have been the same without you."

"Don't sound so sad. This isn't goodbye. We can still keep in touch—still be friends."

She decided to be honest. "I don't know about that. Friends usually have an easier time keeping their hands off each other."

He forced a laugh but didn't deny it.

They both got out of the car and met behind it. No sooner did Zach pop the trunk than Miguel the doorman came out to help her. She was happy to see him. It cut the intensity a bit.

"Welcome back, Miss Nash."

"Thanks, Miguel. I got it, it's just a duffel."

He took it anyway.

Zach and Esme stood about a foot apart and took one last good look at each other.

She felt her bottom lip start to quiver, bit it, and managed, "I'll miss you."

He answered her in a quiet tone, as if he wasn't capable of drawing a full breath. "I'll miss you, too, very much."

Neither made a move to leave until Zach looked down bashfully at his feet. "I hope you find your happiness, Esme Nash."

"I hope you keep yours, Zach Bennet," she replied.

They gave each other a long, sweet hug, and it was obvious neither of them wanted to break away. She purposefully breathed in his scent, trying to put it to memory before the lemon potpourri that pervaded the lobby overwhelmed it and wiped it from her senses. She could feel his heart racing in his chest. It was time to let go.

They stared at each other for what seemed like forever before Esme managed a final and casual "So long for now."

Zach's voice cracked as he responded in kind. "So long for now."

Esme turned and walked into the building. Neither of them saw the other cry.

THIRTY-FIVE

The Stuart Weitzman
Over-the-Knee Tieland Boots

Esme exited the elevator to find Catherine and Elvis waiting to greet her in the hallway like old friends. Catherine looked happier than she had in the pictures in her apartment, her dark black hair pulled back in a neat pony and her blue eyes clear and twinkling at the first sighting of her new friend. She skipped over the formalities of meeting face-to-face and gave Esme a great big hug, which Esme received happily. She really needed it.

Inside, they sat down for brunch—a delicious spread from none other than Katz's. The sight of true New York bagels, baked salmon, and whitefish salad reminded Esme how much she would miss Sy and nearly made her cry again. When she saw the flowers, a beautiful bouquet of gerbera daisies obviously sent by Kurt Vaughn, there was no stopping the tears.

"What's wrong?"

"I'm just overwhelmed. I'm going to miss everyone and everything." She took a bite of her bagel. "Not least of all, this whitefish salad," she said, crying through her full mouth.

Catherine put her hand on her new friend's shoulder.

"You can always come back and visit. And who knows, I may be doing some traveling and need a dog sitter again soon."

Esme smiled at her proposal, but all the unanchored feelings she'd had before arriving in New York came flooding back. She felt lost again. She reached into her purse and covertly pulled out the compass. She placed it in her lap, and it brought her a little peace until she realized that it seemed crazy and worried she was losing her mind.

She hadn't been as covert as she thought, because Catherine came right out and asked her, "What's that in your lap?"

Esme was mortified but showed it to her. "It's a compass that Sy Katz carried around in his pocket for over seventy years until he found what he was looking for."

"Seventy years. I hope it doesn't take *you* that long!"

"Me, too. But I'm afraid I have to figure out who I am first. I'm feeling lost."

"Take it from me, Esme. Find yourself, and everything else will fall into place."

She knew Catherine was right. And after her reaction to learning the details of Jackson Pollock's accident, she knew where she needed to start.

"Can I ask you a question? How did you know you were an alcoholic?"

"Why, do you think you're an alcoholic?"

"No, but I think that my father was."

"I bet Al-Anon could help—it's a group for adults who grew up with an alcoholic."

"Maybe. I don't know if I'll relate to all of that 'God grant me the power' stuff that they preach."

"It's not about believing in God, per se, it's more about a higher power, *your* higher power."

"Well, I haven't believed in much of anything for the past seven years."

"Says the girl holding a compass in her lap hoping it brings her to the right place."

Esme laughed at herself and ceremoniously held up the compass, squeezing it in her fist. "Maybe it will!"

"Maybe it already has. Maybe it's not a coincidence that you came to dog-sit for a woman in rehab for alcohol with a size-seven shoe fetish—maybe it's a God wink."

"I don't think God has been winking at me much lately, but I promise to look into Al-Anon straightaway."

Esme felt better having a plan but apparently still looked upset, because Catherine stood up abruptly and ran to the Temple of Sole. She came out with a huge Stuart Weitzman shoebox. Esme's face lit up.

"What's in that box?"

"A gift."

Esme took the box and shook it, giggling. She opened it up slowly to reveal the iconic over-the-knee boot that was every fashion girl's definition of chic, warm, and endlessly wearable. They were perfect.

"These are for me?"

"They are!"

"But I couldn't, these cost a fortune!"

"That never stopped you before!"

Esme laughed. "Why are you doing this? You've been so generous already."

"Well, I had sex last night for the first time in about ten years, and I think it was due to your meddling, so I wanted to do something nice for you."

"Oh. My. God! You slept with Kurt Vaughn?"

"Maybe."

"I knew it!"

Catherine was smiling like the cat who ate the canary while Esme was busy trying on the boots.

"You think they're too much for the Greyhound home?"

"They may be."

Esme looked at her watch. Her bus was leaving in an hour.

"Talking about home, it's time."

It was time to say goodbye to Catherine and to Elvis, Elvis being the toughest. She pulled Catherine's other shoes out of her bag and thanked her again, while gently finagling the prized boots in their place.

Then she sat Elvis down and told him the deal.

"I'm going home now, Elvis, OK, boy? I'm probably going to stay in Rochester, maybe get a dog and a job—they have art galleries there, too, you know. But I may come back and work here and eat fancy fried chicken and buy my own fancy shoes. If I do, I promise I'll visit you in the park once in a while."

Esme could swear he raised his ears when she said the last part. If he did, it was probably in reference to the park, but she took it as a compliment.

"One day at a time, Esme, one day at a time," Catherine pronounced as Esme hugged her goodbye.

She knew it was an AA saying—who didn't?—but it brought to mind the time she read a card from her father to her mother, attached to a dozen roses. Underneath the printed *Happy Anniversary* message, he wrote *One day at a time*. Esme remembered her twelve-year-old self smiling, interpreting it as some kind of sweet sentiment celebrating their daily love. Now it suggested a long charade.

If stepping onto the Greyhound bus in her old sneakers wasn't enough of a slap back into reality, Esme's first phone call upon leaving New York City certainly did the trick. No sooner did the wheels roll out of the Holland Tunnel than her cell rang. She answered the call with the 505 Rochester area code with resignation.

"Please hold for Ron Fishman," the voice on the other end instructed her. Ron Fishman was her father's lawyer.

The party is most definitely over, Esme thought, remembering his instructions at the funeral, something about paperwork. She had figured it could all wait, but now she was feeling a wave of panic come over her about what she may have been ignoring. His tone confirmed her fears.

"Esme Nash. I've been waiting for you to return the documents I sent you, but I've lost patience."

"I'm so sorry. I'm heading home today. I was out of town."

"For a month?"

"Yes, I'm sorry. I'm staying put until I take care of everything now, though, I promise," she assured him.

"OK. Most important is for you to get a copy of your father's death certificate from the hospital and fill out the life insurance claim form I sent you—you will need it to pay off the mortgage and taxes on the house. Unless you want to sell it."

She thought of the Realtor who suggested selling after her dad's funeral, and answered similarly.

"I don't want to sell my parents' house."

But this time it didn't ring quite true.

The woman in front of her stood up and shushed her as he responded, "Good, then you will own it free and clear. I know your parents wanted that for you."

She hung up, spending the rest of the ride thinking and re-thinking about her future. She knew her life was her own now, but could she give up her childhood home? The willow tree in the back-yard, her bedroom with her canopy bed, even the smell of the place. It was all she had tying her to the past and to her parents. Yet she was filling with dread as each mile brought her closer to it.

There were so many times over the years of caring for her dad that she'd wished she had a sibling to help with the burden of it all, but now she wished she had one for other reasons. If she did, then she might have felt anchored by more than a house—being with her sibling would be the equivalent of being home. She opened up the notes on her phone and started a new to-do list.

1. Fill out paperwork.
2. Get copy of death certificate.
3. Look into Al-Anon.

She paused and realized she could cross that one off right there and then.

She googled Al-Anon in the greater Rochester area and clicked on *Welcome, if you are new to Al-Anon*. It directed her to a quiz titled, "Has Your Life Been Affected by Someone Else's Drinking?"

She didn't want to take the quiz, didn't want to be in this club; she wanted to be in the carefree twentysomething club.

Haven't I sacrificed enough?

She rubbed her thumb back and forth over the compass in her pocket for comfort, somewhat like a rosary, before clicking on the prompt.

From the first question, *Do you constantly seek approval and affirmation?* to the last, *Do you think parental drinking may have affected you?*, she scored a sixteen out of twenty. For once in her life, this was not a test she wanted to ace.

She vowed that she would no longer isolate herself from other people (number 11 on the quiz) and copied down the times and dates of the next few meetings at her local United Methodist church. It was time she faced the truth. She had put it off for long enough.

THIRTY-SIX

The 'Stocks with Socks

Esme was surprised by the lack of mail stuffed into her mailbox until she got to the slip of paper that instructed her that it was being held at the Honeoye Falls post office. She would go down there in the morning, there and the hospital. It had already felt like the longest day in history, and she was rightfully exhausted. And as much as she had loved Catherine's marshmallow bed, there was nothing like being back in her own.

She woke up the next day charged to get down to business. She unpacked her new Stuart Weitzman boots and her old Louboutin Pigalles and placed them in a prominent spot in her closet. They were there to be worn, and she vowed to go places worthy of wearing them. For now she would put her shoe obsession aside and figure out which direction her feet should go in. She threw on her mom's old size 8 Birkenstocks over her fuzzy socks, caring more about fit than style, and left feeling comforted that she was literally walking in her mother's shoes.

Her first stop, the medical records office at Rochester General, filled her with a sense of doom until she realized there was no one left in her life to lose, which instead filled her with dread.

She contemplated which felt worse as she walked up to the counter and quickly proceeded to forget what she was there to ask for.

"Um, my dad's lawyer sent me to pick up records."

"Medical records?" the woman asked while pulling out the necessary forms and placing them on the counter in front of Esme. Esme scrolled through her phone to find the note.

"Actually, I need a record of death for my father, Henry Matthew Nash."

"That's a different form," the woman barked.

This was one of those occasions when Esme wouldn't have minded a little sympathy. She glanced at the medical records form in front of her. The bolded words in the sentence *This authorization may include disclosure of information relating to* **alcohol** *and* **drug** *abuse* jumped off the page like a neon sign.

"I'll take both forms, please."

She filled out the paperwork, and the woman promised that she would email her the information shortly.

Afterward, Esme stopped at the village post office for the mail and headed to the local Wegmans to pick up some groceries. It actually felt good to be home. She chatted with the butcher and took her usual pleasure in the small crumbs he would offer regarding her mom. One couldn't imagine how much conversations that included "your mother preferred angus to prime" meant to her. As the years passed, these types of interactions, with someone who remembered her mom, were becoming rare. They were just the kind of thing that made her never want to leave the area.

It was bizarre to be shopping there for one person after running a household for years that required catering to multiple dietary needs and restrictions. She wouldn't miss buying Ensure but had been yearning for a plate of Selena's Creole jambalaya. She made a mental note to call her and invite herself over for dinner. After all that time together, Selena had never taught her how to make any of her signature New Orleans dishes.

Once at home, she poured herself another cup of coffee and emptied the large bag of mail onto the kitchen counter to sort through. She found the envelope from the lawyer amid a plethora of condolence notes and junk mail. Well, now it was junk; much of it was specific to caregivers or sufferers of spinal cord injuries. She wondered if she would be inundated with medical supply catalogs and whatnot for the rest of her life. If she did choose to move from this house, she would consider not leaving a forwarding address.

She opened the lawyer's letter with the documents inside and slid her arm across the table, pushing everything else out of the way. She completed the forms to attach to the death certificate and sorted through some of the mail. It was a lot to do in one sitting.

She took a break for lunch—a plate of Wushi, as the locals named the supermarket sushi from Wegmans. She worried she'd been too spoiled in the city to ever enjoy Wushi again, but she was happily wrong. It gave her hope that there was indeed a life for her outside of New York City.

She checked her emails and was surprised to have already received one from Rochester General Medical Records Department.

She downloaded the attachment and saved it on her laptop in a new folder: *Dad's Medical Records*. She would look at it later.

Later ended up being all of two minutes.

The medical records of Henry Matthew Nash for treatment at Rochester General were hundreds of pages long and only began on the day of the accident. That was the day Esme was interested in.

Everything else she had witnessed firsthand and, quite frankly, was hoping to forget.

She found the original lab reports. She knew just what she was looking for, as she had already researched the legal limit for drinking and driving—a BAC (blood alcohol content) of .08 is illegal, while a rate of .05 could still render someone intoxicated. She knew that her father's tolerance for alcohol was off the charts. She'd actually heard him brag about it on more than one occasion. It would take more than that to render him intoxicated. She held on to that thought, however warped it may have been.

She thought of the words his doctor had often repeated.

There is no medical reason why your father doesn't speak.

Esme had looked into it further over the years and was aware of all the possible reasons for his silence. They included shock, conscious or subconscious denial, or just a silent right to take the Fifth. It had entered her mind on more than one occasion that for her father speaking may mean confessing. She was sure those same thoughts had entered his doctors' minds, too, but like Esme, none of them spoke those thoughts out loud. At least not to her.

Before reading the toxicology report, she could still hold on to the possibility that her dad was in shock, that he hadn't been drunk that night, that he had really swerved to miss a deer. Esme had once read that Rochester had the highest deer/vehicle collision rate in the state.

She thought of the scenario that she had clung to over the years of caring for her father, picturing her mom and dad sitting together in the front seat of the car, high on nothing else but the excitement of her upcoming graduation. She'd hoped that at the time of the collision they were listening to E Street Radio, as they usually did, singing the words to "Jungleland" or "Thunder Road," when a deer ran out in front of them, decimating all three of their lives. Maybe

she shouldn't read the report—just close the computer and go back
to the mail.

Be brave, Esme.

She ran her finger down the line of results, unsure if the doctor
had even ordered the test at the time. She could swear she remembered the nurse informing the officers that he hadn't. But then there
it was, *BAC*. She took a deep breath, praying it would be .08 or
below. Even at that rate she could convince herself that he wasn't
truly impaired. She found the column and slid her finger from left
to right. BAC—.21.

His blood alcohol level was nearly three times the legal limit.

She ran to the bathroom and threw up her Wushi.

THIRTY-SEVEN

The Brand-New Black Converse Chuck Taylors

EIGHT MONTHS LATER

Esme Nash sat in the front row of her usual Al-Anon meeting at the United Methodist Church of Honeoye Falls, admonishing herself for not wearing socks with her brand-new Converse Chuck Taylors. She already felt a blister coming on. She pushed down the backs of the shoes with her index finger and crushed them under her heels before standing to give her farewell testimony. In typical Al-Anon fashion, she was given three minutes to speak. She slowly inhaled the musty scent of the church basement before beginning. The smell had bothered her when she first started attending meetings there, eight months earlier, but now it brought her comfort. She wondered if the meeting space at the Church of the Heavenly Rest on New York's Upper East Side would smell similarly. She hoped so.

Esme was infinitely more comfortable speaking her truth at these meetings after months of doing so than she had been at the beginning. She had grown very fond of the group that she had settled into and was feeling a bit melancholy about leaving them. She hoped her new group would eventually feel the same.

"Hello, I'm Esme, and I'm the daughter of an alcoholic," she announced.

The routine "Hello, Esme" came roaring back from many familiar faces and a few she had never seen before.

"For those of you who don't know my story, nearly eight years ago, my father killed my mother in a drunk-driving accident. At the time, I didn't fully know that he was an alcoholic. He was left a quadriplegic, and I gave up my life to care for him until his death last summer. It was only then that I allowed myself to address what had happened and the effect that his alcoholism has had on me.

"When I first came to Al-Anon, I was instantly dumbfounded: *How did the words coming out of a stranger's mouth ring completely true for me?* But it turns out that I am the textbook daughter of an alcoholic. A perfectionist and a people-pleaser, I spent my life checking off boxes. *I will be happy when I get to college. I will be happy when I have the perfect boyfriend. I will be happy when I get my dream job.* But I never really was.

"When my parents' accident pushed all those boxes aside, giving up my story was very hard for me. After my father's death last summer, I tried to pick up those same boxes and start over. It was only through new friendships, great introspection, and Al-Anon that I discovered the courage, faith, belief, and hope that I needed to move forward on my own path in an unpredictable world.

"I am the first person on my list of amends. I am proud to say that I sold my parents' house and tomorrow I am moving to Manhattan, the city that I have always dreamed of living in. I got a great new job that I'm confident will fulfill me. And I adopted a dog. Less people-pleasing and more me-pleasing.

"I have finally accepted the fact that I can only see in a straight line, I cannot see around the corner. And that's OK. I've learned to stop my mind from running to the possible wreckage of the future. I know it doesn't serve me, and I know that what's next for me is just as likely to be positive as negative. I no longer worry about when the other shoe will drop!

"Thank you to everyone who has been with me on this journey. This group has been wonderful to me. I promise to come back and visit the next time I'm in town."

Esme stayed a few minutes after the meeting for doughnuts, coffee, and hugs goodbye before heading home for her very last night in her childhood home.

Selena brought over dinner, and they sat on the dining room floor sopping up chicken gumbo with crusty pieces of French bread while laughing over the ridiculousness of Morgan and Liam's wedding gift registry. Esme had first looked it up with the intention of sending them a little something, but as the enormity of their registry registered, she realized there were no little somethings to be had. Now that she was moving to Manhattan, she was thankful she hadn't sent a gift. According to their *New York Times* engagement announcement, it was going to be a spring wedding, and no doubt sending a gift would have led to an invitation. Attending the engagement was more than enough. She returned to the registry every once in a while to bask in its absurdity.

Selena laughed as she weighed the extravagance of the four-thousand-dollar signed David Bowie coffee table book versus the similarly priced James Bond 007 pinball machine versus the iconic five-thousand-dollar Eames lounge chair and ottoman. Esme didn't admit that she had always dreamed of owning an Eames recliner; to her it was the chair equivalent of a pair of Louboutins. She did admit that even when working so hard on herself and training a new puppy and dealing with sorting three lifetimes of belongings, she thought about Zach an awful lot. He had been the first person she had wanted to call when she read her dad's toxicology report and when she had gotten her new job. Both the bad and the good. She tried not to obsess over him, but on more than one occasion she fell asleep dreaming she was back in his arms again.

Selena had good advice on the subject: "Now you know who to look for."

And she agreed. When the dust settled she would find a guy as kind, as compassionate, and as fun as Zach to build a life with. A guy who looked at her the way that he had. She didn't want to be alone, she knew that, but she also knew: *One day at a time.*

Her car was already loaded up for the morning drive with everything she needed for the furnished walk-up apartment waiting for her on the Upper East Side of Manhattan. Aside from her clothes, her shoes, her cherished old poster of Gustav Klimt's *The Kiss*, and a shoebox filled with keepsakes and photos, most everything else worth saving went into storage.

Cleaning out her parents' house had been quite a long, drawn-out task, especially when Esme was feeling sentimental and going through every single thing at a glacial pace. She reread every card from her mom and put them in order from the earliest to the last before tying them up in a ribbon, just as her mother had done at her sweet sixteen. She searched through the pockets of her mom's entire wardrobe before finally giving the bulk of her clothes to Goodwill.

It was then, in the back pocket of a pair of powder-blue Levi's, that Esme found the most telling item of all. A card for a divorce lawyer. Her mother was leaving her father after all, or at least considering it. She remembered something that her mom had written in her graduation card that had left her perplexed. Among the love and the praise, she had written, *Lots of changes coming, for both of us!*

The line, which had always felt like some kind of weird premonition, now took on a totally different meaning. The knowledge that her mother was in the process of taking control of her life inspired Esme more than it saddened her. She felt proud of her.

It was hard saying goodbye to Selena, but she promised to come visit Esme soon enough. Esme fell asleep in about ten seconds that night. Luckily, exhaustion overrode the excitement she felt about finally moving to Manhattan.

THIRTY-EIGHT

The Vintage Nineties Quilted Black Chanel Booties

Esme had laid out her moving-to-NYC outfit the night before while packing up the last of her things. It included a going-away present from Selena. A pair of classic Chanel booties that she had found at a vintage shop on her last trip home to New Orleans.

They were perfect in every way.

She did a final walk-through of the whole house from upstairs to down, each step filled with memories of her parents and her childhood. She stood at the bottom of the stairs and took them two at a time in the mad-rush way of her younger days. As she did, she heard her father yelling his most benign joke—"Anthony, dinner!"—and smiled, thankful that eight months of Al-Anon allowed her to again entertain a pleasant memory of him. On the way back down, she heard her mom calling, "The school bus is here!" and pictured her handing over her brown-bagged lunch with her signature red heart doodled on it, before gathering Esme's face in her hands for a quick smooch goodbye.

She stopped and ran her hand over her mother's prized wallpaper, wondering if the new owners would tear it down. She would never know unless she became one of those people who stopped by with her family years later, the way people do, asking, "I grew up here, would it be OK if I showed my kids around?"

Yes, Esme's dreams now included the possibility of a family and an ordinary long-lived and long-loved life. Not big in Liam's sense of the word—but colossal in hers.

"*Goodbye, Mama,*" she said out loud before yelling up the stairs, "Come on, Clooney, it's time!"

She was glad she was not going it alone. It would surely be easier to fall asleep on her first night in a new place with him lying beside her—even though everyone had warned her that letting a new puppy sleep in her bed was an awful idea.

Her forty-five-pound border doodle, George Clooney, came barreling down the stairs, forcing her mood to lighten on the spot, as he had nearly every day since she'd rescued him.

"Let's go, buddy," she said while clipping on his leash. "We're going home."

And so it was that Esme Nash and George Clooney arrived in New York City on a beautiful spring day with great hope and the keys to her new apartment, a second-floor walk-up on Madison Avenue and Seventy-Seventh Street. She chose it for the brick wall, the fireplace, and the sensational view. The uptown Christian Louboutin boutique sat just across the street.

When she told Catherine the location on one of their weekly calls, a tradition they had happily kept up, Catherine had described it as another God wink. This time, Esme believed she might be right. Catherine was disappointed that Clooney and Elvis wouldn't see each other on the daily, but Esme was happy to be living on the Upper East Side, for now. The staid neighborhood felt predictable in a way that the Village had not—in a way that she hoped her life would be.

The apartment was smaller than it had looked in the pictures, but even more charming. Esme oohed and aahed over the brick wall and wood-burning fireplace before the super took her down a notch with "That hasn't worked in fifty years."

"I'll fill it with candles!" she said, happy for both the curmudgeonly but helpful super and the (nonworking) fireplace.

She had arranged to meet a woman on Craigslist to whom she had sold her car downstairs at six. She had miraculously found a parking spot right in front of the apartment, which was her only regret in giving up the trusty Subaru that had brought her back to the city. Like a true New Yorker, she hated to give up a good spot. But true New Yorkers usually took the subway, and her new job was within walking distance and, more important, lunch break dog-walking distance from her new pad.

The car transaction was seamless, and she climbed back up the stairs an hour later armed with a selection of take-out menus from her charming new neighborhood. She may have been nearly eight years off schedule, but she was happy with where she had landed.

The next morning, she and Clooney ran the outer loop of Central Park with ease. The park was alive with the first signs of spring: crocuses and daffodils rearing their heads and private school kids in gym uniforms kicking up the dusty trail. Even the dogs seemed to have a little extra spring in their step.

Esme had been clocking at least fifteen miles a week as of late, and she was feeling good both mentally and physically. As per usual, she used the time to assess her life. For the first time in a very long while, she genuinely felt happy. It had been a long road to get there, and she knew she wasn't fully there yet, but she also knew she was well on her way.

That afternoon Esme headed to the Hebrew Home at Riverdale to visit Sy and Lena. She squeezed the compass in her hands on the subway uptown and let her mind drift to the excitement of beginning her new job as a docent at the Neue Galerie.

The Neue Galerie was not a gallery in the American sense of the word; it was a small museum set in an elegant Fifth Avenue mansion with an incomparable collection of twentieth-century German and Austrian art. Her old dream job, at the Hudson Payne Gallery, had been hers if she wanted it by the end of October. When Vivian Rococo called and told her so, Esme immediately filled with dread and asked if she could have some time to think it over. She did and called her back the very next day, declining the offer. Ms. Rococo was clearly taken aback and asked why Esme wasn't taking the job that she had seemed to have wanted so badly.

"I'm not sure how to explain it," Esme had answered. "I think I've figured out that I'd prefer laughing on a bus to crying in a limo."

Vivian Rococo burst out laughing at the John Giorno reference, surprising them both, and wished Esme luck.

Esme was unsure of what she wanted to do until about a week later, when she came across a small article in the *Art Newspaper* that took her by surprise.

There is a lot of buzz coming from Vienna regarding the possibility of Gustav Klimt's The Kiss *traveling to America early next year. The Neue Galerie in New York is hoping to charm and captivate the nation with the celebrated Austrian painting in the way the* Mona Lisa *did when Jackie Kennedy convinced the French government to let her borrow the 450-year-old da Vinci painting in 1963. While*

*Klimt's 1907 work is not as old, and many may argue not as famous,
there is no denying the draw of the gold-leafed masterpiece.*

*Another famous Klimt painting, The Portrait of Adele Bloch-
Bauer I, currently hangs in the Neue Galerie. The painting of the
Woman in Gold, as she has been renamed, was famously returned to
its rightful owner long after it was stolen by the Nazis in 1938.
Philanthropist and collector Ronald Lauder purchased it in 2006 for
$135 million, the highest price for a work of art at the time. While
the Belvedere Museum, where The Kiss permanently hangs, refused
to comment, the art world remains hopeful that the loving couple
depicted in the painting will be vacationing abroad sometime soon.*

Esme nearly jumped out of her skin. For her, *The Kiss* was like
an old friend. Aside from the aforementioned poster, which had
adorned her wall since college, she'd spent hours admiring it at the
Belvedere in Vienna. It was the first place she had taken her mom
when she had come to visit during her study abroad program, and
she distinctly remembered the wondrous look on her mother's face
when first viewing the masterpiece in person. It was one of Esme's
most cherished memories. And now the job and her direction felt
mom approved. She was sure that seeing this article was another
God wink, or more so, God hitting her over the head.

She applied for a three-month volunteer docent position, hoping
that she would blow them away and be hired full-time. With the
sale of her parents' house and the life insurance money she'd collected, she would be in a good position financially to do things for
herself, for now at least. She could even go back to school to get an
MFA if she wanted to. It finally felt as though everything was falling into place.

She rubbed her hand on Sy's compass again. She had come so
far since he had given it to her.

When the conductor announced "Next stop, Palisades Avenue," Esme put the compass away and stood by the exit. She was so excited to see Sy and Lena, evident in her quick pace upon exiting the train. When she eyed Sy waiting outside the Hebrew Home for her, she nearly ran to him in anticipation of his warm hug. They headed upstairs to the apartment that Sy now shared with his wife, Lena. They had waited all of two weeks after meeting again to marry in a small family ceremony right on the Hudson. They sent Esme a beautiful photo with the words *All thanks to you* on the back. She had already placed it on the nonworking fireplace mantel in her new place.

Esme filled Sy and Lena in on all the changes in her life, and she could see how proud Sy was of her and her new job.

"I'm kvelling!" he exclaimed. It was a big deal to Esme. There were not many people left who would take such pride in her accomplishments.

"Many of that Klimt fellow's portraits were of fancy Jewish ladies, you know?" he added.

"I do," she teased, "and I'm not at all surprised that you do, too." He smirked in return.

She was curious about Lena's side of the Sy and Lena saga but was unsure whether to bring it up. When Sy left to walk Scout, she couldn't help herself.

"Would you like a cup of tea?" Lena asked, setting the perfect stage for the deep conversation Esme was hoping for.

"That would be lovely, thank you."

They sat down, and Lena pulled out one of those blue tins of butter cookies with the paper cups inside. It made Esme think of her own grandmother. She dipped a pretzel-shaped one in her tea; it tasted like a soggy memory.

"Can I ask you something, Lena?"

"You can ask me anything you want," Lena responded.

"Did you miss Sy over the years?"

"And how!" she beamed.

Esme was taken aback by her answer. Lena obviously noticed.

"Don't misunderstand, I had a good life and a happy marriage. But when Sy put his hand on my shoulder on the bench that day, the years fell away in an instant."

Lena choked on her words a bit before adding, "I was finally home."

Esme blinked away tears. She was unsure if they were for Sy and Lena or for herself. There was no denying that she had thought of Zach every day since they had parted ways on Mercer Street. She missed him terribly and had thought of calling him many times but always chickened out.

"Did you ever think about contacting him?" she asked Lena.

"Of course! I even walked by his store a few times, but I never had the courage to go inside. I was a married woman and would never have disrespected my husband like that. But there were two questions that bothered me all my life—did he think of me, and did he hate me?"

"Hate you? Why did you think that?"

"I never should have listened to him when he said to forget about him. I should have realized that he had been through hell and gone to England to find him. But things were different back then. We were better children. We did what our parents wanted, and my parents wanted me to marry a Schusterman."

She noticed Esme's teary eyes and put her hand on hers.

"Don't worry. I didn't even know I was unhappy until you brought Sy to me that day. I had a second chance, and no one was going to take it away from me."

"Who would do that?"

"You try telling your grown children that you're marrying your old boyfriend at my age and after two weeks."

"Two weeks and seventy-something years!"

They were both laughing when Sy walked in with his familiar youthful swagger.

"What are you two yentas laughing about?" He kissed Esme on the top of her head. "This one's a big yenta, did I tell you that, Lena?"

Esme teased. "I guess you have no interest in finding out what happened with Catherine and Kurt, then?" she asked knowingly.

He quickly sat down next to her. "What happened with Catherine and Kurt?"

Esme laughed some more. "They're basically living together. He sent her those flowers I suggested and boom—that was it."

"You are quite the little matchmaker, aren't you? First Lena and me, and then them."

"I just pushed along the obvious."

"Yes, you can see what's obvious for others but not for yourself."

"You have a big imagination, Sy." She looked at the clock. "I have to get back to my puppy. I don't like to leave him crated for too long."

"Impressive subject change," Sy teased. Esme appreciated him not going deeper, though she knew it wouldn't be the last of it. He wasn't one to keep his opinions to himself.

"Open up your hand," she said, just as he had said to her months before.

He did, and she placed the compass in his palm.

"Thank you, but I don't need it anymore. Maybe give it to someone who does."

"I'm sorry it didn't work."

"It did work!" she insisted. "I'm happy. I found myself."

"That's wonderful, Esme," Lena declared.

Sy wasn't as enthusiastic.

"I'm happy to hear that you figured out *what* makes you happy, but now you should also figure out *who* makes you happy. You think I told you my whole story because *I* was lonely? I told it because I don't want *you* to be."

Esme just nodded, before again thinking the phrase she had heard so often in the past months:

One day at a time.

THIRTY-NINE

The Chloé Scalloped Gold Leather Ballerina Flats

Every day, on the way to work, Esme would traverse a different tree-lined street, taking in its offerings and pinching herself that this was indeed her new life. Everything was a first, from the heavenly coffee served at her new Al-Anon meetings at the Church of the Heavenly Rest to the sweet man on the corner named James, who never failed to say good morning, nothing disappointed.

Within a week of beginning work at the Neue Galerie, Esme felt as though she had been there forever. The walls of the beaux arts mansion and everyone in it were bursting with excitement from the arrival of *The Kiss*. There'd been so much hullabaloo surrounding its New York debut; Esme was immediately caught up in it all. The iconic painting made the cover of the *Times*, the *Daily News*, the *Post*, and the *Wall Street Journal*. *Vogue* reimagined Klimt's golden pair as modern couples visiting different NYC landmarks, banner replicas of *The Kiss* waved from Upper East Side street corners, and

Bloomingdale's, Saks, and Bergdorf Goodman all reported that gold was the new black. It felt like the entire city was awash in gold leaf.

Though she was just a newbie at the Neue, it was immediately obvious that Esme's passion, knowledge, and experience from her time in Vienna were invaluable, making Esme invaluable herself. She had researched and rehearsed every interesting fact about *The Kiss*, Gustav Klimt, and his golden phase, determined to be the best docent the museum had ever seen. Twenty-nine years of perfectionism couldn't disappear overnight, even if she now understood its origins.

Esme found a pair of bright gold Chloé ballerina flats on sale, which made her feel as if she'd stepped right out of a Klimt painting. Aesthetics aside, they were perfect for a job that required her to be on her feet. Even by her last tour of the day, a large and boisterous group, she was feeling good. She had the whole thing down to a science.

She led her group to the second most anticipated work at the Neue—the Woman in Gold—and stopped to explain its infamous Nazi-looted history. She spoke in detail about Klimt's process, explaining how he would apply gold leaf to the surface of a sheet of copper and paint in oil on top of that. The crowd listened but, as usual, seemed anxious to get to the pièce de résistance—*The Kiss*.

The famous square portrait of a man and a woman as they peacefully embrace in a patch of shimmering flowers was given a room all its own. Esme may have done it differently, she thought. She may have united the two works, painted during the artist's glistening golden phase, in one room. Having the authority to make that kind of decision was still, of course, many years away for her. She stepped to the side and watched in delight as the group floated by, one by one, for a much-anticipated look at the painting considered by many to be a love story of two dear friends who secretly became lovers.

She waited before taking questions. She loved this part of the tour and had yet to be stumped.

"Is it true that the picture was once considered pornographic?"

"How does it compare to the *Mona Lisa*?"

"Who were the models for the painting?"

"How much is it insured for?"

And lastly, one she hadn't gotten before—

"Has *The Kiss* inspired any real-life kissing?"

"Great question," Esme responded. "According to the folks at its home, the Belvedere in Vienna, *The Kiss* has been the stage for multiple engagements over the years and inspired many a real-life kiss."

At the back of the huddle, a man shot up his hand.

"Is kissing allowed here at the Neue Galerie?"

"Absolutely. If you have consent to kiss the person next to you, be my guest." Esme laughed at the silly question, but the crowd took it quite seriously.

In a quintessential New York City moment, many in the group took on the challenge.

Esme watched in awe as an elderly couple lovingly embraced, a mother lifted up her toddler overhead and kissed her sweetly on the lips, and two teenagers leaned in for what may have been their first kiss ever. Even the usually stoic security guards eyed each other longingly. It was the kind of spontaneous occasion that made her wish she had someone special to share it with.

Just as Esme had that thought, she noticed the man who had asked the inspiring question weaving his way through the crowd, a Brooklyn Dodgers baseball cap pulled down low, blocking her view of his face. Even with his head bowed, she could feel his gaze, and a fizzing of anticipation began to bubble in her chest as he approached. It suddenly felt like they were the only two people in the room. As he reached her, he took off his hat to reveal the most beautiful sight Esme had ever seen in a museum—Zach Bennet smiling down at her.

Zach's dark eyes were deep with emotion; his simple words, "Hi, Esme," got caught in his throat. He placed his hands on her shoulders and pulled her in for a hug. She soaked in his touch, his scent, the peaceful feeling of his lumbering arms around her—like Lena, she was finally home.

He let go and took a step back. "Would it be OK if I kissed you?"

"I don't know," Esme said hesitantly. "Are you still married?"

"I'm not. I went to see Amara during winter break thinking it would all come back, but it just wasn't the same."

"I'm sorry. How come?"

"We want different things in life, and neither of us was willing to make the sacrifice for the other."

His eyes widened, and he bit his lower lip before admitting, "And also, Sy was right. It's very hard to be married to one woman when you're in love with someone else."

And so it was, at the Neue Galerie, nearly nine months after their first kiss, that Zachary Bennet took Esme Nash in his arms for an encore. She closed her eyes and let the room and the people in it melt away so that all she was aware of was the sensation of his lips on hers. Her heart tightened in her chest, while every inch of her tingled with desire—desire and happiness. They broke for air, and Esme opened her eyes just to make sure it wasn't all a dream. This time she wrapped her arms around his neck and kissed him with a pent-up passion that she knew she had never felt before. Her heart swelled even more. She was indeed finally home.

The group grew quiet, witnessing the intensity of the kiss before breaking out in a cheer for their tour guide and the inquisitive man in the Dodgers hat, the joyous sound overtaking the announcement that bellowed from the speakers: *The museum is now closed.*

Zach and Esme untangled themselves, blushing, laughing, and even bowing as Esme thanked the crowd for coming. They watched in silence as the room emptied. Once they were alone, Esme took a long look at Zach before pulling him lovingly toward her and asking, "How did you know where to find me?"

Zach reached into his pocket, pulled out the compass, and placed it in the palm of her hand. She squeezed it tightly and felt its magic.

"You are my north," he said with such certainty it took her breath away.

Esme looked into Zach's glistening eyes and took his hands in hers, the compass now felt by them both.

"You are my north, my south, my east, and my west," she said, her eyes filling with her own happy tears.

Zach and Esme walked out of the museum, hand in hand, onto the sidewalk of the city that they both now called home. They promised each other that they wouldn't let go—for at least the next seventy years.

ACKNOWLEDGMENTS

To Amanda Bergeron, I am blessed and humbled to be the beneficiary of your editorial brilliance. Thank you for your belief in me and my stories and your tremendous contribution to them. And to Sareer Khader for lending your fresh eyes to this project and for stepping in to see it through. Thank you!

Thank you to my agent, confidante, and dear friend, Eve MacSweeney. Your genius and thoughtfulness make for a priceless combination.

To Jin Yu, it has been such a pleasure to work with you again. Thank you for your enthusiasm, expertise, and for always giving my crazy ideas a chance!

To Danielle Keir, I was so excited for the chance to work with you and am happy to say that you went beyond my expectations. And to Tina Joell, a fantastic new addition to the team. Thank you both so much!

To Claire Zion, thank you for your invaluable input and treasured support.

And to the rest of the team at Berkley, including but not limited to Ivan Held, Christine Ball, Jeanne-Marie Hudson, Craig Burke, Lindsey Tulloch, and Christine Legon. Thank you, thank you, thank you!

To my trusted (and loved) first readers, Linda Coppola, Andrea Levenbaum, and Melodie Rosen. Endless thanks for your time, your grammatical prowess, and your insightful commentary. I truly couldn't do it without you. An extra shout-out to my middle daughter, Melodie—you got mad skills—thank you for sharing them with me.

And to the rest of my family, my loving husband, Warren, and my other daughters, Raechel and Talia, thank you for putting up with living with a writer. I know it's not always easy. I hope my endless love for you all makes it worth it.

To my fellow authors who have been so supportive of me and my novels, I feel so lucky to have connected with you. And extra thanks to Adriana Trigiani, Elin Hilderbrand, Emily Henry, Katie Couric, Jo Piazza, and Zibby Owen for all that you have done for me and the book community in general.

And a great big shout-out to the Bookstagrammers. You saved me when poor *Eliza* came out during COVID, and once again shouted your love for Esme from the social media rooftops. Thank you for your incredible and selfless support.

This novel took me to many places of which I had little personal knowledge. I would like to thank the following people for sharing their expertise.

My brother, Andrew Levenbaum, for sharing his nautical know-how, in addition to a lifetime of love and support! And to my sister-in-law, Lori Semlies, for the legal lingo in all my novels and for being more of a sister than a sister-in-law.

Thank you to Rita Schrager and Zach Bleckner for all your insight on Cuba and to Charles Leigh for sharing his lifelong knowledge of Cape Cod. To Shaul Magid for the scoop on Dartmouth College and to Dr. Evan Goldstein for his expertise on the emergency room and spinal cord injuries. To Karen Avrick, Ellen Crown, and Heidi Siegel for their shoe insight. And to my dear friend Julie Laub, whose love of shoes (and life) was infectious. Some of Esme's best parts come from my memories of you.

To Marsha Bogen Schtierman, thank you for sharing your inner thoughts and feelings about reconnecting with Monty, your first love.

Thank you to Helen A. Harrison from the Pollock-Krasner House and Study Center for the most memorable private tour and for sharing your incredible insight on the artists, their marriage, and the intricate details of Pollock's death.

To Sol and Carole Zabar, the mavens on all things appetizing, thank you for making sure I got it all right. And a little extra to Sol, for inspiring Sy Katz's character to begin with. A special shout-out to all of the long-gone appetizing shops and dairy restaurants of the Lower East Side, where my mom would take me for sustenance in between scouring the neighborhood for pickles and bras and needlepoint canvases. And, of course, to the ones still standing, specifically Russ & Daughters. Thank you for the inspiration and the Hopjes candies with the check that taste like memories.

And, in the true spirit of Al-Anon—I would very much like to thank Anonymous for her immeasurable help.

To my mother, Florence Hammer Levenbaum, for sharing her memories of growing up in Brooklyn and especially for the beautiful story of how she met my dad. And to my uncle, Seymour Hammer, for helping me flesh out some of the details after my mom passed away.

And finally, the entirety of Sy's time in the service is that of my father's, Seymour Levenbaum. Not only his journey but some of his words are taken directly from his letters home to his mother. I never had the chance to speak with my dad about his time in the Coast Guard. Aside from the fact that he didn't talk much about it, he passed away when I was just eleven. Piecing together and sharing his story has been my greatest honor as a writer. I love you, Dad, and I remain endlessly proud to be your daughter.

A Shoe Story

JANE L. ROSEN

BEHIND THE BOOK

People often ask if there is a lot of me in my characters, and until now, the answer has really been no. Of course there is always some transference between the author and their protagonist, but while Esme and my life stories are very different, a lot of her personality and experiences can be traced right back to me. While I grew up on Long Island and spent a lot of time in Manhattan, it was far different from actually living there. That young girl eating sushi in the Village and realizing that she could actually live in the city was all me. I also felt a lot of the same awe and excitement that Esme did when moving into my first NYC apartment a few weeks after college graduation. It was that fake-it-'til-you-make-it, anything-is-possible time in life, and I loved it.

The camp boyfriend dumping Esme before Thanksgiving—all me. Her first time quietly exiting a frat house just to be outed through the window—me. The quote at the start of the book, from the NYC cab driver—precipitated by me.

As a writer and a general yenta, as Sy would say, I have always had an affinity for talking to taxi drivers. When I'm nervous, I tend to spill my current anxieties as if the cabbie has an advanced degree in psychology or whatnot (it often feels like they do!). Between COVID and the advent of Uber, taxi confessions feel like a lost practice, but after a lifetime in the back seats of NYC cabs, I have quite the collection of tales. This time, I was late for a meeting at Little, Brown and my driver was an older man from Senegal with a French accent.

"Is traffic very bad?" I asked. "I'm late for an interview." It wasn't really an interview, but it felt like one. I was meeting the editor of the

Gossip Girl series regarding a young adult book I was working on. So it felt like someone deciding whether or not they would work with me, ergo, an interview—ergo, my nervousness.

"It's not so bad," he responded.

"OK, good. I'm nervous—and my feet hurt already."

I was wearing my black patent Lanvin Mary Jane heels (chapter 5) and they pinched at the instep. Anyone who owns them is probably well aware of my sacrifice. And that's when he shot back with, "I hope you're not wearing those shoes with the red bottoms; they won't think you're hungry enough!" I laughed at his spot-on advice and his surprising knowledge of designer shoes. But I wasn't really that surprised. I knew that the narrative of the red-bottomed shoe ran deep.

There was a famous ad campaign for the furrier Blackglama back in the seventies with the slogan "What Becomes a Legend Most?" It featured a host of feminine icons, including Sophia Loren, Diahann Carroll, Julie Andrews, Judy, Liza, and even Barbra—all wrapped in mink. If that ad campaign had been created a decade later, I have no doubt we would all have been looking down at their feet.

By the nineties, it was all about the shoes.

While bringing up my now-grown daughters on the Upper East Side, like many moms, my days were bookended by school drop-off and pickup. In between, I would fit in exercising (usually yoga or walking the reservoir with a friend), writing (screenplays at the time), household stuff, and errands. For the errands, I wouldn't stray far from a ten-block radius: Madison Avenue between 86th Street and 96th Street, familiarly known as Carnegie Hill. One day, while conquering my to-do list, I met a lonely old man. I have no memory of how we met, but after we did it was as if he was always there when I left the house. His wife had recently died, and his sons lived in other cities, so he liked to be outside, among the living. His palpable loneliness and my tendency to feel responsible for the world collided, and soon he was accompanying me on nearly all my errands. At the time, I had come down with designer shoe fever—albeit a mild case when compared to my Upper East Side neighbors—and had treated myself to a few choice pairs. My foray began with black satin Louboutin slingbacks whose bottoms I happily scuffed on the dance floor of every black-tie event I was invited to, a pair of denim Gucci loafers which I am still annoyed that I gave away, and a pair of black Prada ballet flats with mesh inserts and rubber bottoms. The Prada flats were my absolute favorites—I lived in them, until one day when I made the mistake of kicking them off at a garden party, where they met a new puppy and an early demise. I would say I was devastated, but I don't want you to find me shallow . . . let's just say I was very upset.

But, just like Sy, my new-old friend Robert had the answer. He took me over to a little shop called Berger's Shoe Repair that I had never even noticed, right down the block. Like many of the old narrow storefronts on Madison, it's not there anymore. Mrs. Berger assured me she would make them as good as knew. And she did. It was a real treat going to Berger's, and just like the cobbler in *A Shoe Story*, she was filled with unsolicited but welcome advice on a host of non–shoe related subjects. I used any excuse to visit, and my shoes benefited immensely—they never looked better.

So, as you can see, the famous words of Nora Ephron's mother, "Everything is copy," really ring true on the pages of *A Shoe Story*. I hope you enjoyed the read and that we can get together in person or online and chat about it one day soon. And please, don't forget to wear your favorite shoes. I will be wearing mine!

—Jane

PS. There are many organizations nationwide that facilitate partnering with older adults for companionship and to combat loneliness. My family and I volunteered for an organization called DOROT in NYC for many years and always found it be a beautiful and rewarding experience for all. If you are interested in making a friend like Sy, check out dorot-usa.org, ncoa.org, or voa.org, or just google "volunteer to visit local elderly near me." I promise you will be glad you did.

DISCUSSION QUESTIONS

1. Do you remember your first special pair of shoes?

2. Esme makes a choice to care for her dad instead of following her dreams. Have you ever made a choice that changed the course of your life? Do you think it was the right choice?

3. Liam was Esme's first love, and Lena was Sy's. All four admitted that they never really stopped loving this first partner. Can you pinpoint your first real love? Do you still think about them?

4. Did you have a favorite between Zach and Liam? Who would you have chosen? Did you think Esme would end up with Zach, with Liam, or on her own?

5. There is a lot of talk in the book about matching thought bubbles. Do you think it's better to think similarly to or differently from a partner?

6. Some people spend a lot of time thinking about the past and what could have been, while others never look back. Which camp are you in and how does it affect your life?

7. When reading a book with multiple stories, many prefer reading one over the other. Between Esme and Sy, whose story did you connect with more? How come?

8. Zach and Liam look at the world and NYC quite differently. Whose NYC would you fit into? Why would you choose it?

9. We all face regrets when it comes to love. Have you ever lost a love and then encountered them again? If not, do you wish you had? What does that conversation look like to you?

10. What did your twenty-one-year-old self think is important that you don't think is important now?

11. The shoes in this book are a metaphor for trying on new lives. What life would you try on for size if you could?

12. What was your guiltiest shoe purchase? How did those shoes make you feel?

WHAT'S IN JANE'S BOOK BAG

- *Going There* by Katie Couric
- *Island Time* by Georgia Clark
- *Modern Comfort Food* by Ina Garten
- *Last Summer at the Golden Hotel* by Elyssa Friedland
- *Moms Don't Have Time To: A Quarantine Anthology*, edited by Zibby Owens
- *We Are Not Like Them* by Christine Pride and Jo Piazza
- *The Shoemaker's Wife* by Adriana Trigiani
- *Zabar's: A Family Story, with Recipes* by Lori Zabar
- *Crying in H Mart* by Michelle Zauner

Jane L. Rosen is an author and screenwriter whose debut novel, *Nine Women, One Dress*, has been translated into ten languages. Her second book, *Eliza Starts a Rumor*, won the Zibby Award for best sophomore novel. She and her husband have three daughters and live in New York City and on Fire Island.

CONNECT ONLINE

JaneLRosen
JaneLRosenAuthor
JaneLRosen1